The Wisdom of Sally Red Shoes

Also available by Ruth Hogan

The Keeper of Lost Things

The Wisdom of Sally Red Shoes

A Novel

RUTH HOGAN

NEW YORK

Copyright © 2018 by Ruth Hogan

All rights reserved.

Published in the United States by Crooked Lane Books, an imprint of The Quick Brown Fox & Company LLC.

Crooked Lane Books and its logo are trademarks of The Quick Brown Fox & Company LLC.

Library of Congress Catalog-in-Publication data available upon request.

ISBN (hardcover): 978-1-64385-209-6
ISBN (ePub): 978-1-64385-210-2
ISBN (ePDF): 978-1-64385-211-9

Cover design by Melanie Sun
Book design by Jennifer Canzone

Printed in the United States.

www.crookedlanebooks.com

Crooked Lane Books
34 West 27th St., 10th Floor
New York, NY 10001

First North American edition: June 2019

Originally published in Great Britain by Two Roads, May 2018

10 9 8 7 6 5 4 3 2 1

To Duke Roaring Water Bay.
My blessing.

*. . . and one has gone right away and will never,
never come back, and we shall be left alone to begin
our lives again. We must go on living, we must.*

Anton Chekhov, *Three Sisters*

*Etiquette may be defined as the technique of the art of social life.
For various and good reasons certain traditions have been handed
down, just as they are in any other art, science or department of life,
and only very thoughtless persons could consider unworthy of notice
that set of rules which guides us in our social relations to each other.*

Lady Troubridge, *The Book of Etiquette*

The old woman fills her lungs with the crisp autumn air, throws open her arms and exhales a perfect top C.

The note soars, pure and clear, above the gravestones that are scattered down the hill in front of her. There is no one to hear the astonishing power and perfect pitch of her voice except the crows perched in the pines that punctuate the landscape, and a squirrel excavating acorns from his stash beside a crooked stone cross.

The woman thrusts her hands into the pockets of her well-worn tweed coat, remembering with a smile a scarlet silk gown she wore in another life, many years ago. Almost the same shade as the scuffed, red shoes she is wearing now. Beneath the crackling of lines and wrinkles on her weathered face, there remain the traces of extraordinary beauty, and her eyes sparkle, brimful of curiosity, as she surveys the scene before her. She begins a slow descent, zigzagging across the rimy grass between the graves. The squirrel springs bolt upright, twitching his tail in alarm at her approach, but refuses to abandon his supply of nuts.

As the woman approaches the path at the bottom of the hill, she finds a solitary tattered rose, its pink petals fringed with frost, lying at her feet. She picks it up and inspects it closely, marvelling at its fragile beauty before placing it carefully on a nearby head-stone. Life is full of small joys if you know where to look for them, and the woman's bright eyes are forever seeking them out and finding them, even in the darkest of times and places.

A black shape falls from the sky and lands beside her, rearranging its feathers and cawing loudly. Another crow joins it, and then another and another. Their number grows as they follow her through the rusty, wrought-iron gate into the park, some hopping behind and beside her, and others swooping around her head. The park is almost empty, save for a few dog walkers and a handful of children taking a shortcut home from school. She takes a paper bag from her coat pocket and begins to scatter its contents.

As the crows grab and gobble their daily bread, the woman looks up in wonder at the sky where dark clouds are haloed with the copper light of an impending sunset.

Small joys.

Chapter One

Masha

Several years ago . . .

Today's pool temperature is 6.3; little warmer than a mortuary, but then I am not quite dead yet.

Mist hangs low over the blue slab of water like dry ice on a lighted disco floor, but deep below the bright, shimmering surface this is going to be my last dance. A *danse macabre*. The bitter cold is soothing like an ice pack on exquisite pain and is lulling me to sleep. The body's instinct is to fight to stay alive and I can feel my lungs burning; screaming for air.

But my mind, like David Bowie's Major Tom, is feeling very still.

They say that just before you die your entire life flashes in front of you, but for me it is a single fragment. That instant when I woke up and he was gone. These are the final moments when my body and soul are still united in the fragile alchemy we call being 'alive'. But my spirit is exhausted by grief too almighty to bear and so my soul is bidding farewell to the flesh and bones it once called home.

It is such a relief simply to let go.

Chapter Two

～

Alice

Several years ago . . .

The rich, sweet smell of toffee and fruit filled the kitchen as Alice opened the oven door and carefully removed the hot tin. Pineapple upside-down cake. It was Mattie's favourite. Alice checked the clock on the wall. He would be home soon and starving hungry as usual after an afternoon at the pool. Today Mattie was being tested for his Bronze Medallion award that involved all kinds of challenges, including basic life-saving skills. Alice had no doubt that he would pass with ease. Since he was a toddler he had always been completely fearless in the water and had learned to swim before he started school.

Alice tipped some potatoes into the sink ready to peel for their supper of shepherd's pie – another of Mattie's favourites. She wanted to spoil him today, not just for the swimming test but because she loved her son beyond measure and always worried that she didn't say that enough. Waiting for him to come home from school was the highlight of her day. Once the potatoes were ready, she set them to boil and turned the cake out of the tin and onto a plate. She checked the clock again. Any minute now. She wiped the condensation from the kitchen window with the back of her hand so that she could watch for him walking down the road, and soon his dishevelled figure appeared, blazer unbuttoned despite the cold, tie at half mast and one shoelace undone. He had a satchel over one shoulder, a sports bag over the other and a wide grin plastered across his face. Clattering in through the back door he dumped his satchel on a kitchen chair, his sports bag on the floor and made a beeline for the cake.

'Not so fast, young man!' Alice said, smiling at his eager face. 'How did it go?'

'I passed!' said her son with a triumphant fist pump, his eyes still fixed firmly on the cake.

'I always knew you would,' said Alice, ruffling his still-damp hair. 'Now, get changed and put your wet swimming things in the bathroom, and *then* you can have some cake.'

'Muuum!' Mattie protested good-naturedly, but he snatched his sports bag from the floor and galloped up the stairs. By the time Alice had cut a slice of cake, he had changed out of his uniform and was back in the kitchen.

Chapter Three

〜

Masha

Present day

Today's pool temperature is 10.4 and a bitter wind grazes the surface of the water. The Charleston Lido opened in 1931; a thing of beauty and a place for pleasure. But by the mid-1980s the sounds of splashing water and children's laughter were no more than ghostly echoes. For the next twenty years the tiles in the empty pool cracked and flaked and sprouted weeds. The walls of the changing rooms grew soft with mould and the poolside bunting flapped frailly on the ground like fishes slowly dying. The lido's resurrection was a small miracle performed by a determined neighbourhood band of ordinary, extraordinary people, some of whom had learned to swim here as children. I, for one, am very grateful. The pool where I learned to doggy-paddle, clutching a rectangle of grubby polystyrene and wearing a saggy-bottomed nylon swimsuit, was trapped inside a grim, concrete box where the air was thick with the warm stench of chlorine, and the threat of verrucas lurked on every surface. The Charleston at sunrise is an ethereal beauty. But it is also my penance.

Every week I come here to drown. Almost.

I'm an authority on drowning and I've studied well. I have an intimate knowledge of Francesco Pia's work. Frank is a silver fox with two master's degrees and a broad smile. He was also a lifeguard for over twenty years and is an internationally recognised expert and legend in his field. Drowning. His specialist subject is drowning. I can recite his 'instinctive drowning response' word for word. It's saved in my YouTube favourites.

Today the ground glitters with frost and the water will be punishingly cold, but it welcomes me, as ever, with a siren's embrace and lures me deeper and deeper. At first I just used to put my head under the water in the bath. But it wasn't enough. My bathroom is a place too cosy to properly play 'chicken' with death. At the lido, I swim underwater to the steps at the deep end and then I hold onto the handrail until my lungs implode and I drown. Almost. Japanese pearl divers can hold their breath for up to seven minutes in pursuit of underwater treasure, but the average person can only manage thirty to forty seconds. My personal best so far is just shy of two minutes. It's self-inflicted waterboarding.

After my swim (because I do actually have to swim a bit as well, otherwise it might look odd) I go home to a comfortable Edwardian house with high ceilings and commensurately high heating bills – a generous legacy from my maternal grandmother to her only granddaughter. I am greeted with undignified enthusiasm by my wolfhound Haizum. He is a long-legged, hairy affair of a dog with the eyes of an angel and the breath of a goblin. He is also my reason for living. Literally. He has an appetite for all things disgusting and inappropriate, and his diet to date has included most of the contents of the compost bin, bird poo, whole cloves of garlic, a bar of soap, a dead frog and a pair of rubber gloves. My vet bills are prodigious.

After a lunch of salt-and-vinegar-crisp sandwiches, which I share with Haizum, I settle down at my desk and pretend to work. I'm fortunate that my job allows me to work from home when I'm not seeing clients, and provides me with somewhere to see them so I don't have to have them in my home. God forbid! Haizum slumps sulkily onto his bed, disappointed that a walk is not next on the agenda. I scan through some emails, look up the word of the day on my favourite dictionary website ('tatterdemalion' – *ragged, unkempt or dilapidated*) and inevitably stray onto You-Tube. How on earth did we manage to waste time before the Internet? I persevere for an hour or so and then give up. Usually a visit to the Charleston calms my inner demons for a while. But not today.

At the sound of his lead being lifted from its hook, Haizum leaps into action; a maelstrom of limbs and hair skittering perilously across the tiled kitchen floor. The cemetery is just a short walk across the park and the cold, crisp air, still tinged with the earthy undertones of autumn, is intoxicating to breathe. If the pool is my penance, then this place is my sanctuary and today it is fairytale beautiful. It is a fine example of a Victorian garden cemetery, and the Victorians did death so beautifully. Towering trees stand guardian over the rows of imposing headstones and graceful sculptures. The angels are my favourites and there are a whole host of them here. Some, on children's graves, are small with unfledged wings and hands softly clasped in prayer. Some stand in silent vigil with downcast eyes, guarding those who lie beneath their feet; and others have stretched their arms towards the sky and spread their wings ready for flight.

But one is very special. I am spellbound by each elegant sweep and curve of her polished marble figure and the expression of serenity she wears on her face. She is the Cate Blanchett of angels and she kneels on a grave here in the oldest part of the cemetery, quite close to the chapel. But should she ever choose to unfold her magnificent wings, I am certain that she would fly straight up to heaven in the most elegant fashion.

I hope that heaven exists. Because when the person that you love the most is already dead, it is the one place where you might be reunited, and if heaven is just wishful thinking or an urban myth, the hope of finding them again is gone forever.

'But if it does exist, will I ever get there?'

I know the angel can't answer me, but I always find some consolation in her exquisite face. I don't really support any particular religion. I'm not much of a joiner; I'm more of a soloist. The thought of complete strangers hugging me and telling me they love me and that God does too makes me want to run for the hills. How do they know? He might not. I'd consider myself blessed if he could be persuaded to offset my occasional blasphemy, pathological intolerance of wimps and bad drivers, and skipping Holy Communion classes aged thirteen, against my kindness to animals and reasonably consistent – although not always successful – attempts to be a fairly decent sort of person. Because surely that's more important than following someone else's arbitrary religious rules?

'What do you think?'

The angel doesn't look like a jobsworth to me. I'll take her silence as assent. And although I may not be a joiner, there are plenty who would like to be who are simply not made welcome. I prefer to think of myself as freelance religious. I like angels, so I'm inclined to look more favourably upon a religion if it includes the angelic element. If it discourages gratuitous hugging, even better.

The ground is covered with damp leaves, rotting now and

losing their bright-jewel autumn hues to winter's sludge of grey and brown. Haizum pushes through the leaves with his nose, greedily inhaling the scent of hedgehogs, foxes and Lord only knows what else. I can only smell the scent of freshly dug soil and decay. A lone crow stands sentinel on a cross-and-anchor head-stone, watching our progress with nervous suspicion. He caws a protest when we get too close before casting his black wings wide and sweeping up into one of the dark, soaring pines. A pair of squirrels scrattles up and down the rough bark of its thick trunk like over-excited children playing chase, and Haizum watches them intently, frustrated that they are out of reach. The golden afternoon light is slowly bleeding away and now I can smell smoke from a bonfire. Soon all my angels will be shrouded in shadows.

But there will be no angel to mark my grave. No one will come to my funeral except the undertakers and the vicar. There will be no flowers, no hymns, no tear-jerking music. No tears at all, in fact. Because there will be no mourners. The care home – or Happy Endings, as I have nicknamed it – where I shall have spent my old age waiting for death in inappropriate frocks and shoes, smelling of cheap rose talcum powder and wee and wear-ing smudged red lipstick on my teeth, will be very glad to be rid of me. The vicar, who will no doubt be short and skinny, with a weak chin and a lisp, and wearing beige Y-fronts under his vestments (or, in these days of fledgling ecumenical equality, thousand-wash-grey big knickers and a bra with as much 'come hither' as a dentist's chair) will probably dismiss my coffin to the burner with the words 'Thunderbirds are go!'

I might get a prayer if I'm lucky.

Of course, this is not my funeral of choice. I should choose a glass-sided hearse drawn by two magnificent black horses, and have 'Casta Diva' from Bellini's *Norma* playing as my coffin is carried into a splendid gothic church. I'm tempted to include a Jean Paul Gaultier model dressed in a sailor suit. The vicar would be tall, dark and charismatic; holy enough to suit God's purpose, divine enough to suit mine. The congregation would be elegantly dressed and their grief would be evident, but dignified. My coffin would glide through purple velvet curtains to the sound of 'La Vie en Rose', and of course, my beloved boy would be there to see me off.

In my dreams.

By the time we leave the cemetery, the daylight is dwindling into a crepuscular shadow world and the park resembles an Arthur Rackham illustration with tall, black trees stretching their spindle limbs across a purple bruised sky. The bandstand is a haunting silhouette against the orange and crimson mottled clouds that veil the full splendour of the late autumn sunset. We cut across the muddy grass which is already stiff with frost, Haizum loping in all directions in pursuit of imaginary small creatures and revolting smells while I stride purposefully so as not to resemble an easy target for a mugger looking to steal a mobile phone. As we approach the path I can see the small, tatterdemalion figure of the old woman who feeds the crows. She brings a bag of bread every afternoon for the noisy black birds who loiter in the treetops on the side of the park that shares a boundary with the cemetery. As they jostle restlessly on the grass waiting for the bread to be thrown, the birds look like a gang of sulky teenagers hanging around on a street corner. The woman is bundled up in a patched tweed coat that is several sizes too big, a red woolly hat with a pom-pom and red Mary Jane shoes with brown socks. My grandma always used to say, 'Red hat, no knickers!' In my head, I call the woman 'Sally Red Shoes', but I have no idea of her real name or the presence or otherwise of her underwear.

11

'Hello,' I call to her as we reach the path. 'It's going to be chilly tonight.'

'Fuck off,' she replies with a smile. 'Bloody blackbirds eat all my bread.'

Her vocabulary belies her demeanour. Her manner is unfailingly gracious and she enunciates her expletives beautifully. Their literal meaning is incidental. 'Fuck off' is her version of 'Good evening'. It is as though the dictionary in her brain has been scrambled, and all the words and their meanings have become mismatched. She has periods of clarity when her communication is more conventional, but now is not one of them. Perhaps it is simply a reversal of the process we go through when we are very young – learning new words and uniting them with their meanings, like playing that card game where you lay all the cards face down and take turns to choose two cards until you find a matching pair. As a child I was always keen to keep an interesting word by me until I could match it up with its meaning. I kept 'fuck' to myself until one day when I was about nine and I slipped it into a conversation I was having with my mum. She failed to supply me with its exact meaning, but the slap round the back of my legs gave me a general idea. Perhaps Sally's matching pairs simply keep drifting apart.

She throws the last of the bread onto the grass and Haizum gobbles a few pieces before I hastily restrain him on his lead. My 'goodbye' is lost in the clacketyflap of the crows' wings as they scrabble and squabble over the few remaining crumbs. We follow our usual route around the back of the bowling green, tracing the perimeter of the cemetery, and then head back down the main avenue towards the bandstand. A blackbird's alarm call echoes through the dusk as he is startled by Haizum's diligent investigation of the bushes and undergrowth. I can smell smoke again now as people come home from work and the lights go on and fires are lit in the large Victorian houses that face the park.

As soon as he is through the front door, Haizum makes a bee-line for his water bowl from which he slurps noisily and then leaves a trail of slobber and water across the kitchen floor that I immediately walk through, having removed my boots at the front door. I always think that I shall have a cup of tea when I get back from our evening walks.

Tonight, as usual, I pour myself a glass of wine.

Chapter Four

～

The rocking horse is all that's left. I waited a year exactly. Three hundred and sixty-six days. It was a leap year that year. And then I cleared the room.

From the garden, I can see it in the upstairs window: a handsome dappled grey creature, with flared nostrils and a red saddle. The garden has succumbed to its customary late autumn chaos. The last of the blackberries are hard, black knobbles dusted with mildew, and the windfall apples ooze, sticky and sweet, beneath the trees – a generous feast for hungry birds. A few hardy dahlias and chrysanthemums still bloom in the raggedy flower beds, but the last of the roses have shattered and their fragile petals lie strewn across dark soil.

I have been working in the garden all day; sweeping leaves, pruning trees and bushes, planting bulbs and moving pot plants into the greenhouse for their winter hibernation. Making everything tidy. Ready. My back aches, a film of sweat and soil coats my face, my fingernails are black and my hands pierced a dozen times by rose thorns. But soon I shall have my reward. The mobile phone in my pocket buzzes and I fish it out and peer at the screen. Dad.

'What's the name of the bloody useless article who calls himself the Chief Constable?'

My father doesn't believe in the introductory niceties of tele-phone conversation, such as 'Hello, it's Dad'.

'I don't know off-hand, but I'm sure I can find out. Is it urgent? Is a ram-raid on the postbox in progress or an illegal rave rampag-ing at the bowling pavilion?'

'You may mock, my girl, but the very fabric of society is unrav-elling when a senior citizen is unable to pull out of his own drive-way because it is blocked by the four-wheel drive of some silly woman who can't walk five yards to pick up her bone-idle children from school. What's more, when I asked her to move it, she told me to "Eff off, you silly old bastard!" That's trespass aggravated by verbal assault and I'm not standing for it.'

Dad could never be accused of being a moderate. The high standards he sets for himself in both behaviour and attitude are his benchmark for humanity, and he takes a pretty dim view of those who fall short.

'I'll find out for you, but I do know the Chief Constable is a woman.'

'Bloody hell!'

He doesn't hold with female chief constables either.

After a very late lunch, shared, as usual, with Haizum, I reward myself with a bonfire. I'm not sure if it's really allowed – it's probably contrary to some by-law or another – but I'll happily risk the wrath of the bonfire police for the crackle and spit of burning leaves, flame-warmed face and hands, and the scent of wood smoke clinging to my clothes and my hair. Besides, at this time of year they're commonplace. Yesterday was Halloween, and there'll be an endless cacophony of firework displays this week-end. But whatever happened to 'penny for the guy'? When we were kids, half the fun of Guy Fawkes Night was the painstaking construction of a ramshackle effigy of the man himself, using a pair of old trousers, a shirt, a pair of tights (for the head) and a great deal of screwed-up newspaper. We then paraded it round the streets on a makeshift go-cart attempting to extract money for fireworks from kind-hearted neighbours. But back then, it was a very genial affair, quite unlike the 'demanding money with menaces' that trick or treat has become. Last night Haizum managed to scare away from my door a gaggle of teenagers dressed as zombies and vampires, but the price I paid for their empty-handed exit was half a dozen smashed eggs on the windscreen of my car.

The fire takes a while to catch. Some of the leaves are damp and I fan the faltering flames with an empty potting-compost bag. My efforts are repaid with a sudden spit and flare. Upstairs, in the bedroom window, the wooden horse rocks gently back and forth. Or is it just a trick of the smoke-hazed light? Today is *Día de los Angelitos*. Day of the Little Angels. One of the three days of the Mexican 'Day of the Dead' celebrations, *Día de los Angelitos* is when families gather to remember the children who have died. They invite their spirits to visit, and they celebrate their lives, however short. And we keep this day, every year.

But I wish we didn't always have to do it alone. I wish we could share the memories, both happy and sad. The 'firsts' that still make me smile, and the 'lasts' that make me crumple and weep.

I have never had the courage to ask my family and friends to join me. They might think it mawkish, or morbid, or just plain weird. Edward is the only one who really understands and so Edward is the only one who joins us. Edward and Lord Byron, his dog. I make my *ofrenda* in the garden and decorate it with sugar skulls, lanterns and paper marigolds. Earth, wind, fire and water are represented by fruit, tissue-paper bunting, candles and a glass of water, and I surround my little angel's photograph with dishes of his favourite sweets and biscuits (chocolate buttons and custard creams), and the white rabbit. It was his favourite toy. His bed-time comforter, battered and balding from a thousand cherub-lipped kisses and chubby-armed cuddles. The fire is blazing now and Haizum is squinting at the flames and sniffing at the smoke. I will sit by this bonfire with Edward and a couple of bottles of wine and will the rocking horse in the window to rock. I will draw back the veil between me and the past and force myself to remember. All of it.

Hours later, the wine bottles are empty and my head is resting on Edward's shoulder as we huddle close to the mound of smouldering embers – all that remains of the fire. My hands are as cold as a corpse, but I can't bring myself to move.

'Masha?'

Edward whispers my name softly, but I don't answer. He strokes my hair and sighs.

'She sleeps.'

He shifts uncomfortably and then kisses the top of my head.

'I sometimes wonder, my darling girl, if all we're doing here is keeping the grief alive.'

The tears squeeze out from under my eyelids.

Haizum and Lord Byron have finally given in to temptation and are eating the custard creams.

Chapter Five

～

Alice

Present day

Alice inspected her shopping list again to make sure that she hadn't forgotten anything before unloading her trolley at the checkout. She smiled to herself thinking how the items on the piece of paper in her hand had changed over the years, reflecting the transformation of her little boy into a testosterone-tormented teenager. After the endless paraphernalia of babyhood, his requirements had distilled into a simple bill of fare. Blackcurrant squash, cheese balls, fish fingers and shepherd's pie. He would eat almost anything she cooked except mushrooms and swede, but fish fingers were a twice-weekly mainstay. How times had changed! Fish fingers were still on the list, but food was fast being eclipsed by a panoply of personal hygiene products. Deodorants, facial cleansers, cologne sprays, spot creams and disposable razors were the new essentials. Razors! What on earth were they for? Mattie's chin was almost as smooth as Alice's. Perhaps he was shaving his legs.

As she unloaded the contents of her trolley onto the conveyor belt, she wondered if Mattie might have a girlfriend. He was only thirteen, but they started so young now. Alice had been sixteen and a half before she'd had her first proper kiss, and even then she hadn't liked it much. It had been with a boy called Gareth Blood- worth after the school disco. He had walked her to the bus stop and kissed her while they were waiting for the number 19. She remembered that it was raining and she had snagged her tights on the seat in the bus shelter and that she hadn't really fancied him, but thought that he might do to practise on. All her friends had already been kissed by then – even Deborah Dickey who wore braces. Alice was beginning to feel left behind; out of kilter with the rest of the world. But kissing Gareth Bloodworth hadn't helped. It wasn't dreadful, just vaguely disappointing – like biting into a powdery apple. And she had kept her eyes open. She had watched the raindrops trickle down the dirty plastic walls of the shelter while Gareth tried to put his hand on her bum.

'Do you need any help with your packing?'

The girl on the checkout had purple hair and a nose stud. Alice was pretty sure that 'Courtney' – as her name badge pro- claimed her to be – had been kissed by the time she was sixteen and a half. She'd probably had sex, a tattoo and some serious hangovers by then too.

'No thanks,' said Alice, smiling. 'I'll be fine.'

She shook open the plastic carrier bags that she had brought with her and began filling them with the items Courtney scanned and then flung in her general direction at breakneck speed. Alice hoped that Mattie's first kiss would not be with a girl like Court- ney. Or Deborah Dickey for that matter. Courtney handed over the receipt and a money-off voucher for fruit-flavoured tea bags, and then expressed the hope that Alice would 'have a nice day' with as much indifference as she could muster.

Outside, a bitter wind blew across the car park, making the

heavily loaded trolley treacherous to steer. As she reached the boot of her Nissan, a sudden gust slammed the trolley into the car's rear door, chipping the deep red paintwork. Alice rubbed the dent with her fingertip, more curious than concerned. It was an old car anyway. A dependable workhorse. So long as it got her and Mattie safely from A to B, and the radio and heater worked, she was content. As she drove out of the car park, the roads were beginning to fill with traffic; parents going to collect their children from school. Mattie caught the bus from their village to his upper school on the edge of town. After a while the houses thinned and trees and fields filled the horizon. Above it a bleak and bloated sky began shedding sleet that blurred the dirty windscreen. As the wipers struggled to clear Alice's view she wondered if Mattie would tell her if he had a girlfriend. She switched the radio on for company, and while the smooth voices of pop duo Charles and Eddie asked 'Would I lie to you?' Alice answered her own question. Of course he would tell her.

There were never any secrets between them.

Chapter Six

~

Masha

All I can hear is the sound of water dripping. Dropping softly onto grass and earth, splashing hard and bright onto path and stone. In the sixteenth century, Chinese water torture was used to drive its victims insane simply by dripping water onto their foreheads. Drip, drip, drip. Or sometimes – drip. Drip, drip. An inconsistent pattern, but consistently torturous.

This morning a fine drizzle shrouds the monuments and mausoleums in the cemetery, making the marble glisten and the leaves of the holly bushes shine. And everything drip.

I have come to visit the children. After a busy morning of consultations at work with an insomniac, a hypochondriac and a middle-aged man who believes he is the reincarnation of Elizabeth Taylor, I need some peace and quiet. In a sheltered corner of the cemetery, beneath the protection of a copse of ancient conifers, is where the children 'sleep'. Here there are always fresh flowers and fresh tears. Windmills and teddy bears and shiny foil balloons. These are the piteous mementos of a childhood cut short or, for some, never begun. Today, in the drizzle, I could almost pretend that it's a playground. That the children have simply gone inside, leaving the toys behind in their haste to escape from the rain. But these children will never return. Emma Grace Spencer was just three years old when she died. The only child of Walter and Marie, she loved to dance and her favourite food was jam sandwiches. Strawberry jam. She had a tabby kitten called Popsy and when Emma Grace giggled she wrinkled her nose. Her parents moved to the coast and opened a tea shop. They couldn't bear to continue living in the house where their daughter had died. I wonder if they ever returned to visit her grave with its two little angels hand in hand. Emma Grace was dancing too close to the hearth when her new dress caught fire.

It's always a living hell for the parents who are left behind. Billy Band was a lively boy with a mischievous streak. Or a 'right little sod' according to his dad, but the apple of his eye nonetheless. Billy's gravestone has a football carved into the granite to remind us of all the goals he scored in his short life. He was seven years old when he chased his football into the road and was hit by a bread delivery van.

You need to know that it was my fault. My beloved boy died twelve years, seven months and eleven days ago and it was my fault. He had a tangle of dark brown curls and eyes the colour of delphiniums. I can still smell the soft sweetness of his skin and feel his small and perfect hand in mine. Almost everyone said that it was a tragic accident; that I couldn't possibly blame myself. But of course I do. Every day.

As I turn away from the children's graves to walk up the hill towards the predominantly Polish section of the cemetery, I am startled by a small figure darting in and out between the gravestones. A little boy in a blue coat is playing by himself, swinging a grubby-looking teddy bear by the paw. Grief can be the gateway to its own kind of madness, and for the briefest of moments my reason is overruled by a desperate, ridiculous fantasy. My little boy? My gut twists. Of course not. He would be a gangling youth by now, battling with teenage acne, raging hormones and the agonies of dating. I used to bring him here. Some might say it's a strange playground for a child, but he loved it. He would chatter away to the angels and crows and try to feed the squirrels with pine cones.

Haizum has spotted the child and is straining on his lead to reach him and say hello. I pull him back and look round for the boy's mother, or any other responsible adult, but there is no one else in sight. Seeing Haizum, the boy squeals happily and rushes towards him, slipping on the wet grass and banging his head on the border stone of a grave. I lift him to his feet and gently stroke the red mark on his forehead where a bump is beginning to form. His sudden bawling is testament to the fact that he is more frightened than hurt, and I brush the tears from his cheeks and try to comfort him as best I can. The scent of his skin and the soft feel of his hair unravel me, even after all these years. How could it be that nobody is watching over this beautiful little boy?

'Where's your mummy?'

He shakes his head, buries his face in his teddy. I stand up and look around again. A woman with a baby in a pushchair is yelling and hurrying along the central path, her footsteps jerky with panic and her words sharp-edged with fear.

'Jayden, you little bugger! Where have you been?'

At the sight of her, Jayden starts wailing again and lifts his arms up towards her. He is rewarded with a smack on the bottom followed by an embrace tight enough to leave him breathless. The woman is now sobbing as hard as her son and she covers his head in angry kisses.

'He fell. He's got a bit of a bump on his head, but I don't think it's anything too serious.'

I try, but probably fail, to keep an accusatory tone from taint-ing my reassurance. Where the hell had she been? She looks up at me, wild-eyed, through her tears, but I don't think she's heard a single word, and when the baby in the pushchair decides to join the chorus, I force a smile and walk away before I say something I might regret. But I can't resist stroking the little boy's head as I go. Dark brown curls. I head back down the hill towards the gate and even when I reach the bottom path I can still hear them crying.

When my boy died, some people seemed to think that my grief was insufficient. Not clamorous enough. But drowning is a quiet affair. According to silver fox Frank, the truly drowning are rarely able to call out for help; unable to shout or wave their arms in the air. They are fighting too hard simply to keep their heads above the water. And so it was with me. There were awful but necessary practicalities to deal with, and I had no strength to spare for embarrassingly public displays of grief. There was screaming loud enough to tumble the walls of Jericho – inside my head. But people need to see grief. It must be on show to give them a role to play; tears to dry, flowers to send, consolation, however meagre, to offer. Stoicism stymies sympathy. Too often and too readily mistaken for cold-heartedness, it discomforts the would-be com-forters and marks the mourner as strange. Untouchable.

But left alone I was a danger to myself. I have survived, but only just. And now I am caught in a rip current of grief and strug-gling against it gets me nowhere. The fight is exhausting and some-times it takes all my strength to simply stay afloat. I'm not fond of the person I have become, but I don't know how to be anyone else.

Haizum is desperate to get back into the park. He often has to stay on his lead in the cemetery to prevent him from stealing teddy bears, and weeing on headstones and floral tributes. He has scant respect for the memory of the deceased and cannot be trusted with anything small and fluffy. As we pass under the canopy of fir trees that guards the gate in the iron railings, I unleash him, and he bounds off like a catawumpus (word of the day – *something very fierce*) in pursuit of some fat pigeons who will have flown off long before he reaches them, leaving me to walk alone.

Alone is who I am. I have no child, so I am no longer a mother, and no man, so I am neither a wife nor a lover. I have wonderful friends whom I love and I know love me back, but no one for whom I am the centre of their world, and they of mine. Except Haizum. Which is why I am terrified of growing old. I shall finish up in the Happy Endings home because there will be no one else to have me and it is probably exactly what I deserve.

The path from the gate is littered with the skeletons of pine cones that have been eaten by squirrels, and then dropped from on high, in the hope of hitting some unsuspecting passer-by. The crows are gathering in anticipation of Sally's arrival with their supper. They jostle one another restlessly and squawk loudly with hunger and impatience. In the distance I can see her shuffling along in her huge coat looking like a parcel that is coming unwrapped. I wave half-heartedly at her, unsure if she can see or recognise me, and set off after Haizum. Having seen off the pigeons, he is now barking furiously at the bottom of a tall tree, no doubt chastising some squirrel who has cheated in the game of chase by disappearing up the tree. The drizzle is heavier now, and despite my hat and scarf and coat I am cold enough to shiver. Perhaps it is the thought of those teddy bears, flowers and windmills lying in the wet grass on children's graves.

Chapter Seven

'Darling Masha! How are you?'

Epiphany air-kisses me near both cheeks, and then stares me straight in the eyes whilst holding me by the shoulders at arm's length. She raises her eyebrows knowingly.

'Hmm. I'll get you a drink.'

Epiphany is a true friend. The kind of friend you'd take to war with you, should the need ever arise. We met at school, travelled after university and eventually worked together. She has stood by my side unflinchingly through the good, the bad and the unspeakably ugly times. She sweeps up to the bar of The Cock and Curtain and flutters her eyelashes vampishly at the delicious-looking barman, who is twenty years too young for her and about as camp as Butlin's. Epiphany swears the name of the pub refers to the interior decor, which is a heady blend of Victorian brothel and musichall dressing room. There are crimson swagged curtains with as many frills and flounces as a cancan dancer's skirts, and bottle-green velvet, button-backed sofas with the odd beer stain and cigarette burn for added character. Burgundy and cream flock wallpaper provides a backdrop for framed black and white photographs of silent-film stars and music-hall artists, and a signed photograph of Barbara Cartland. Above the open fireplace is a gruesome arrangement of tiny, bright-coloured stuffed birds, dried flowers and foliage, beadwork, ribbons, and a stuffed mouse all trapped under a large glass dome. A mesmeric monstrosity, it looks like a collaboration between Damien Hirst and Laura Ashley. Hanging from the ceiling is a collection of china chamber pots, and the whole place smells of stale beer, wood smoke and furniture polish.

Masha is not my real name. It's a nickname Epiphany gave me years ago and it stuck like toffee. She says she named me after Chekhov's character in *The Seagull*, whose first line in the play is, 'I'm in mourning for my life', alluding to the fact that I spend an inordinate amount of time loitering in the cemetery. She returns from the bar with glasses of white wine, one of which she plonks down in front of me with a grin.

Epiphany takes an enthusiastic swig from her glass and leans back in her chair. Her auburn hair is cut in a short, sharp bob and her lips are a slash of shiny plum on her pale high-cheekboned face. She works for the local council in the personnel department, which is now called the Ministry of People Development, Deployment and Dispatch (Orwell would heartily approve), where I was once her colleague, and is obviously desperate to share some highly inappropriate gossip with me. The pub is gradually filling up with people like us – friends meeting for a couple of drinks on their way home from work – and Epiphany glances round theatrically before announcing in a stage whisper, 'The Deputy Chief Fire Officer has been arrested in a gentlemen's public toilet dressed as a woman!'

The Deputy Chief Fire Officer is a florid-cheeked six-footer with curly red hair and a definite predilection for steak and kidney puddings and pints of Guinness.

'He was quite rightly released without charge because he wasn't actually committing any offence, other than in the fashion sense. An A-line skirt, chiffon blouse and a rather boring twinset. Honestly, darling, what was he thinking! A Diane von Furstenberg wrap dress would have been so much more flattering. And it's not as though he can't afford it on his salary.'

I sip my wine, trying to keep up with Epiphany's rather erratic train of thought.

'But if he was released without charge, what's the problem?'

Epiphany puts down her glass and sighs. Her expression changes, momentarily betraying her true feelings. 'Some stunted-dick smartarse at the local nick took photographs on his phone and now it's gone missing. The Chief Exec's desperate to keep a lid on the whole affair, and has been closeted – ha ha! – in his office all morning with the Chief Constable, reading the riot act about the unprofessionalism of her officers and exploring avenues of damage limitation.'

I smile at the thought of the stuffed shirts having to cope with such an unexpected chiffon blouse.

'Apparently he was just out for a walk one evening and was caught short. Actually leaving the house in women's clothes is quite a new venture for him, and when nature called he didn't have the confidence to use the Ladies. Unluckily for him, a local busybody with nothing better to do saw him go into the Gents and called the police.'

When I worked at the council the gentleman in question was a young, moderately ambitious and strictly by-the-book station officer, and whenever I'd had any dealings with him I had found him pleasant enough. I now had a sneaking admiration for this middle-aged individual whom I had hitherto assumed to be as sensible and dull as baked-bean-coloured tights and bran-based breakfast cereal. I'm a sucker for hidden depths. But I could also see why my new-found approval might not be widely shared.

'Presumably the concern is the potential for a lurid scandal in the tabloids unfortunately timed to coincide with a recent review of Chief Officer salaries, which has left most of the local electorate believing that their recent hike in council tax bills is paying for holiday homes in Tuscany for the council's most senior officers.'

'Exactly! And it makes his choice of outfit even more indefensible.'

There were many reasons why I stopped working in local government. I'm surprised I lasted as long as I did. I was like Ginger Rogers at a Morris Dance. The current situation was sadly typical. The council had trumpeted the launch of its Managing Diversity policy years ago. It outlawed discrimination against just about everything and everyone, including transvestites. But with a real life lipsticked ladyboy in their midst, six foot four in his white stilettos and found in possession of a fully superannuated local government salary, the policy makers missed a golden opportunity to prove that here was a council not just talking the talk but also walking the walk. If the walk, however, turned out to be more of a totter in size ten stilettos, they fell at the first hurdle.

Epiphany's many and varied talents are indisputably wasted in her current job. But as she once explained to me, it suits her well enough. Her real life is outside of work. She lives in a fabulously decadent flat where she imagines herself to be one of the women in Giovanni Boldini's paintings. It is furnished with plush chaises longues, gold-framed rococo mirrors, ostrich feathers, jardinières, aspidistras and antimacassars. There is a baby grand piano covered in an embroidered silk piano shawl and an Edwardian tailor's dummy wearing a satin corset and a green tin helmet in the sitting room. A beautiful Edwardian gramophone is regularly used to play 78s, of which Epiphany has an extensive collection.

She shares the flat with a pair of Siamese cats – who shred the antimacassars, dig in the jardinières and look elegant and slightly disdainful – and her boyfriend, an artist called Stanley.

Epiphany drains her glass and gives me one of her looks.

'So, tell me, darling Masha, have you been swimming lately?'

She knows about my regular visits to the lido, but even she doesn't know why I really go.

'I went on Wednesday.' I give her a bright smile, knowing full well that it will look like a party hat on an undertaker.

'Well, I really hope that all this swimming is for the benefit of some gorgeous man in Daniel Craig trunks who scythes up and down the pool like an Olympian while you pose prettily on a sun lounger.'

This time my grin is genuine.

'It's November! There was frost on the ground!'

Epiphany treads a fine line with the expertise of a high-wire walker. Her expression betrays that she has more to say on the matter, but she remains silent. I know she wants to help, but I can't let her. And even if I did, what could she do?

On this occasion, she opts to change the subject.

'Well, I spent today preparing for a disciplinary at work. Riveting stuff.'

'Do tell! But let me get another round in first.'

Once the wine is on the table, Epiphany begins.

'Of course, if I tell you, I'll have to kill you.'

'Absolutely. So, come on, spill the beans. Who's done what – allegedly?'

'A member of staff from the canteen has been spiking some of the coffees for the Rationalisation of Resources Sub-Committee with Viagra. Allegedly.'

'Good for them. I can think of a few members who might be grateful!'

Epiphany laughs out loud.

'That's not the best of it. The Chief Executive stood up to address their meeting and found he wasn't the only thing standing up. He didn't know whether to be proud or embarrassed!'

We finish our drinks and wrap up against the bitter cold outside.

'Oh, by the way, I forgot to say. Roni has a new boyfriend.'

'Blimey. What's this one like?'

Roni is Epiphany's younger sister and her absolute antithesis.

'No idea whatsoever, but we'll soon find out. He's coming to dinner two weeks on Saturday. And so are you.'

Chapter Eight

❦

Alice

The dripping tap was keeping time with the painful pounding in her head. They had had a row and she had lost her temper. The freshly baked chocolate cake mocked her from its blue and white plate on the table.

'I don't want your stupid, shitty cake!'

Had Mattie really said that? Her Mattie? No, he hadn't. He'd yelled it, just inches from her face. She could see the livid, mottled rash left by the scrape of that morning's razor on the edges of his chin, and smell the musk of teenage boy that no amount of cologne could hide. Alice sat down wearily and rubbed her temples with the palms of her hands. He had been late and it was dark and she was worried. That was normal, wasn't it? Any mother would be. But deep down she knew her fear was greater than that every time Mattie left the house. She was always afraid she would never see him again. She had found herself caught in a pendulum trance between the clock on the wall and the window. By the time he got home he was almost an hour late and her head was ready to explode. He had stopped at Sam's to see his new guitar. He hadn't rung her because he was THIRTEEN! He wasn't a kid.

Sam's mum was cool. She let Sam go into town on his own and *she* wasn't watching at the window for him to come home from school every day like some sort of nutcase stalker. And he didn't want her stupid, shitty cake!

Alice wiped the tears away with the back of her hand. This was new territory for her. Mattie had always been a sweet, biddable boy, but now she found herself living with a fractious, unpredictable teenager. She didn't even recognise his voice any more. He growled and squeaked alternately like a duet between a grizzly bear and a guinea pig. And tonight she had come very close to slapping him. Instead she had walked away. Into the garden and down to the fence that kept the brambles at bay. Mattie had stamped upstairs to his room, venting his fury onto every step of the stairs. From the garden, she could see him in the light of his bedroom window, dragging off his uniform and hurling it onto his bed. It was too cold to stay outside for long and so now she was back in the kitchen with the shitty cake wondering what to do next. She was the parent. She should know what to do and there was only her. No grandparents, no aunts, no uncles. No fairy godmothers. She checked the lasagne in the oven. It was beginning to burn around the edges, and the filling was starting to bubble over the sides. Perhaps he wouldn't want her shitty lasagne either. Alice turned the oven off.

A few moments later the kitchen door opened and Mattie shuffled in wearing his favourite old jogging bottoms and a sheepish smile. He looked so young again, more like her little boy. She took a deep breath.

'Mattie, I was worried. It gets dark so early, and there are only a couple of street lights out there. If you had rung me and asked, it might have been different. That's what your mobile is for. But you didn't and so I was afraid that something bad might have happened. To you.' She waited a while for her words to sink in before adding, 'Can you understand that?'

He nodded, keeping his eyes fixed on his feet.

'I'm sorry, Mum. I didn't mean to make you worry.'

When he was little he would have hugged her, but now he was too embarrassed. He stroked her arm roughly with the back of his hand; an awkward, loving gesture that made everything suddenly all right. Alice ruffled his hair – he was still her boy – and shook her head in mock despair.

'Well, I suppose I'll just have to chuck this away.' She picked up the plate with the cake on it and made towards the bin.

'Nooooo!' Mattie howled and swiped his finger through the chocolate icing before smearing it onto the tip of her nose.

After dinner, when Mattie's homework had been done, they sat together on the sofa watching *WALL-E* for the umpteenth time. It was a film about a small, sweet-natured robot left alone to clean up a post-apocalyptic Earth and Mattie had loved it ever since she had first taken him to see it at the cinema. The fact he still loved it reassured Alice that the spirit of her small, sweet-natured boy remained somewhere inside the body of this gangling youth beside her, and when the familiar happy ending played out as it should, she could have sworn he brushed a tear from his razor-sore cheek.

Chapter Nine

⁓

Masha

My parents' neat 1930s semi is a time machine. Each room transports me back to a different point in my past. On the wall in what used to be my bedroom, the poster of *Red Roofs* by Pissarro still clings resolutely to the wall. A little curled at the corners and tattered around the edges now, it was a present on my fourteenth birthday and back then was flanked on either side by Madonna and Boy George. The single bed is bare but I can still picture the rose-strewn eiderdown that used to cover it. It was the kind that, with its shabby chic credentials, would now fetch a fortune on eBay. I can still feel the prick on my skin when one of the feather quills poked through the silky material, and smell its powdery, Parma violet embrace when I snuggled beneath it on winter nights. Mum tried many times to persuade me to change it for a duvet, but it had come from my beloved grandma's house, and I refused to part with it. My white dressing table used to stand under the window, cluttered with the usual magpie miscellany that was the lifeblood of a teenage girl. Flashy bottles of perfume and gaudy nail polish, Maybelline mascara and eyeshadow, and a wooden music box containing a real silver charm bracelet and a tangle of cheap costume jewellery. It's all gone now, except for the empty bed and the poster, but these four walls still hold the essence of my teenage self.

Mum and Dad had planned to redecorate the room as a place for their grandson to stay. But before the stepladder could be brought in from the shed and the pasting table erected, their plans had been made obsolete. I never asked what happened to the Peter Rabbit wallpaper and matching bedlinen.

On the landing is a low, glass-fronted cabinet containing a collection of tiny animal ornaments that my dad bought for my mum while they were courting. The dogs were always my favourites, and when I was about six or seven I was occasionally allowed to take them out and play with them. Carefully. I used to re-enact *The Hundred and One Dalmatians*, or at least a rather loose interpretation of it, with a pair of pugs, a dachshund, a Great Dane and an indeterminate specimen, my preferred playmate, who looked like a cross between a sheep and a weasel. He's still in the cabinet, despite having lost a foot in one of our adventures. He was parachuting to the floor attached to a plastic rain hood to rescue one of the pugs from the evil clutches of a ferocious daddy-long-legs, and he miscalculated his landing, ricocheting off the edge of the coffee table during his descent. I stuck his foot back on with a tiny piece of bubble gum. Mum probably doesn't know, even now.

In the kitchen, the back wall of the pantry still bears patches of the wallpaper that is one of my earliest memories – a hideous brown, cream and orange repeat floral pattern – that once covered all the walls and was home high fashion when I was still in my high chair. Also in the pantry, somewhere at the back – probably hidden behind a dusty packet of cornflour, or tucked inside an empty cocoa tin – is a white china pie funnel in the shape of an elephant. It was originally my grandma's and Mum used it every time she made one of her apple and blackberry pies. As a little girl I loved it. And so did my little boy. Which is why it is now hidden out of sight for fear that it might summon up painful memories. But I know it's still here – somewhere. They couldn't bear to part with it, but nor can they bear to look it at.

Haizum bounds in through the back door, tail lashing furiously, and sets off in search of Mum, who is a soft touch when it comes to the contents of the fridge. Before I can wipe my feet on the doormat, she follows him back into the kitchen.

'Here's my big boy!' she greets him, cupping his head in her hands. 'I expect you're hungry, aren't you?' She opens the fridge and feeds him half a dozen cocktail sausages that he wolfs down without even chewing.

'Would you like a cup of tea, love?' She addresses me more cautiously.

'Thanks, Mum. Just a quick one. I've got loads to do. I just popped round with the name of the Chief Constable for Dad.'

I always do that. Pave the way for my departure when I've barely set foot in the door. I don't have to be back at work for at least an hour, but I can't be here without having a clear sight of the way out. I need to see the EXIT sign lit up in the dark, just in case I have to escape the other memories that resonate relentlessly here. I didn't have to come round. I could have phoned, but I do like to see them. And I know how much they love having Haizum around. But. I go through to the sitting room, leaving Haizum in the kitchen begging Mum for more sausages. This room seems closest to the present, but still feels as though it is snagged on the hook of that terrible moment that changed all our lives forever. It has a dual aspect, looking out onto both the front and back gardens, and today it is bathed in the tawny light of a sunny winter afternoon. I sit, as I always do, on the sofa that faces the front window, overlooking the closely cropped lawn and the privet hedge that shelters a flock of garrulous sparrows.

The photos used to have pride of place on the mantelpiece, but now they sit on top of the bureau in a shady corner of the room beside the back window. There are three of them. One was taken when he was just ten weeks old. He is in my arms, looking up into my face, and the tiny fingers of his left hand are curled around my thumb. If I look at the photo, my arms remember the warm, breathing weight of him, and the grip so hard on my thumb, as though he would never let it go. But I don't look. There is another of him in the back garden of this house, sitting on a blanket, legs splayed, playing with a ball. The third was taken just a week before he died. It is a studio shot of the proud grandparents with their precious grandson. The happy smiles before the heartbreak. It has never been mentioned – the migration of the photographs. There are lots of things we don't talk about now.

Haizum trots in looking very pleased with himself, followed by Mum carrying two mugs of tea.

'I've called your father twice now, but he's messing around with something in the garage, so if his tea gets cold it's his own fault.'

She hands me a mug and nudges a coaster nearer to me on the side table next to the sofa. As soon as she sits down in an armchair, Haizum plonks his head in her lap and stares up at her adoringly.

'How's my handsome boy, then?' she asks him, stroking his ears.

'Probably full of sausages, judging by the amount of time he spent with his head in your fridge,' I tease.

Haizum sighs contentedly, basking in the attention he is

receiving. Or perhaps he has indigestion. I wouldn't be at all surprised.

'He's a great big fella, so he needs to keep up his strength.'

Haizum demonstrates Mum's point by whacking her knee with one of his giant paws.

'This tea's cold!' Dad marches in, still wearing his cap and overalls, his nose red-tipped from the chill of the garage.

'I called you twice to come in, but either you're going deaf or you had the radio on too loud. In any case, there's more in the pot if you want a fresh one.'

Haizum trots after Dad, back into the kitchen, where I can hear the fridge door being opened again.

'You'll make him fat!' I call, but either Dad *is* going deaf or – much more likely – he is choosing to ignore me.

Mum plumps the cushion behind her and then picks up her mug from the table and takes a sip. 'Your father's going daft as well as deaf,' she mutters. 'This tea's still plenty hot enough. So, how's work? Are you busy?'

Nice and safe. These are the things we *do* talk about – work, Haizum, the weather. Whether it's garden rubbish bin collection this week, or orange recycling. These things we are comfortable with. The other things are always just a whisper away, but we never give them oxygen.

'Busy enough. I've had two new clients this week, which always helps.'

The mantle clock ticks steadily, marking the nearly but not quite comfortable pauses in our conversation. Mum is silently counting the ticks, but stops when she catches me watching her barely moving lips.

'Peggy next door is having her cataract seen to next week. I've promised to make her Ronald a chicken casserole to tide him over while she gets used to wearing a patch. She's worried she might not be able to cook without dropping things.'

'She'll have an eye patch, not her arm in a sling. She just fancies one of your home-cooked dinners instead of that microwave mush she usually serves up.'

The neighbours are a lovely couple, but cooking isn't something that Peggy has ever got the measure of.

'Don't you feed this hound of yours? He's starving.' Dad comes back in, minus his cap and with a fresh mug of tea in his hand. Haizum is following him, nudging at Dad's trouser pocket.

'He's clearly not starving; if anything he's getting a tad portly for a wolfhound. He just knows that you and Mum will spoil him rotten whenever he comes to visit.'

Haizum pushes his nose into Dad's pocket, causing him to slop tea over his hand onto his trousers. I grab Haizum's collar and address him sternly.

'Now that's enough, my lad. Sit down nicely or you'll be waiting for me outside!'

My attempt at discipline is wasted as Dad immediately springs to his defence with 'Oh, leave the daft bugger alone. He was only after the humbug that's in my pocket.'

He pulls the boiled sweet out to prove his point and Haizum is immediately by his side looking hopeful.

'Absolutely not!' I warn the pair of them. 'Especially as you never let me brush your teeth,' I add, to a crestfallen Haizum.

I drain my mug and stand up to hand Dad a piece of paper.

'Here are the Chief Constable's details. Now, don't go causing any trouble . . .'

I kiss each of my parents on the cheek. 'Don't come out. Stay and finish your tea.'

'What's left of it!' says Dad, ruffling the fur on Haizum's head.

On my way out through the kitchen, I pause at the back door and glance over towards the pantry. For a moment I'm tempted to go in and fetch the pie funnel. To hold it in my hand and feel the smooth, cold china on my skin. But I don't. I leave the bitter-sweet sepia world that my parents' home has become exactly as I found it.

Chapter Ten

Today's pool temperature is 8.7. In other words, absolutely freezing. I was in the pool for a grand total of ten minutes. Partly due to the icy water and partly because of the nosey parker in the wetsuit. I know that most people would find my behaviour in the pool a bit odd and I fully understand why. I swim to the deep end, disappear under the water, stay there for as long as I can and then swim back down the pool and get out. It's strange, I grant you, but I'm not doing anything wrong. It's not as though I'm taking a pee in the pool or ogling passing packages in Speedos. I don't expect to be questioned. This is England. But the woman in the wetsuit was Australian.

'Blimey, what's your game? It's a bit chilly to be playing fishes, isn't it?'

She must have got into the pool just after me and she is the reason why I am now sitting in the car park pretending to sing whilst Edith Piaf is throwing a wobbly. Edith Piaf is my car – a green and white Citroën 2CV. Like her namesake she is small and French, with huge eyes (headlamps) and can be a bit of a diva. Currently she is objecting to the cold and refusing to start, which is why I'm having to perpetrate this ridiculous charade while the Australian takes an age to unlock her bicycle from the cycle rack.

'I'm a singer. The underwater thing is just a way to improve my breathing technique.' As lies go, I was rather pleased with it at the time. She caught me on the hop. It was the first thing that came into my head and I thought it sounded pretty plausible. But I couldn't sustain it in conversation. I know nothing about 'proper' singing. So now I'm over-compensating in case the Australian is watching, whilst willing Edith to get her derriere in gear and start. I've even chosen 'Waltzing Matilda' as my pretend song. Finally, Edith gives a grudging splutter and shudders into life. *Merci beaucoup!*

Back home I leave Edith in the drive and walk to the corner shop. I didn't trust her to start again if I stopped at the shop on the way. Inside, Elvis is sitting on the floor, carefully examining the tins of tomato soup. Not the swivel-pelvis Elvis of Graceland, Memphis, Tennessee, but our local reincarnation of him. Our Elvis is in his late sixties and has slicked-back black hair and red cowboy boots. Today he is wearing a peaked leather cap, crushed velvet trousers and several coats of mascara. And our Elvis rides a bicycle. But not just any bicycle. It is a magnificent machine with coloured tassels attached to the end of the handlebars, a large wicker basket and an assortment of mirrors on long stalks that look like strange futuristic flowers. As a small girl I distinctly remember having two things at the top of my wish list before the days when the desperate longing for a pony eclipsed any other desire. I wanted a swimming costume with a little frilly skirt attached and coloured tassels for the handles of my bike. I was disappointed on both counts. Every time I see Elvis's bicycle I feel a ripple of envy and, on occasion, gently stroke the tassels as it stands outside the shop. I have even once contemplated grand theft bicycle. But then, I'd never get away with it. Everyone knows this is Elvis's dream machine.

Elvis is a discerning shopper. Today his list includes tomato soup, which means each tin must be removed from the shelf, scrupulously inspected, and then set down on the floor. Once all the tins have been examined, a selection will be made and the chosen tin will be placed in his shopping basket. Occasionally someone will tut ungraciously as they are forced to manoeuvre themselves around his seated form and selected groceries to reach the cornflakes, but regular customers take it in their stride. Literally.

The corner shop is a microcosm of the neighbourhood it serves. The shopping baskets filled with its products are small windows into the lives led by its customers. The tinned prunes and denture cleaner are for the inhabitants of the retirement flats on the corner. The sweets, crisps and fizzy drinks are bought by the younger pupils of the private girls' school just down the street; boisterous, self-assured creatures with Alice bands and ankle socks. Celebrity gossip magazines, bottles of flavoured water and lip gloss cater for the fifth and sixth formers; willowy adolescents, quieter, less assured but more disdainful. Cigarettes, cheap cider and Pot Noodles are favourites with the tenants of the nearby Housing Association flats, largely occupied by young, single, unemployed men. The smart, thirty-something professionals who live in the streets that run off the main road, in large houses brimming with newly acquired period features and bespoke furniture, buy lemongrass, truffle oil and goat's cheese for their dinner parties with other smart, thirty-something professionals with names like Hugo and Olivia.

Or perhaps I misjudge them.

Maybe the woman in top-to-toe Ted Baker, who is carefully selecting a ripe avocado to add to the crème fraîche, pimento-stuffed olives and organic chocolate already in her basket, is having a post-children, premenopausal, passionate affair with her snake-hipped, wet-lipped Zumba instructor. Maybe she is going home to change into her Agent Provocateur underwear. Maybe this woman and her afternoon lover will paint one another with the organic chocolate and then lick it off during the throes of wild and sweaty sexual intercourse. Maybe. But I'm definitely right about the people from the retirement flats. The tinned prunes are for digestive rather than sexual purposes. I am here to buy a bottle of wine, a custard doughnut, dog biscuits, a packet of mints and some tissues, which probably makes me a boozy, lonely, comfort-eating dog-lady with bad breath and chronic rhinitis.

Elvis is behind me in the queue, quietly singing to himself. The elderly woman at the counter is struggling with gnarled, arthritic fingers to prise a couple of pound coins from her purse to pay for a pint of milk and a packet of fondant fancies. I wonder if they will have fondant fancies at Happy Endings. The thought makes me feel ever so slightly sick. Coins flick out of the poor woman's uncooperative fingers and spin across the floor. Elvis retrieves them and places them gently into her veined and crooked hand with a flirty wink that brings a smile to her face.

On my way home I catch sight of him again, flying along on his beautiful bicycle. He is smiling at everyone he passes and singing loudly, the tassels on his handlebars fluttering in the wind. These simple pleasures make him a very rich man and it is the kind of wealth I envy. Happiness. I want to be happy again.

The wine I bought is for Epiphany's dinner party tonight. But thank God there is absolutely no danger of any Hugos or Olivias being there. There would be more chance of seeing Elvis – the one who died in 1977 – in attendance.

Chapter Eleven

～

Dinners are one of the most important forms of entertain-
ment. It is a greater compliment to be asked to dinner than to
a luncheon or afternoon or evening party.

Lady Troubridge

'Meet Hugo!' Sophronia, Ephipany's younger sister, is clearly besotted with her smirking companion. 'He's the love of my life!'

God help us.

Sophronia, which she prefers to be shortened to the more 'cool' Roni, is a startling contrast to Epiphany in every possible way. She is tall and voluptuous with a luxuriant mane of jet black hair, most of which used to belong to small orphan girls in India. Her hair extensions are complemented by eyes that are today so astonishingly turquoise that she is either wearing contact lenses or she has had cosmetic eye surgery (which is becoming increasingly popular, apparently – another fascinating nugget I picked up from Google). She has completed her latest very striking look with acrylic nails that could easily qualify as offensive weapons, more make-up than Boots sells on a busy Saturday morning and enough hairspray and perfume to asphyxiate an entire flock of coal-miners' canaries. She is what my grandma, with a disapproving 'tut', would have described as being very attractive in an 'obvious' way. Her dress is neither here nor there – literally. It is at least a size too small. For a twelve-year-old. Roni works in a call centre, but given her appearance I'm amazed she manages to do anything at all. Her cosmetic reconstruction must take hours each morning and then she has the formidable task of keeping it all intact. How she manages to get through the day without bits of her falling off, I can't begin to imagine.

I have a sneaking suspicion that Hugo is an estate agent and – this is just a hunch – a complete arse. He is wearing a bright pink shirt with comedy collar and cuffs, designer jeans, and a smile as sincere as a politician's promise. Still, he may just be nervous at meeting a group of new people.

'Nice place you've got here, Fanny,' he says, rather too loudly, to Epiphany. 'Sold one like this just last week for a small fortune to a couple moving out of London. Of course, it was interior-designed by a professional, not like yours, and didn't have all this old-fashioned clutter' (this said gesturing towards all Epiphany's treasured possessions), 'but with a bit of work and some top-quality fixtures and fittings, yours would shift for almost as much. Let me know if you think of selling, and I'll be happy to give you a few pointers.'

So, I was right on both counts. Epiphany swallows hard and replies with admirable self-restraint 'Thanks, I'll bear that in mind. And by the way, I much prefer Epiphany.'

Hugo is too busy assessing the market value of her home to reply.

Epiphany, looking gorgeous in a 1930s black and gold embroidered kimono, air-kisses me in her usual fashion and supplies me with a welcome glass of Sauvignon Blanc. She rolls her eyes in Hugo's direction, and I gurn sympathetically in return. Epiphany loves her sister dearly but is frequently obliged to resist the urge to throttle her. Roni is a sweet girl with beautiful teeth, astonishing breasts and no common sense whatsoever, which seems to leave her vulnerable to disastrous relationships with rather unpleasant men, and subsequent disappointments in affairs of the heart. Her back catalogue of boyfriends has led to a justifiable apprehension, for both Epiphany and me, about meeting any new ones, and Hugo's certainly not making the best first impression.

My fellow guests include Helen, a mutual friend and work colleague of mine, and her husband Albert, who is an astrophysicist. They have a delightful daughter, Julia, who at eleven years of age is already frighteningly beautiful and wise, and I am privileged to be her godmother; fairy or otherwise. I am very happy to see that my Edward and Lord Byron have already arrived and are elegantly sprawled across a chaise longue. Edward and I met on a training course years ago when I still worked for the local authority. The gentleman delivering the training had an unfortunate personal hygiene issue that might easily have been solved by washing, and possibly a clean shirt, but which he instead attempted to disguise with something that smelled suspiciously like pine disinfectant and a posture that kept his arms clamped ferociously to his sides. The course was held in a small, prefabricated classroom on one of the hottest days of the summer. Unable to bear the interminable monotony of the trainer's voice combined with his peculiar body odour, and completely uninspired by the complexities of compulsory competitive tendering, we spent a good part of the day bunking off and smoking Edward's cigarettes behind the wheelie bins. Fortuitously united by equally sensitive noses and low boredom thresholds, we have been inseparable ever since. Edward is a librarian of antiquarian books who has a particular interest in rare and precious historical volumes. He is a passionate collector of vintage children's books, a voracious reader of early twentieth-century literature and the man I love the most in the whole world. He is funny, clever, witty, acerbic and deeply in lust with Michael Bublé. Lord Byron is his small but perfectly turned-out smooth-haired English fox terrier. Lord Byron and Epiphany's cats have an understanding. They ignore each other totally and then probably bitch about each other horribly the next day. I join them on the chaise longue and scrounge one of Edward's cigarettes, which he smokes through a silver-tipped amber holder, flicking the ash into the aspidistra.

'I see Sophronia has come in her *fille de joie* outfit this evening. She obviously doesn't hold with the *ars est celare artem* school of thought when it comes to face painting.'

'Oh, come now Edward, don't be a spoilsport. If you're going to be insulting at least do it in English so I can understand.' Helen has joined us and leans in conspiratorially.

'How do you know I was being insulting if you didn't understand?' Edward replies, feigning offence.

'Because you were talking.'

'What I said was that Roni has come dressed as a lady of the night and doesn't believe in "less is more" when it comes to make-up.'

'Or cleavage, evidently. I bloody well hope I don't have to sit next to her. Her perfume is so strong I might just suffocate.'

Hugo has finished casting his professional eye over Epiphany's flat and swaggers over to join us.

'So, Edward, what car do you drive?'

'Actually, I don't.'

I don't think Hugo is really interested. He just wants to tell us about his.

'Just taken delivery of a brand new Beamer; dark blue; soft top; goes like shit off a shovel.'

I am struggling to find something polite to say in response, but for Epiphany's sake I dig deep. Bicycles with tassels on the handlebars are much more my specialist subject when it comes to transport, and the best I can manage is, 'That sounds very *practical.*'

But I needn't have worried. It soon becomes apparent that Hugo is very content with an audience rather than a conversation. Within ten minutes we have a comprehensive inventory of Hugo's prized possessions, including detailed information regarding his fully integrated, state-of-the-art home entertainment system, holiday apartment in Ibiza and signed copy of Kylie Minogue's *Showgirl: Homecoming Live* CD. We also know that he's a brilliant skier, can drink almost anyone under the table, has met Liam Gallagher, and can get free tickets to the local cinema because his cousin's the manager. Hugo is obviously a mover and shaker.

Stanley emerges from the kitchen and announces that dinner is ready. I am relieved to discover that I am not sitting next to Roni, and am therefore in no immediate danger of suffocation nor condemned to a conversation debating the merits and misdemeanours of various soap stars. She has been sandwiched between her new man and Epiphany. However, I am disheartened to find myself seated between Hugo, whom I'm afraid will spend the whole evening confirming his prize arse credentials, and Edward, who will spend the whole evening encouraging him. This seating arrangement has left me in something of a quandary.

Many years ago, Epiphany gave me *The Book of Etiquette (The Complete Standard Work of Reference on Social Usages)* by the gracious lifestyle icon Lady Troubridge as a birthday gift. I have been an ardent fan of the fabulous Lady T ever since. Her book provides invaluable guidance on all manner of thorny issues, such as the removal of gloves at the dinner table; when to bow or not to bow; how to treat one's servants, and what to wear for a stay on the Riviera. She has a particularly comprehensive set of rules relating to behaviour at mealtimes that includes how to eat various dishes – 'Birds should not be turned over and over on the plate, and no attempt should be made to eat the legs' – and how to ensure the entertainment of all one's guests. Lady T advises that 'the hostess must do her best to place a man who enjoys the sound of his own voice by a dull or silent woman'. Now, I'm fairly certain that Hugo will turn out to be a man who enjoys the sound of his own voice more than any other, but I am also aware that this is the first time that Epiphany has met him, so I shall not assume that I have been cast as silent or dull. However, Lady T goes on to say that 'the guest who accepts a dinner invitation should realise his responsibility to his hosts, and put himself to some trouble to entertain his neighbours, even though they are not such as he would have selected to sit by'. Bugger. That means I shall have to try to talk to him.

Lord Byron is seated at the table on the other side of Edward, and has his own linen napkin attached by a silver clip to his collar. He has a small silver bowl in front of him and waits with perfect manners for his dinner to be served. Having girded my loins and mustered all my powers of graciousness (which, it must be said, are limited at the best of times) by taking several swigs of wine, I turn to Hugo.

'So, tell me, Hugo, what made you become an estate agent?' Not very original, I know, but better than 'So, tell me, Hugo, why is it that you feel compelled to behave like a complete arse?'

'Well, to be honest' (now *that* would be a novelty for an estate agent), 'I just have a natural gift for dealing with people. They seem to trust me and I work really hard to be the best that I can be. I don't mind what I have to do to make sure I beat my targets.

I've won salesman of the month more times than anyone in our branch and the more I win, the more I earn.'

'That must be very rewarding,' says Edward.

I kick him under the table – sideways, which is a bit awkward. Hard.

'That's why I do it. The things I like to do cost money, and lots of it. "Work hard, play hard, stay hard", that's my motto.'

Hugo turns to me and winks at the 'stay hard' bit. Edward pinches my leg under the table. Hard. I take another swig of wine. The thought of a 'hard' Hugo is more than I can stomach. A change of subject is urgently required.

'What type of thing do you like to read, Hugo? Edward has a wonderful collection of antiquarian books. He's a librarian.'

Hugo laughs loudly as though I've just told a joke and replies, 'Books don't really do it for me; dust collectors as far as I'm concerned. If the story's any good, I'd rather wait 'til it comes out on DVD.'

I have a feeling that Edward is beginning to lose patience. His tone remains civil but his words betray just a whisper of rancour.

'Well, that's understandable, considering how much you spent on that fabulous home entertainment system of yours.'

'Damn right, Eddy. Come on, it must be as boring as hell shuffling books all day. It's not exactly the cut-and-thrust career a man really wants. Books look great in the library of some bloody great house that I'm trying to sell to people who want to pretend that they've got a bit of culture. But even they won't actually read them. They just want their friends to think they do.'

Hugo has just reduced one of Edward's greatest joys to the status of an interior design accessory and I am fighting the urge to spill something hot onto his crotch. Right on cue, Stanley serves the soup. And for Lord Byron there is a fat pork sausage cut into slices. He sniffs his food appreciatively and begins to eat. Hugo's soup spoon pauses in the dangerous drip zone midway between bowl and mouth, and I know at once that this is the defining moment. This is the moment when Hugo's fate will be sealed; the moment when he couldn't keep his mouth shut. Cometh the hour, cometh the arse.

'I can't believe you let your dog eat at the table. It's not very hygienic, is it?'

Houston, we have a problem. I watch a large drip of soup fall inevitably from Hugo's spoon and splosh onto his lurid pink shirt. The soup is blood red borscht, and he now looks as though he has a small puncture wound to his chest. Given time, Hugo's mouth and the selection of cutlery on the table, he may soon actually have one.

'Lord Byron always dines with us, at the table, and don't worry – he's had all his inoculations, so he's unlikely to catch anything from you.'

Edward's expression is friendly, but his tone is glacial. His patience has finally run out. At this point most people would have taken the hint; changed the subject; just shut up. But not Hugo. And he chooses the least appropriate person to serve as his ally. He turns to me.

'Don't you find it ridiculous the way some people treat their animals as though they're people?'

'Indeed I do, Hugo,' I reply. 'I find it astonishing that otherwise perfectly sensible people can believe that it's appropriate to treat their dogs or cats as derisively as though they were mere humans. It is perfectly clear to me that Lord Byron is far more intelligent than many people I've met, and his manners are unquestionably superior.'

Hugo cachinnates (word of the day – *to laugh loudly or immoderately*), which is not a good response.

'Roni warned me that her sister's friends are somewhat eccentric. I think you're all barking mad.'

I'm pretty sure Lady T would take a very dim view of biffing a fellow dinner guest, so I may have to sit on both my hands if this continues.

'Let me assure you that nothing I have said was with the intention of deliberately amusing you.'

Once again Hugo finds my reply immensely diverting and snorts with laughter like a truffle pig with a cocaine habit. Edward has been watching this exchange with barely concealed fury at Hugo's rudeness, but now I see mischief glinting in his eyes. His tone is almost genial as he asks Hugo, 'And in what way, exactly, do you find us "eccentric"?'

'Well, for starters, the clothes you wear are what most normal people would consider to be fancy dress!'

Hugo clearly believes himself to be a wit and a wisecracker. The word I'm thinking of also begins with a W. Bearing in mind his hideous, soup-splattered shirt, this man has got more front than Blackpool. But he hasn't finished yet.

'And you express views that you obviously can't really believe, just to be shocking and entertaining.'

I wonder at this moment if he would find a sharp blow to the testicles shocking and entertaining in equal measure.

'For example?' Edward encourages Hugo to open his mouth a little wider, so that he can shove his own foot even further inside. Hugo leans back in his chair, preparing to deliver some further considered words of wisdom.

'For example, the whole doggy thing. I mean, I suppose they're quite cute, those pampered little pooches,' he gesticulates condescendingly in Lord Byron's direction, 'but they're too small to be proper dogs.'

'And what about Masha's wolfhound? Is he a "proper" dog?' asks Helen, who has been listening to the conversation with increasing irritation.

'Well, that's a whole different ball game!' Hugo turns to me with a lecherous grin.

'Size really *does* matter.' He holds up his empty wine glass to indicate that it needs refilling and then continues: 'But of course, most of these spoilt doggies are simply child substitutes, for people who can't handle the real thing.'

There is a brief but exquisitely awkward silence, before Roni explains.

'Hugo has a little girl, Sophie. She lives with her mum, but comes to stay with him every third weekend.'

I feel rather than see the anxious glances, all in my direction, and under the table, Edward takes my hand and gives it a little squeeze. At this point I excuse myself. In the safety of Epiphany's wonderful downstairs loo, I try to blink back the guilty tears that are threatening to embarrass me. The walls of this little room are covered in strange and wonderful pictures cut from magazines, inspirational and hilarious quotations, and anything else that takes Epiphany's fancy. The windowsill is full of kitsch knick-knacks and the tiny window is framed with coloured fairy lights in the shape of flowers which are reflected in the mirror on the back of the door. The woman I see reflected in the mirror is a selfish, self-pitying fool, little better than horrid Hugo. That exquisite silence was entirely my fault.

Today would have been my son's fourteenth birthday, and for all these years, this is what I have put my friends through. I have condemned them to a crippling carefulness in order to spare my feelings, and it has taken Hugo's big mouth to make me realise it. My grief has become an addiction; a bad habit like a tattered comfort blanket that I have hung on to for far too long. It has to stop. I look in the mirror again, and try to see my face as a stranger would see it. It has all the requisite physical components to make it reasonably attractive; green eyes, full but well-shaped lips and a strong, straight nose. But there is no spark or spirit behind those eyes, and there is an expression of ingrained defeat haunting every gaunt contour of that woman's face. That woman in the mirror is not me. She is the spectre that I have allowed myself to become and I don't want to be her any more. I want to be the old Masha; the one I pray to God is still hiding inside me somewhere, hanging on by the tips of her fingernails. On the way back to the dining room, I meet Epiphany taking soup bowls back to the kitchen. She looks worried.

'Are you okay?' she asks.

It has to stop.

Back at the table, Stanley is serving pea and mint risotto. After a few mouthfuls Hugo blows his nose on his napkin. Lady T is fearfully hot on 'ugly tricks at meals', and I'm pretty sure this would qualify. But Epiphany is clearly determined to be a gracious hostess to the bitter end and turns to Hugo.

'So, Hugo, what's been the most difficult house you've had to sell?'

She does a reasonable job of sounding genuinely interested, considering the fact that Hugo has talked incessantly, enthusiastically and exclusively about himself since he arrived. The only relief from this relentless, self-congratulatory monologue has been the occasional insult or derisory remark fired at one of her other guests.

'I never have a problem selling any property.'

Why are we not surprised?

'It's a gift,' he continues, 'that I happen to have. You just have to know what to tell the buyers and what to leave out.'

'But isn't there some sort of code of practice now, designed to protect us mere mortals from the wily ways of estate agents with their beguiling descriptions, and craftily cropped and airbrushed photographs?' asks Helen, who has recently been thinking of moving.

'It's rumoured that such a document exists, but I certainly don't lose any sleep over it.'

Hugo's ability to mind his manners is deteriorating in direct proportion to the amount of wine that he is pouring down his throat. Never mind that politeness didn't appear to be his forte in the first place. He continues with his mission to enthral us with the glamour and excitement of his job.

'I've had a few dodgy moments in my time, I can tell you.'

'And I'm sure he's going to,' I whisper to Edward.

Hugo pauses dramatically for a moment to adjust the huge cuffs on his horrid pink shirt, and I notice that his cufflinks bear the words 'shaken' and 'stirred'; 007 would be so proud.

'One time, I arrived at this house a bit early for the viewing. While I was waiting for the prospective buyers to turn up, I thought I'd check out the lingerie department in the master bedroom. I'd met the vendors, and the wife was really fit. My guess was La Perla, Agent Provocateur, and a little bit of Ann Summers for those saucy weekends away. I'm a bit of an expert on ladies' underwear; especially getting them out of it.'

Hugo winks at me. Again. But this time it is accompanied by a sweaty hand squeezing my thigh. At this juncture I want to punch Hugo very hard indeed. My reserves of graciousness are completely drained and I am now running on vapour. Edward is choking with laughter and Epiphany swiftly draining her wine glass. Albert is staring intently into his risotto, and Roni is gazing adoringly at Hugo, oblivious to the fact that everyone else thinks he's an arrogant, lecherous oaf. Hugo clearly believes that we are all in awe of his daring and continues, 'Anyway, I was just getting started and the wife came home unexpectedly and nearly caught me.'

'That's appalling!' Stanley leans back in his chair and shakes his head in disbelief.

'I couldn't agree more, mate!' Hugo isn't quite following Stanley's line of thought here. 'I'd only managed a quick rummage in one drawer before she barged in.'

Stanley leans forward and fixes Hugo with a hard stare. 'Are you seriously suggesting that it's acceptable for someone in your position to rifle through the personal possessions of one of your clients?'

'I like to call it perks of the job, mate. Perks of the job.'

For the briefest of moments there is an embarrassed silence where each of us, excluding Roni, tries to fathom whether we are still obliged to be gracious, or whether the line in the sand has been crossed and, regardless of Lady T's advice, the gloves are now off. Stanley is the first to decide.

'Well, I'd call it sleazy knicker-fiddling,' he says quietly, shaking his head in disgust.

Hugo is now slightly confused. It has never occurred to him that someone could seriously question his complete fabulousness, especially as the more wine he drinks the more convinced of it he becomes.

'You need to lighten up a bit, mate. Live dangerously for once.'

Hugo is speaking just a tiny bit more slowly now in a valiant attempt to stop his words slurring together, but his sentences are sliding off a tongue made dangerously slippery by excess alcohol, and his efforts are in vain.

'I'll fetch dessert,' says Stanley through grimly gritted teeth.

Moments later, Hugo looks uncannily like the former Soviet president Mikhail Gorbachev. Having drunk himself into a state of semi-consciousness, he has fallen forward into his dessert of blackcurrant fool – how apposite – and, having been propped back up by the solicitous Roni, is now sporting a rather jaunty purple birthmark across the front of his head. He snores loudly through cigars and coffee, listing and swaying precariously in his chair. He is saved from falling only by Roni, who checks and steadies him like a ventriloquist with her dummy.

Lady T advises that should any accident occur at the table it should be 'ignored as far as may be by host, hostess and guests'. We are all, with the possible exception of Roni, delighted to ignore Hugo. Roni tells us all about her new hobby, Raq Sharqi, which is apparently a form of Egyptian belly dancing, and offers to perform for us next time we are all together.

'Heaven forbid,' whispers Helen. 'I'd rather have cystitis.'

Eventually Roni orders a taxi and attempts to rouse Hugo and get him on his feet. Albert gallantly comes to her assistance and holds him up while Roni drapes his coat over his shoulders. As Albert leads Hugo to the door, Roni clutches my arm.

'I'm so sorry. He didn't mean anything by it – the dogs instead of children thing. He's just drunk.' She looks genuinely upset and I feel terrible. Edward steps into the breach.

'Don't be daft, darling!' he says, throwing his arm around her shoulders and giving her a comforting squeeze. 'It was the wine talking. We could barely make out what he was saying anyway.'

I give her a hug before she follows Hugo and Albert down the drive.

'That's the most animated Albert's been all night. And it's all down to Hugo's departure!' Edward remarks to Epiphany and me, as we are trying and spectacularly failing not to giggle at

Hugo desperately clinging to Albert, who is looking increasingly uncomfortable and irritated. Lord Byron, who is surveying the situation with obvious disdain, calmly walks up to Hugo and cocks his leg. Nobody else appears to notice, so I feel Lady T would advocate that on this occasion, discretion is the better part of valour. I say nothing.

Following Hugo's and Roni's unsteady departure, we all congratulate Epiphany on her extraordinary graciousness in the face of extreme provocation, and thank both Epiphany and Stanley for their hospitality. Another taxi arrives for Helen and Albert, and amid the affectionate farewell hugs and kisses, Albert, who as usual has hardly uttered a word all evening, winks at me and mutters, 'That Hugo! Bloody man's a complete arse.'

Edward and Lord Byron are walking me home. It is clear, cold and still, and our footsteps echo along the street as we stroll, arm in arm, under the vast starry sky.

'Are you okay?' Edward asks me as we reach my front gate.

'Of course I am.'

I kiss him on both cheeks and the top of Lord Byron's head. Edward hugs me hard and then looks straight into my eyes, as though he is searching for something. For a fleeting moment I feel that there is something else he wants to say. The words, unspoken, hang between us like a breath in the night air, and then they are gone. Perhaps I have frightened them away. Edward waits until my key is in the door, and then sets off to complete their short walk home.

'By the way,' I call after him, 'your dog weed up Hugo's leg.'

I can hear him laughing all the way down the street.

Chapter Twelve

Today's pool temperature is 8.5, the sky is the colour of cement and it is raining hard. And today I need pain to punish me. Because tomorrow is Christmas Eve and it is therefore the law that everyone must be happy. We must all wear scratchy jumpers emblazoned with snowmen or penguins or reindeer. We must eat our own body weight in seasonal poultry, pies and puddings. We must pull crackers, watch *Doctor Who* and pretend that we love the padded, scented coat hangers that our stingy colleague has re-gifted to us in the secret Santa. And we must drink snowballs. It's the law. And I will, I promise. I will try to be happy and not notice when guilt comes tapping on my shoulder as it always does. But to pay for tomorrow, today I must drown. Almost.

There are only two other people in the pool and no sign of the Australian, but if she does appear, this time I'm ready for her. My lungs squeeze and burn while the cold, deep water soothes my mind, but I'm careful not to stay too long. I learned that lesson the hardest way several years ago. After one minute and fifty-five seconds timed on my diver's watch I burst back onto the surface and swim to the shallow end. The rain stings my goosebumped skin as I hurry back to the changing rooms. Dried and dressed I emerge clutching the book. The book I carry in case I meet the Australian. You see, I'm an addict. And like most addicts, I'm devious. I cover my tracks. The book is called *Techniques to Improve Your Singing.*

In the empty car park, Edith Piaf starts first time and I praise her fulsomely. On the radio a children's school choir is singing 'Rudolph the Red-Nosed Reindeer'. I switch to another channel. My little boy never made it to school. He only had two Christmases. His first was as a tiny baby and his second when he was still barely old enough to know what was going on. That was when we gave him the rocking horse; Edward and I. He was too small to ride it alone, but when we held him in the saddle he kicked and squealed with delight. He had no idea it was Christmas, but he loved his present. I coax Edith into first gear and then into second and head out of the car park. It has finally stopped raining and the pale winter sun is a faint smudge of brightness behind the glowering clouds. I need to get a move on. Haizum is due at the vet in half an hour to get his nails clipped. I had the back seat removed from Edith Piaf when I bought her, to accommodate Haizum. He is delighted with his customised mode of transport. I'm pretty certain he thinks that the car is his and I'm merely the chauffeur.

Patience behind the wheel is not one of my virtues and the woman in the car ahead is already annoying me. She is a ditherer, barely nudging twenty-five miles an hour. Edith is spluttering in third gear. The woman needs to stop chatting to her passenger and concentrate on her driving. The traffic lights ahead are green but we'll never reach them before they change. My knuckles are turning white on the steering wheel and I'm itching to blast the horn, but I manage to restrain myself. I do shout, however. She can't hear me, so where's the harm? And it makes me feel better. Sure enough, the lights change to red as we pull up in front of them, and I finish my remonstrative tirade with a delicious triple expletive. The man in the lane alongside me is agog. I hope he can't lip read. Perhaps I should pretend that I'm singing again. I bet the woman has put her vehicle into neutral and applied the handbrake, and I bet she's never done a handbrake turn in her life. It was one of the first things I attempted having passed my test and been trusted to drive Dad's Mini by myself. He didn't notice the scratch from the collision with a bollard for two days. The car in front has a small dent in the rear wing. Someone probably drove into it while the woman was having a dither.

We make it to the veterinary surgery with a couple of minutes to spare and then spend half an hour in the waiting room while the two vets on duty battle through their lists, overfilled with the pre-Christmas rush of pet owners reluctant to risk an exorbitant bank holiday call-out fee. Haizum would rather not be here. He is making his feelings known by howling and trying to climb into my lap. Behaviours that, when performed by a quivering wreck of a wolfhound weighing 180lbs, can be a little disturbing. The woman who was sitting next to me holding a perky-looking miniature dachshund has moved to the opposite side of the room and is tutting disapprovingly. There is a brief hiatus and then *someone's* dog passes wind. At first it is hardly noticeable; a transitory pungent puff barely troubling the nostrils. But it soon develops into something much worse. It has a definite twang of Brussels sprout. Very festive. Of course, nobody says a word but I blame the dachshund, whose owner appears to find the smell exceedingly sternutative (word of the day – *causing sneezing*). But I think that's a diversionary tactic that simply confirms the dachshund's guilt. Haizum's appointment lasts little longer than five minutes and is a painless procedure, rewarded, as usual, by a handful of biscuits. On the way out he swaggers jauntily past the nervous patients still waiting to go in, before lunging through the revolving door out into the car park.

Back home he settles down in front of the fire to recover from his ordeal while I decorate the small Christmas tree that I bought on impulse yesterday; a living one because I love the smell, and because it is proof that I want to change my life. I'm not sure how I'm going to do it just yet. I don't have a plan, just a feeling. A feeling that this, the way I'm living now, is not enough. Not any more. And only I can change it.

This is the first tree I have bought since my little boy died. That first Christmas without him, Mum and Dad wanted me to spend the day with them, but I refused. I told them I'd be fine. That I just needed to be by myself. High days and holidays were like a dentist's drill on a tooth with an abscess. And Christmas was the worst. Because Christmas is all about children – advent calendars, carol concerts, visits to and from Santa, nativity plays. Jesus Christ – you can't get away from it. So, that first 25 December, soused in self-pity and furious with the relentless festive cheer, I killed Christmas. I lit a fire in the sitting-room grate and, one by one, I burnt every single Christmas decoration in the house. I threw every Christmas card into the flames, followed by every unopened gift I had received. I stared into the inferno I had created and watched paper curl and crumble, plastic melt, foil dissolve and glass pop and shatter. And I drank vodka. A lot of vodka. Edward came and found me halfway through the bottle and about to set fire to a large poinsettia – a gift from a well-meaning neighbour. He never told a soul. But he also said that if I ever did anything like it again, he would tell everyone that not only had he found me drunk and setting fire to things, but that I had wet my knickers and been sick on the carpet. I don't think I had, but I've never been completely sure, and so I took Edward at his word and stick to outside bonfires now.

When I was a little girl the Christmas tree was always my

domain. Dad would wind the fairy lights through the branches first and put the angel on the top and then the tree was mine. I am the only child of two only children. My parents were delighted and, I suspect, a little over-awed when I was born. I wasn't spoilt exactly, but I was raised on a very long leash. A spirited child full of strange ideas and vivid dreams, I would single-handedly put on plays and pantomimes for my parents and an audience of assorted dolls and teddy bears, and my imaginary friends far outnumbered my real ones. I expect my lovely, sensible, conventional parents were rather startled by the wild and whimsical daughter their combined genes had conspired to create. By the time I had finished with the Christmas tree it usually looked like an explosion in a tinsel factory, and one year I covered it in clothes pegs. To their credit they never changed it. They never waited until I was safely tucked up in bed before tweaking it a little to resemble more closely a customary Christmas conifer.

This year I'm going to decorate this tree for Gabriel, to fill a little of the void left by the memories we never made of the Christmases we never had. But also in the hope that, just maybe, some Christmas in the future might be truly happy.

Chapter Thirteen

～

Alice

Alice was a very careful driver. Especially when Mattie was in the car. And today she wasn't sure where they were going, which made her more cautious than usual.

'Come on, Mum! I'm going to be late.'

Mattie was leaning forward in the passenger seat as though his posture might quicken their progress. They were on their way to a football match at a school on the other side of town, and Mattie was on the team. Kick-off was in forty-five minutes but Mattie had to be there at least half an hour before that. Alice peered at the street signs through the grubby glass of the windscreen, trying to get her bearings. At least it had stopped raining. As they pulled up at a set of traffic lights, Alice asked Mattie to read out the directions again. Finally! Just ahead she could see the name of one of the streets they were looking for. Mattie was drumming his feet impatiently in the footwell. He longed to be old enough to drive, but he certainly didn't want his mum to teach him. She was too slow; far too careful. She would probably make him drive round and round a car park for the first six months.

They arrived at the school with just minutes to spare and Alice had barely parked before Mattie leapt out of the car and sprinted off, lugging his sports bag over his shoulder. Alice stayed in the car. There was no point getting out now and standing in the cold. Besides, she might bump into some of the other parents and be forced to make small talk. Alice preferred her own company. She switched on the radio. A children's choir was singing carols. Mattie had had a lovely singing voice but he'd dropped out of the school choir last year when his schoolboy soprano began to misbehave with the onset of puberty. In any case he was growing up fast, and hanging around with his friends kicking a ball or riding bikes was far more appealing these days than practising a three-part harmony for the local music festival. Alice switched the engine back on and turned up the heater. It was getting really chilly. She searched in her bag for her gloves and caught sight of the brown envelope that she had shoved in there without opening when it had arrived with that morning's post. Her stomach tipped like a seesaw when one child dismounts. She was afraid that her old life had finally caught up with her. That it was time to pay for what she'd done. But it was Christmas and she didn't want it ruined. She would open it after Boxing Day. Besides, it would probably be nothing. Everything would be fine.

The rain had started again; not heavy, but enough to make you thoroughly wet if you were out in it. It rattled on the car roof and doodled watery squiggles down the windscreen. Alice checked her watch and sighed. Twenty minutes to kick-off and then another ninety minutes standing on the touchline in the cold, cheering Mattie on. Alice had much preferred it when Christmas had meant coming to watch him in the nativity play or Christmas concert. Unlike Alice, Mattie was a natural performer and loved being centre stage. His innkeeper had brought the house down with his ad lib to Joseph of 'Don't you know it's Christmas? It's our busiest time of year!' She pulled on her gloves and buttoned the neck of her parka.

Never mind. She consoled herself with the thought that this evening, after tea, they were going to decorate the tree. It was artificial, but looked every bit as good as a real one without the annoyance of needles dropping all over the carpet or the inconvenience of finding a way to dispose of it after Twelfth Night. They always decorated the tree together and Alice loved sharing this special Christmas ritual with her son. When Mattie had been small, Alice would wait until he was in bed and then rearrange the ornaments in a more even distribution over the tree. He tended to hang them in a cluster dictated by how high he could reach, but now he was taller than Alice, and it was his job to place the star on the very top of the tree.

The match was a nil-nil draw. Mattie had scored the only goal, but it was disallowed by the referee, who was a teacher at the home team's school. He was still fuming at what he perceived to be a terrible injustice when he flung his sports bag onto the back seat and slammed the car door. Alice had no idea whether the referee's decision had been justified, but she was pretty sure that the yellow card he had shown to her son as a result of his subsequent prolonged and aggressive protest was completely fair. She had been aware of some of the other parents glancing furtively in her direction and had felt her cheeks redden. The man standing next to her, who was the father of one of Mattie's team mates, shook his head in disbelief.

'Bloody ref should have gone to Specsavers! There was nothing wrong with your lad's goal.' Alice was ridiculously grateful for his support.

Mattie slumped into the passenger seat beside her, glowering. She didn't want to fight with him tonight.

'Bloody ref should have gone to Specsavers!' she repeated. Mattie very rarely heard her swear, and knew full well that she understood next to nothing about the rules of football. The grin he fought so hard with his teenage pride to keep from his face eventually defeated him and the storm broke.

'Can we have fish and chips for tea?'

Alice fastened her seat belt and turned the key in the ignition.

'Of course we can.'

Chapter Fourteen

～

Masha

Now more than ever seems it rich to die
To cease upon the midnight with no pain
In loving memory of Marie,
cherished daughter of Maud and Francis
Delivered from her pain at last
and sleeping peacefully with the angels

I often wonder about little Marie. I rather hope that having finally escaped her pain, she is doing something a little more exciting than sleeping peacefully with the angels. I like to think of her as dancing or trampolining or riding ponies with them. Hers is one of the many graves I visit regularly, with its carved lilies on a headstone that, this afternoon, glints in the silver sunlight of the last day of an old year. On the grave itself there is a white marble figure of a sleeping child watched over by two angels. Each delicate curl on her head has been lovingly coaxed from the cold hard stone until it seems as if it would be ruffled by the softest of breezes. Today, as always, I cannot resist stroking her sleeping head. She looks as though the gentlest touch could wake her; so close to life yet so long dead.

Of course, Keats has been taken out of context. Actually, he is contemplating suicide. He says in the same poem, 'I have been half in love with easeful Death'.

Me too.

There have been times since my beloved boy died that I have thought about it. Not in the fanciful and romantic way Keats describes it, but simply as the most practical option. Just to stop living a life I no longer wanted. I never wanted children. My son was not planned, nor was his father the love of my life. They were both mistakes. But whilst one lost his sparkle as quickly as Christmas tinsel on New Year's Day, the other lit an unexpected spark of fear and excitement. I double-dared myself to see it through. I needn't have worried. My fear, like grit in an oyster, turned into a love as pure and perfect as any pearl as soon as I saw his crumpled face. He was an angel and I named him Gabriel. But I wasn't reborn or transformed into a *Blue Peter* presenter overnight. I had no intentions of 'settling down' to a sensible life and I still wasn't that fond of children, but this tiny boy became my life. I loved him fiercely to make amends for the fact that I hadn't wanted him enough at the start.

His death was my apocalypse.

After the initial, searing pain, there were days of dark, falling, numbness and then the agony would return. And so began the endless, uncontrollable merry-go-round. Excruciating days of hell on earth when I retched and cried until my throat bled, followed by senseless days of living death when I couldn't even crawl out of bed. When Gabriel died, I wasn't there. I failed him at the last. I will never know if he screamed for help or if he struggled. If it was quick and painless, or slow and agonising. It was the things I didn't know that tortured me and threatened to unravel my sanity, and so I found out as much as I could. I became an expert on drowning.

Next year I must try harder at swimming.

This wonderful cemetery, where little Marie is buried, was opened in 1855. I know this because I've been swotting up. I spend so much time here that I've decided to make myself useful. I intend to volunteer as a Friend of the cemetery. Given my natural aversion to joining things, I don't want to be on any committees; I just want to do something, preferably on my own, to be helpful. I quite fancy myself as a tour guide, showing people around the cemetery and pointing out graves of particular interest. But before I offer my services I want to make sure that I'm up to the job. So I'm practising what I might say. For example, I might introduce my tour by explaining that the cemetery was designed to look 'natural' with its meandering paths and informal tree-planting, and that the aim was to create a landscaped park, but with aspects of the cosy and familiar churchyard to accommodate the Victorian notions of the contemplative tomb and the domesticated dead. Although I'll probably have to find a slightly slicker way of saying it if I don't want to bore my tourists to death before they've got through the gate.

Marie's parents probably visited her every week to keep the grave pretty and tidy. It must have brought them some comfort and I can't help but envy them that. But now she belongs to my family too. She is one of my 'Family on the Other Side', as Edward calls the people whose graves I visit regularly. I have adopted them, one by one, over the years, for a variety of reasons. Some because I am touched by the brief details on the headstone; others because I am drawn by the beauty of the monument; others simply because they look forlorn and long forgotten, and in need of a visitor. All because I have no grave for my own son.

My second visit today is to Dear Little Colin who died aged eleven in 1913 and was at least spared the pain of losing his father just two years later in the desperate trenches of the First World War. His headstone is crowned with a daisy chain carved into the stone, and bears the inscription 'The souls of the righteous are in the hands of God'. Let's hope so.

Sapper W. W. Ralph is buried near the bottom of one of the rows of graves that run vertically from the chapel towards the park. I visit him on behalf of his mother, Sarah, who will certainly be dead herself by now, just in case she has not been reunited with him. Sapper Ralph died in Mesopotamia in 1917, of heatstroke, aged twenty-two. He was interred in the British Cemetery in Baghdad, and I think it unlikely that Sarah or his father, Thomas, were ever able to visit him there, which is why they had a memorial erected in my cemetery. I picture their young son delirious with fever, dreaming of his mother's cool, comforting hands on his face and a glass of ice-cold, home-made lemonade, whilst dying beneath the sweat-soaked sheets of an Army hospital bed thousands of miles from home. Of course, it's entirely possible that Sarah was a dreadful fishwife and Sapper Ralph dreamed of a large glass of beer and a final night of passion with a big-breasted woman called Gloria. But I'm basing my opinion of their characters on the only clues I have, which are the tasteful design of the headstone and the poignant words written in his memory.

It is getting chilly now and I'm ready for home. Edward is throwing a party tonight and Haizum and I are both invited. For once, I'm looking forward to New Year's Eve. In fact, for once, I'm trying to look forward instead of longing for the past. Another wasted year has almost slipped away, but I'm determind that next year is going to be different. Haizum cocks his head as a disembodied snatch of music floats past. He turns and searches for the source of the sound, pulling me with him. There is a distant figure standing in a higher part of the cemetery with her arms flung open and her head held high. Singing. She is singing. It looks like Sally. I am too curious to walk away but approach using a circuitous route, so as not to intrude or (heaven forbid!) appear nosey. It *is* Sally. She seems to be directing her performance towards a group of Italian graves covered in lanterns and bright silk flowers, and is engaging with the headstones exactly as if they were her audience. I recognise the tune, but the words are in Italian, apart from the odd, random English expletive. It is a bizarre scene, but strangely beautiful. I don't know whether to stay or try to slip quietly away. As Sally hits a particularly high note, Haizum decides to harmonise, throwing back his head and howling like a banshee, which soundly scuppers any chance we had of making a discreet exit. Sally sees us and acknowledges me with a slight nod, but she is totally immersed in her music and Haizum continues as her enthusiastic accompanist As they reach their final crescendo, a scattering of crows bursts skyward from the canopy of one of the firs and Sally bows deeply to the sound of their wings' applause.

As the crows fly off into the park Sally grabs a red rose from one of the graves, picks up her bag from the ground and heads towards us. The sun is low in the sky now, and the leaden clouds are backlit with gold. Haizum greets Sally with the affection that he reserves for those whom he associates with food, and tries to push his nose inside her bag, searching for bread.

'Daft silly fucker.' She rubs his head and fishes out a crust for him. She hands me the rose and takes my arm – which catches me by surprise – and she walks me towards the gate.

'Your singing was lovely,' I tell her.

'Him too!' she replies, nodding at Haizum.

This woman should, by rights, scare the bejesus out of me. She shouts and swears, sings to dead people, steals flowers from graves and is clearly as mad as a jumping jack. *And* she's touching me (remember my aversion to gratuitous hugging?). But I think I like her. She is like a naughty best friend at school who will lure you into mischief but will always have your back. Maybe we could form a double act and my guided tours of the cemetery could include musical interludes courtesy of Sally. In the park the crows are waiting on the grass and Sally flings the bread at them as though she is sowing seeds. By the time her bag is empty, it is getting dark and the silent park is falling asleep under a blanket of shadows. As I leave her at the bus stop I wish her a happy New Year. She bends and kisses Haizum on the head and then turns and salutes me.

'Bugger my boots and knees up Mother Brown!'

I couldn't have put it any better myself.

Chapter Fifteen

⟋

Today's pool temperature is 6.3 degrees, and this morning I'm swimming not drowning. I'll do ten lengths and then treat myself to a flat white coffee and a blueberry muffin before heading off to work. Since my epiphany at Epiphany's dinner party, I've been trying to change. Christmas was hard, as it always is, with memories divided into 'befores' and 'afters'. Even the happy ones, when my boy was still alive, are now bordered in black, like mourning stationery. But it's a new year and things are going to be different. It's not easy. I'm still an addict and some days I succumb to the merciless cravings. Then, once again, I can be found crouching underwater at the deep end. But not today. Today the sting of cold water on my bare skin is exhilarating, reminding me with every stroke I take how very much alive I am. And lucky to be so. There are only a handful of other swimmers in the pool. Epiphany would very much approve of the man I keep passing in the lane next to mine. With his broad shoulders and powerful legs, he is, to borrow her words, scything through the water like an Olympian.

The high from swimming in such cold water is intoxicating and I am disappointed when my ten lengths are done, but my fingers are beginning to go white at the tips and it is time for me to get out. Dried and dressed, I order my breakfast from Flo, the woman who serves in the lido café.

'You ought to be having a bloomin' great fry-up after swimming in that freezing pool,' she exclaims, as she tops up my coffee with steamed milk. Flo is everyone's mother, dispensing advice, whether it's wanted or not, to all her customers in the same no-nonsense tone.

'I expect that's what you'll be having,' she says to the person waiting behind me to be served. It's the Olympian.

'Next time, Flo,' he answers with a grin.

'That's what you always say. Let me guess – Americano to go?'

I take my order over to a table overlooking the pool while Flo prepares his drink. I hate to admit it, but I'm disappointed that his order is to go. He looks just as good with his clothes on as he does without them, and there is something very warm about the tone of his voice. And by warm, what I actually mean is sexy. I suddenly realise that I'm staring and turn my attention to the singing book I have with me just in case the Australian turns up. As I flick idly through the pages I'm reminded of Sally singing to the Italians in the cemetery. I'm certainly no expert, but from what I could tell, she can sing very well. I'm inexorably drawn to Sally. Every time I go to the park or the cemetery, I find myself seeking out her raggedy figure through the dark trees or amongst the gravestones, hoping that she'll talk to me or, if her words are ferhoodled (word of the day – *mixed up, muddled*), simply walk with me. Her idiosyncrasies are strangely comforting, as though they somehow excuse or at least diminish my own.

When the Olympian has gone, coffee in hand, Flo comes over to wipe the top of the perfectly clean table next to mine.

'He'd just do for you,' she says to me, with a wink. As I said: advice given, wanted or not. And now I'm blushing.

Chapter Sixteen

~

Alice

As the cold, velvet drugs slunk into her plump vein, she leaned back into the softness. This was the terrible place where the brown envelope that she had refused to open until after Christmas had led her. This could be the beginning of the unravelling of her carefully constructed world. She would try to hide it from Mattie for as long as she could, but her past had finally caught up with her and now she would have to pay a catastrophic price. The here and now slipped away and her mind was sucked backwards into a vacuum until it was caught in a net woven by memories of the distant past.

Kissing the crown of dark, damp curls and counting the ten tiny fingers and toes as she held Mattie in her arms for the first time. The nurse had smiled and said that he weighed 7lbs and 4oz . . .

A spring morning so long ago and Mattie crying by the river. She had kissed away his tears, hot and salty. Scraps of bread to feed the ducks were still squashed in his baby, chubby fingers, and a tiny white feather . . .

Mattie in a school blazer, too big; his first. Shiny black shoes and grey socks that folded over just below his bony knees. So excited to be going to school at last. Until then she had kept him close; too close, perhaps. Just him and her. But when that day came she knew she had to let him go. She spent the whole day waiting for him to come back . . .

Mattie's sixth birthday party. His friends from school came over and there were games – Pass the Parcel and Musical Chairs – and the little girl in the blue dress who cried when she didn't win. Or was it a red dress? She had made cheese straws and a cake with a train on it.

Back in the real world her arm was cold and she shifted in the chair, pushing herself further back, but her mind stayed where it was, clutching at the memories as they drifted past.

Learning to swim at the local baths. She had held his hands while he kicked like fury with his strong little legs and laughed with joy. Blue swimming trunks with a red stripe. Armbands at first, but soon he didn't need them. He could swim on his own like a big boy . . .

He was always such a good boy; a happy boy. She must have been a good mother because he was always happy. She made him a birthday cake and taught him to swim. And he hadn't died like all the others.

Chapter Seventeen

~

Masha

Most people would call this a fine spring morning, but not me. I hate the spring. I don't want to. I want my heart, like Wordsworth's, to dance with the daffodils. But instead I fall morosely into step with Pooh's friend Eeyore. As soon as the trees flaunt fresh leaves and lanterns of blossom and the sun begins to warm as well as illuminate, my world is cast into shadows. As new life emerges all around, I can only see how fragile and vulnerable it is. For me spring is always a harbinger of doom.

In the park baby ducklings, merest wisps of feathers and air, are buffeted across the pond by the gentlest of breezes. I am terrified that they will become separated from their parents and gobbled up by a passing Canada goose or a predatory pike. The fields are full of knock-kneed lambs; woolly, button-eyed babies trotting unsteadily after their mothers. Children on school visits to friendly farms will coo and fuss over them, and in a few short weeks they will be herded, frightened and bewildered, onto trucks and driven to the slaughterhouse (no school visits here). Baby white fleeces stained red, lamb chops on a plate. Spring lamb. No wonder I don't eat meat. And then there's the Grand National. A field of noble equines; fiery eyes, gleaming coats and rippling muscles. But legs of glass. Long, fine, brittle legs of glass. Easily broken, rarely mended. The Grand National; always the last race for some. You can bet on that.

I hate the spring.

My place of work is one of those large Victorian houses that face the park. The gravel crunches beneath my feet as I walk up the drive to the huge front door, immaculately painted in British racing green and resplendent with original brass letter box, door-knob, knocker and bell pull. Helen, who is our receptionist here, takes a perverse pride in keeping them polished to military stan-dard. She regularly grumbles that she is not employed to do the cleaning, but refuses to entrust the brass to Dorothy who is.

The impressive hallway is tastefully decorated in muted Far-row & Ball, and has an intricate mosaic tiled floor. The stained-glass panels on either side of the door filter the sunlight onto the tiles to produce a dance of pattern and colour. A large, gothic hat and coat stand lurks against the wall to the left of the front door, and there are two lushly verdant aspidistras (affectionately known as the 'maiden aunts') in ceramic pots enthroned on mahogany plant stands on either side of the central staircase. To the left of the staircase is the waiting room, which houses a selection of grand, wing-backed leather chairs, a square glass-topped coffee table flaunting copies of *Homes & Gardens*, *The Lady* and *GQ* (under which Helen hides the copies of *Hello!*, *OK!* and the *People's Friend*) and a large rectangular aquarium containing a shoal of languid, jewel-coloured tropical fish. At the far end of the room, opposite the window, is a polished wooden counter, behind which Helen is seated. She is on the telephone.

'I'm sorry to hear that you're in so much pain . . . and you can come anytime?'

'Well, we could squeeze you in at 2.30 p.m. today if it's urgent.' The change in her tone is almost imperceptible, but her face makes her irritation very clear. 'You're going to be at the hairdresser then?' She covers the mouthpiece and hisses in my direction 'So, not so much "indescribable agony", as "a bit of a twinge"?'

The Park Clinic offers three types of therapy: psychotherapy, physiotherapy and acupuncture. Helen says we should be called 'Needy, Kneading and Needles'. I'm the psychotherapist. I retrained after leaving the council; finally made use of my degree in psychology. Epiphany said it was like an arsonist becoming a firefighter, but in truth it was part of my plan to stay alive. When Gabriel died and I began my education in drowning, there was one time when I went too far and almost died. The water was very cold and I stayed under too long. Someone dragged me out just in time and I made out that it was simply a foolish accident. But I knew that it was more than that, and I learned a valuable lesson from it. I'm a survivor – I don't want to die. The problem was that I was at the mercy of my emotions – I lacked control, and some-times my grief could override my will.

So, I came up with a survival plan. Firstly, I got Haizum. I would never leave him – he is now the love of my life. Secondly, I trained to be a psychotherapist. I learned to understand my emo-tions and with that knowledge came a certain degree of control. I have never told anyone about how I nearly drowned, not even when I was in therapy myself as part of my professional training. To be honest, I'm ashamed and rather embarrassed. I may be many things, not all of them pleasant – impatient driver, erstwhile fire-setter, biscuit-dunker – but one thing I'm not is a quitter. And to drown, whether deliberately or through carelessness, would definitely count as quitting. My survival plan has been enough to keep me alive. But now, I want more. I don't want my life to be defined by someone else's death, even if it was my only son's. Hai-zum has stopped me from dying, but now I want to live again instead of just surviving. Even in spring.

The clinic is owned by Georgina, the physiotherapist, who lives in a large apartment upstairs with a tarantula called Marion and an African grey parrot called Moriarty (she says they are much better company than her ex-husband, and far less trouble in the bedroom department). Georgina is an impressive Amazonian sort of woman in her late fifties, with silver hair hacked into an unruly bob and piercing blue eyes. She strides about the clinic like an over-enthusiastic hiker, talks like an old-school BBC Radio 4 announcer, and is Brown Owl to the local Brownie pack whose pixies, imps and sprites idolise her. I have never seen her dressed in anything other than her clinic coat and/or combat trousers and Dr. Martens boots, and, in winter, a selection of enormous jump-ers that look as though they have been customised by a gang of angry mice.

By way of contrast, the acupuncturist, Fennel, is a nervous, bird-boned woman who looks like a bean stick with a hat on. Her dreary twinsets and long, narrow corduroy skirts are accessorised with brightly coloured stripy tights (just visible above her crêpe-soled, sensible shoes) and dangly ethnic earrings, which she believes add a certain joie de vivre to her style. She is mistaken. She looks like a demented rag doll and I avoid her as much as pos-sible. I wouldn't trust her to sew on a button, let alone stick needles in me.

My consulting room is behind the waiting room and has a beautiful view of the garden. It is what I like to describe as a 'comfortable' room, and what Helen prefers to call 'messy'. But the randomness is deliberate, and carefully constructed. I know exactly where everything is, and no one is allowed to move anything. If they did, I would know. There is a large walnut desk whose polished surface is almost totally obscured by a laptop marooned amongst books, piles of paperwork, a bowl full of old glass marbles, photographs of my beloved boy and Haizum and a heavy Bakelite telephone. There is also a baby aspidistra, a niece of one of the maiden aunts, in a chipped, blue-glazed planter, decorated with rather luscious-looking cherubs, and a large glass snow globe containing a scene of Paris. When I am feeling stressed after seeing a particularly difficult client, the cold, smooth dome is soothing to touch, and a few turns of the key and a couple of gentle shakes produce a magical, musical world in which I can lose myself until the scowl on my face fades away. I have also been known to invite exceptionally troublesome clients to gaze into its depths and take a few moments to relax, to buy myself some time to dredge up something even remotely constructive to say to them when the only words that immediately spring to mind are 'For goodness' sake, bugger off and get a life!'

Facing the door is a grand open fireplace with lustrous green and deep blue tiles, and a carved wooden surround. Above this is a large, framed print of a windswept woman in a billowing dress and a wide-brimmed straw hat striding out with two greyhounds on a leash. There are hills in the background, and a luminous blue sky filled with cream cushiony clouds. It is a glorious painting by Charles Wellington Furse called *Diana of the Uplands* and I never tire of looking at it. I have a rather battered swivel chair behind my desk, and two comfortable, high-backed chairs and a squashy sofa. There are a box of tissues, a jug of water and a glass on a small round side table between one of the chairs and the sofa. And there is a bottle of vodka in the bottom drawer of my desk.

The intercom on my desk buzzes and Helen announces the arrival of my first client. The people I see come to me for a wide variety of reasons. I even see some to help them with bereavement. Those are the clients I feel least comfortable with. Having failed so spectacularly to deal with my own, I always feel like an obese dietitian or an ambisinister (word of the day – *clumsy or unskilful with both hands*) brain surgeon. I am a tired but veritable cliché, like the builder who never finishes his own kitchen extension, or the hairdresser who never finds time to blow-dry his own hair. Today's client is Errol Greenman and the only problem I have with him is trying to keep a straight face. I open the door to greet him, and he comes in and sits down on the squishy sofa. As usual, he is wearing a plain grey shirt, flared jeans and a sleeveless pullover which looks as though it has been knitted by his mother. He is forty-three years old, still lives at home with his parents and has never had a girlfriend. Or boyfriend. Or friend. He collects Action Man dolls and enjoys attending Action Man conventions. He only eats food that is white, red or brown and never mixes two types of food on the same forkful. Astonishingly, none of these things are the reason why Errol comes to see me.

'So, Errol, tell me: how have things been this week?'

Errol sighs and shakes his head. 'Terrible. It's happened every night. I'm so sore I can barely walk and I'm worried that my parents are going to find out. They'd be horrified!' When he speaks, two globules of cottage-cheese-like spit form in the corners of his mouth and stretch like string hinges when he opens it.

I nod encouragingly and ask him to go on.

'I'm beginning to wonder if I should handcuff my hands to the bed before I go to sleep,' he announces, dramatically.

I bite my bottom lip to discourage the smile that is threatening to sabotage my professional demeanour.

'Well, it might help, I suppose. But I'm not sure it's advisable. Tell me exactly what happened.'

'It's the same as usual. It's always the same. I have my milky drink at 10 p.m., go to bed and read for fifteen minutes, and then I turn out the light. The next thing I know, they've taken me and done horrible, unspeakable things to me and when I wake up I'm in the hall, or the kitchen or the bathroom. One of these nights, they'll leave me in the garden, or they won't bring me back at all!'

'And what makes you think they've done terrible things to you?'

Errol looks coy and wrings his hands theatrically.

'The bruises. They're so sore, and they weren't there when I went to sleep. And on Tuesday night, when I woke up,' his voice drops to a whisper, 'I'd had an accident in my pyjamas.'

At this point I'm forced to look away and pretend to be making a note of something. I *do* genuinely feel sorry for poor Errol, I promise I do, but he's a very difficult man to help. His mother has confirmed to me that the bruises are caused by Errol colliding with the furniture in the dark. I spoke to her with his permission (on the proviso that I didn't mention his specific problem) and she told me that he had done it since he was a little boy. But it's very difficult to help a chronic somnambulist who insists that, rather than sleepwalking, he is abducted nightly by aliens. I could suggest the installation of closed-circuit cameras, which would prove to Errol that the furthest he goes on his nocturnal travels is the downstairs of his parents' home, rather than the outer reaches of space. But I suspect that alien abduction, albeit imaginary, is the most exciting thing that happens to Errol, and it might be cruel rather than kind to deprive him of it, until he finds something equally thrilling to replace it. Mine is not an easy job.

There are days when I wish I were Diana of the Uplands.

Chapter Eighteen

Haizum bounds excitedly across the park towards me with something red clasped between his jaws. He skids to a halt just in time to avoid body slamming me, and proceeds to murder his prey at my feet. It is Sally's woolly hat. I scan the park anxiously, searching for her untidy figure, and see a group of youths in a circle over by the pond, jeering and pushing at a victim I can't see, but know immediately to be Sally. I grab Haizum and march over to them (less Diana of the Uplands, more Attila the Hun). There are five of them: boys aged about fifteen dressed in low-slung jeans and hoodies, and flashy trainers that demonstrate how 'sick' they are. Sally staggers around in their nasty little ring-o'-roses circle, red-faced and incoherent with rage. Her hands and arms are flailing furiously, but the slaps and punches she is throwing are easily dodged by her much younger assailants.

My voice is calm and steady, but with what I like to think of as an indisputably steely 'don't fuck with me' undertone. My absolute fury renders me absolutely invincible.

'What the hell do you think you're doing?'

'Wot the fuck's it got to do wiv you, bitch?'

This from the ringleader. He wasn't obvious at first. He looks much the same as the others. Perhaps a little more attractive – slightly taller and with a bit of a swagger. But then I noticed his eyes. Dull, ice-blue, dead-fish eyes. As though his life has already leached away any emotion he may once have been capable of feeling, and all that's left is a corpse-cold automaton. I can almost hear the duelling banjos. This boy is straight from *Deliverance* country. Haizum doesn't like his tone. He places himself between me and the boys and raises his lips to display his potentially dangerous dentition. This is accompanied by a rumbling growl guaranteed to loosen the most constricted of bowels. The other youths begin to break the circle, backing away. The ringleader remains, his eyes still fixed on mine. Haizum moves forward and I place a restraining hand on his collar. Conversation is pointless.

'Just fuck off before my dog rips your throat out.'

I sense he is not used to this type of reaction. He is used to fear, abuse or anger from his victims. Loss of control. As he turns to follow his fellow hoodies, he spits back at me, 'I'll remember you. Fuckin' whore!'

'Good. You should.'

Sally is in a dreadful state. I fix what I can with soothing words, the return of her hat (with a few ventilation holes in it courtesy of Haizum) and a mug of sweet tea from the café in the park. Surprisingly her scrambling switch is off, and once she has blown her nose with prodigious force several times, swallowed some of her tea, and smoked a rather scrawny roll-up, she is able to tell me what happened.

On her usual afternoon visit to feed the crows she had noticed the boys gathered by the edge of the pond, and could hear the ducks flapping and squawking loudly. She went over to investigate and found the loathsome little shits throwing empty beer cans and lumps of rubble, taken from the park warden's yard specifically for this purpose, at the ducklings on the pond.

'I shouted at them to stop and threatened to call the police, but they took no notice. The nasty-looking one – thinks himself King of the Crap Heap – he simply laughed in my face.'

She takes a sip of her tea and Haizum rests his head consolingly on her lap (he is probably also looking for food).

'But then I could see he was going to turn his attentions to me. He'd thought of a new entertainment.'

Her voice quavers slightly and she begins to roll another cigarette. She had been right. Sensing another vulnerable victim to amuse himself with, Deliverance Boy had turned his pack on her. They had snatched her hat and thrown it to one another over her head before discarding it on the grass. They had grabbed the bag of bread she had brought for the crows, and two of them held her arms whilst the ringleader held her nose and force-fed her the bread until she was afraid she would choke. Finally they surrounded her and pushed her roughly between them, shouting insults and obscenities, revelling in her distress.

'If you hadn't turned up, my dear, with the Big Fucker here, I'm sure something horrible would have happened to me.'

Sally insists on buying me a second mug of tea, and Haizum gets a Scotch egg as a reward for his chivalrous behaviour. She asks me my name.

'Masha.'

Sally smiles and pats my hand.

'That explains why you are always in the cemetery! You're Mr Chekhov's young lady – in mourning for your life, no doubt.'

I need to change the subject. This is uncomfortable territory for me.

'And what's your excuse?' I ask. 'Your beautiful singing is wasted on dead people.'

Sally laughs. 'It's the best audience I've ever had! Besides,' her face was serious again now, 'singing is never wasted. And it is the only music you can carry with you everywhere and always.'

I try to persuade Sally to report the incident to the police, but she insists that there is no point.

'They won't listen to me once my words start playing silly buggers. They'll simply think I'm some batty old tractor with a wheel missing. And I'm dreadful when I get worked up. I shall be effing and blinding all over the department store. They'll end up charging me with breach of the peace!'

Sadly, she's probably right. And even if the culprits were by some small miracle charged and found guilty, their so-called punishment would probably only amount to 'accountability' counselling sessions or twenty minutes' community (dis)service. I manage to scrounge some stale bread from the girl behind the counter at the café. I walk with Sally across the park to feed the crows, and then we part at the bandstand to make our separate ways home.

'Thank you so much, my dear. You and your wonderful hound are my guardian angels.' And with a wave and a smile she is off to wherever is her home.

The sun is still warm, and the trees are frothing with pink blossom.

I hate the spring.

Chapter Nineteen

Her caramel faux-fur coat is unfastened and through her cream chiffon blouse a tantalising glimpse of leopard-print bra is just visible. The magnificent breasts it shelves jiggle saucily as she prowls the aisles in her kitten-heeled boots. Having dropped Haizum at home, I have continued to the shop to buy some cigarettes. I rarely smoke these days, but I am still raging about poor Sally and feel the need for a medicinal glass of wine and a couple of cigarettes. I am now transfixed by this vintage sex-siren, who must be seventy if she's a day. She is a woman who looks as though she is starring in a movie of her own life, and loving every minute of it. She is dazzling. Her long, platinum-blonde hair is twisted into a sexily dishevelled chignon, she wears several strings of pearls and even more make-up than Roni. Her eyes are heavily lined in black, her foundation could support a small bungalow, and her lips are painted into a perfect red pout. But somehow, on this woman, the effect is less lady of the night and more old-school Hollywood glamour.

I cannot help but follow her. I am caught in her backwash. Her basket contains fresh salmon steaks, crème fraîche and dill. I copy her shopping. I wish I could copy her full stop. I want to be her. She will never end her days in a Happy Endings home. I follow her to the wine counter, trying to keep my distance, but irresistibly drawn. She selects a bottle of prosecco. As she moves on, I take a bottle of the same wine from the shelf. Suddenly she turns round and catches me. I can feel the colour rising in my cheeks. In a few short moments I have turned from shopper to stalker.

She takes another bottle and places it in her basket. 'It's always good to have one in reserve,' she says with a smile. I feel like a schoolgirl facing her prefect infatuation. I can only nod in reply. As she moves away once again, I stay where I am, pretending to study the Italian reds and trying to recapture my composure. I wonder where she has been hiding. In all the years that this has been my corner shop, I have never seen her. If I had, I would remember. Definitely. As I dither by the dog food, another cus-tomer comes in. Elvis.

It is immediately apparent that he is equally transfixed by the mystery woman. She is now standing at the counter waiting to pay and smiles at him with enough sizzle to set a fire. At once his cheeks are burning. With obvious reluctance, he takes an empty basket and walks away. The woman apologises to the cashier and explains that she has forgotten something.

'Do go ahead and pay,' she says to me, leaving her shopping on the counter. 'I'll just go and fetch it.'

Once outside the shop, I allow myself a moment or two of covetous gazing at Elvis's bicycle before heading home. I need a cigarette.

Chapter Twenty

Today's pool temperature is 12.6 and sunlight flashes and sparkles on the broken water as I begin my fifteenth length. The lido is becoming busier with the warmer weather, but it is too early in the day for any children to be in the pool. During the school holidays I shall swim as soon as the lido opens its doors. Children in the water make me nervous.

I am swimming more and more these days; further and more often. The deep underwater still calls to me to atone, but I'm trying not to listen. I speed up to overtake the woman who is swimming in the lane next to me. She is an untidy swimmer with thrashing limbs and splashing strokes. Demonstrating more enthusiasm than efficiency, she ploughs through the water with all the grace of a lopsided pedalo. As I manage to pass her I get a faceful of water from a particularly vigorous kick-stroke before I escape into the open water ahead of me.

The Olympian is standing at the edge of the pool adjusting his goggles. I can't help but notice, as I swim towards him, that he looks just as fetching in his trunks as Daniel Craig did in his. I must remember to report this to Epiphany. Or maybe not. I wouldn't want her to get the wrong idea. Or perhaps that should be the *right* one. After twenty lengths I climb out of the pool and peel off my swimming cap. I have a lot of hair, and, squashed under a skin-tight dome of Lycra, it gives my head an odd, mis-shapen appearance, a bit like a cauliflower. Set free, it is a long skein of dark curls. The same curls that my son inherited from me and refused to let me brush if ever he could help it. The Olympian is now scything through the water, sleek as a seal, and the pedalo is having a break, puffing and blowing as she clutches the side at the deep end of the pool.

In the café Flo is being kept busy by a group of young mums and their toddlers. As I wait to be served the woman in front of me is struggling with a small boy, who is doing his best to escape from her, and a buggy containing a fractious baby who has pulled off both her socks and thrown them on the floor. The little boy yanks his hand from the woman and makes a break for the door, causing her to drop her purse, scattering change everywhere. One of the other mothers, already seated, jumps up and gathers the wriggling escapee in her arms, while I help his mother to retrieve the contents of her purse from the floor. As I hand the coins back to her our eyes meet and I see a young woman whose face is ashen with exhaustion. She, however, sees someone she recognises.

'I know you.'

This is going to be awkward. I have no idea who she is. I smile uncertainly, playing for time to try and remember, but knowing full well that I shan't.

'You've got that big dog.'

That's me. But who's she?

'You found my little boy when he ran off in the cemetery. He fell and hit his head?'

Jayden's mum. She asks Flo for a cup of coffee and a glass of milk.

'You probably thought I was a bad mother, losing my Jayden like that.'

Guilty as charged, but I'm hardly going to admit it.

'Let me bring your tray for you.'

I carry it over to the table where Jayden is happily drawing with his finger in a mess of spilt sugar. His mum places the glass of milk in front of him.

'Say hello, Jayden. This is the lady with the big dog.'

He won't remember. It was months ago. Jayden's eyes light up and he claps his hands.

'Doggy! Doggy!'

His mum wearily scrapes back a chair across the floor and sits down.

'He loves dogs, does Jayden. But we can't have one. Not in the flat.'

Judging by the bags under her eyes and the pallor of her skin, she could barely muster the energy to care for a goldfish, let alone a dog. As I turn to leave them to their drinks, she touches my arm.

'I'm not a bad mum.' The words are delivered in a quiet voice with a steely edge and I can see a flash of defiance in her eyes.

'I didn't say—'

She interrupts me. 'You didn't need to. It was written all over your face.'

She takes a gulp of her coffee before she continues.

'I was visiting my mum's grave. We'd only buried her the week before, and I had a bit of a . . . moment.' The catch in her voice tells me the pain is still raw. 'He was there one minute, and then when I looked up . . . Well, you've seen how quick he is.'

I can feel my face flushing. I smile, but I'm embarrassed. Ashamed. I have used my grief as an excuse to be judgemental and I have strayed onto the path of self-righteousness. This woman has called me out on it.

'I'm so sorry about your mum' is all I can think of to say. Jayden's mum nods an acknowledgement and then turns to her friends and I am mercifully dismissed. I want to go straight home, but Flo has been watching and I know she won't let me go without comment, so I go back to the counter and order a large mug of tea.

'I'll bring it over to you.'

I sit down at the table furthest away from the group of women and their children, carefully arrange my book in front of me and stare out at the pool where the Olympian is still swimming. I wonder if he's single. It crosses my mind to eke out my tea and hang around in the hope that he might come into the café after his swim, but I quickly dismiss the idea, as I'm already perilously close to being late for work. Besides, the jumper I'm wearing is about as flattering as a tea cosy. It shrunk in the wash and now the sleeves are far too short. If, and that's a gargantuan 'if', I'm going to attempt to engineer an encounter with a man as indisputably hot as the Olympian, I should at least make sure that I don't look like a walking jumble sale. Flo bustles over and plonks a mug of steaming brown tea on the table.

'I'm doing you a teacake as well. You look like you could do with it.'

'Thanks, Flo.'

She picks up the book and inspects the title, clearly surprised and more than a little amused.

'*The Victorian Way of Death*. Blimey! That's not very cheerful. You should try something a bit more Mills & Boon.'

'It's research. I'm going to be a cemetery tour guide.'

Flo's face is a picture of consternation. The smell of burning drags her back to her counter before she can articulate her dismay, but she soon returns with my teacake.

'It's a bit black round the edges, but I've put plenty of butter on it.' She hovers. 'What happened there then?' She tips her head ever so slightly in the direction of Jayden's table.

The price of a teacake.

I sigh. 'We had a bit of a misunderstanding. It was a while back now, but I think I upset her. I was probably a bit rude.'

Flo pats my hand.

'Never mind, love. Water under the bridge now.'

There is a queue forming at the counter and Flo returns to her post with a final word of advice.

'Eat your teacake before it gets cold.'

Chapter Twenty-One

~

Alice and Mattie

In a cottage in a wood,
A little old man at the window stood,
Saw a rabbit running by,
Knocking at the door

Alice woke up sticky, shivering cold. The nausea washed over her in waves, small but constant, with the occasional breaker thrown up by a particular taste or smell. Her limbs felt leaden – bloated and blighted by the noxious cocktail that was sneaking through her veins. But in reality she was little more than skin and skeleton. Her clothes hung pathetically on the jutting bones of her hips and shoulders, and her face was the colour of uncooked tripe. Why the hell was she putting herself through this? Was it really worth it? And what about Mattie? He tried to act as though he was fine with typical teenage bravado, but she could see the fear in his restless eyes.

'Elpy, elpy, elpy.' The words floated into her head, like driftwood cast ashore from long ago. When Mattie was a little boy he used to play a game. His eyes would open wide and he would pretend to be afraid. He would draw pictures in the air with his forefingers and whisper the words 'Elpy, elpy, elpy.' It was always the same and she never understood what he meant. Over and over, always pausing at the same place, desperate for her to join in, to fill in the missing pieces. But it was a puzzle she never solved, just like the tiny white feathers that she sometimes found in his pockets.

Looking back, maybe sometimes even then his fear had been real and not pretend.

*　*　*

Mattie sat down at the base of a tree and reached into his pocket for a cigarette and a box of matches. Sam had given him a couple. He had nicked a whole packet from his mother.

'She won't even notice,' he boasted. 'She's always got loads knocking about the house.'

Sam had taught him how to smoke. He didn't really like the taste of it, but it made him feel cool. Well, it did when it didn't make him cough. It made him feel more like the other boys at school. Because often he didn't. It was hard to explain, but he felt slightly removed, as though there was one tiny piece of him that was missing or mutant in some way. A rogue gene, like a rough edge on a jigsaw piece that prevented a perfect fit.

Mattie could see his house from here. These were the woods at the bottom of their garden, but to get here he'd had to come via the track down the road. The last part of the garden was impenetrable, a vicious tangle of nettles and brambles. He'd once suggested that they could clear it. It would give them more space and then maybe he could get more rabbits, but his mum had dismissed the idea. He tucked the cigarette between his lips and struck a match. He sucked tentatively until the end of the cigarette glowed and then blew the smoke out without inhaling. Mattie came here to smoke *because* he could see the house from here. It somehow underlined his defiance of his mother and enhanced his crime with a daring frisson. He puffed again, this time taking a little of the smoke down into his lungs.

His mum was the problem. He felt guilty even thinking it, but it was true. She was the one who made him feel different. She wasn't like the mums of other kids at school. He flicked ash onto the mossy ground and watched the grey flakes flutter and settle. It wasn't that he didn't love her. Of course he did, and she loved him. He knew that without any doubt. But it sometimes felt like she loved him too much, too desperately, as though he were her only reason for living. She still waved him off to school every morning as though she might never see him again, and was watching at the window for him when he came home each afternoon. He was too old for that now. It wasn't normal. It was irritating, and though he would never have admitted it to anyone else, somehow just a little bit creepy.

It had been a hot and sticky afternoon, and the cool shade and quietness of the woods was soothing. He drew again on the cigarette, harder than he intended, and his coughing clattered through the silence, scaring a nearby pigeon into flight. Mattie stubbed the dog-end out and shifted uncomfortably against the rough bark of the tree. He was late now, but still reluctant to go home. Maybe today she wouldn't be watching for him. Over the past couple of weeks, something had changed. She had changed. She looked different and Mattie worried that sometimes she seemed muddled, as though she were unsure about even the most mundane aspects of their domestic routine. Meals had been late and he had twice found her putting unwashed laundry into the tumble dryer. He kept asking her if she was okay, and she always said she was fine. Mattie checked his watch. Five more minutes and then he would go. He took a deep breath. The cigarette had made him feel slightly sick. Or maybe it was the thought of going home.

Chapter Twenty-Two

Masha

The woods are dark and cold, and gunshots crack the silence. I am inside the cottage and the rabbit is cowering outside; flattening itself against the ground, making flesh and bones and fur as small as possible. I can't get the door to open. I scratch and scrape and kick and scream. My fingers are bleeding and my nails are torn. My breathing is fast but ineffectual; the air made too thin by fear. One final shot and then silence. The door opens. The huntsman made the perfect shot straight through the back of the head. But the body is not of a rabbit, but a little boy. Gabriel.

And then I wake up.

The details of my nightmare are always the same, but the horror is never diminished by familiarity. The luminous numbers of the clock on my bedside table tell me that it is 3.37 a.m., and Haizum's snoring is the only sound that ruffles the dark stillness. I climb out of bed and he is instantly awake and by my side. My fingers reach for his warm head and he sighs dolefully and licks my salty hand. I am drenched in cold sweat and my pyjamas cling to my now shivering frame. Across the landing, the door to Gabriel's room is open and I can see the rocking horse silhouetted against the moonlight. I wish it would rock. The ghost of Gabriel would be better than no Gabriel at all. Haizum follows me across the landing and I sit down on the bare floorboards next to the horse. As I set it in motion I close my eyes and try to see my little boy sitting on its back, using the metronome creak of its rocking to summon pictures of the past. Not the flat, frozen images of photographs, but living, breathing memories – trailers of a past life. When Gabriel died I gathered up and treasured even the tiniest scraps of anything that proved he had been here. I found a half-eaten custard cream under one of the cushions on the sofa. It still had Gabriel's teeth marks in it. I kept it until it was covered in blue mould and crumbled away in my hand. It would never have lasted that long if I'd have had Haizum then. He has settled down at my feet, but shifts his considerable bulk restlessly on the uncomfortable floorboards.

Eventually, I allow the horse to rest. I am cold and stiff, but still reluctant to move. And then I hear it. The throbbing, bouncing, joyful notes of the T. Rex song I used to play to Gabriel when he was still kicking inside my belly. 'I Love to Boogie'. I have loved it ever since I saw the film *Billy Elliot*. And so did Gabriel. As soon as he was old enough to stand he would wobble and jiggle and wave his hands when he heard it. He too loved to boogie. I know that the music is only in my head, but it doesn't stay there. Moments later I am downstairs with T. Rex blasting from four speakers. I only wish that I could bring myself to dance in my pyjamas.

Chapter
Twenty-Three

Edward was Gabriel's father. He was the one who came to ante-natal classes with me and held back my hair when, stricken with morning sickness, my head was down the toilet. It was Edward who paced the corridor outside the delivery room when I was in labour, and he was the first person to hold Gabriel in his arms and welcome him into the world. He changed nappies, read stories, did midnight feeds, and told me that everything would be all right when I was giddy from lack of sleep and covered in baby sick. Edward was Gabriel's father in every way except biologically; a minor detail that held no significance for any of us.

Edward is also the brother I always wanted but my parents failed to provide. We are very alike; as emotionally complicated as one another. Not in a sophisticated, glamorous 'I want to be alone' Greta Garbo way, but in an awkward, frustrating and sometimes self-alienating way. For example, we both find the admission of any kind of personal vulnerability as embarrassing as tripping in your high heels and falling flat on your face in front of millions on the way to collect an Oscar. Stiff upper lip doesn't even begin to cover it; rigor mortis is more like it. I have seen Edward weep unashamedly and very publicly at the end of the film *The Railway Children*. You only have to say the words 'Daddy, my daddy' in Jenny Agutter-esque tones and his eyes fill with tears. But six years ago, when the love of his life and partner of fifteen years, Rupert, left him to go and open an antiquarian book shop in Hay-on-Wye with his reiki practitioner, Edward's upper lip remained as stiff as Prince Charles dancing the rumba. And so it was when Gabriel died. Drowning is a quiet affair and we kept our grief tightly swaddled in suffocating self-restraint. It seems that we each independently entered an unspoken pact to protect one another by refusing to discuss our devastation. I think now that it may have been a mistake, but it is a mutual flaw born from mutual love that binds us together and makes our friendship so precious.

Today I'm meeting Edward for lunch, but I have some visits to make first. Most people are uncomfortable about being in a cemetery if they're not there to attend a funeral or visit the grave of a loved one, but he is happy to meet me here. Unlike the Victorians who built this place, people nowadays seem to think that cemeteries are morbid places and to visit them for recreational purposes is at best creepy and at worst, tempting fate. But perhaps it is the confrontation of their own mortality that really unsettles them. After all, it is the only certainty that we all share. However fit, fabulous, rich, double-jointed, brilliant, brave, funny or fastidious about cleaning our teeth we are, we are all going to die. It may not seem fair, but there it is. As Thomas Gray reminds us, 'The paths of glory lead but to the grave'.

Or perhaps it is fear of the dead themselves. When I was a little girl we used to go out on Sunday afternoon drives in the country with my grandparents. Whenever we passed a cemetery or churchyard, my granddad used to wind down the window and shout, 'Any complaints?'

He never received a reply and said this was a fair indication that the dead were a pretty contented lot, and when his time came he died peacefully in his own bed with little pain and with no fear.

I am here to visit more members of my Family on the Other Side. The sun is high and bright and the trees scatter dappled shade across the path. The gravestones cast crisp shadows, chequerboarding the grass, and high in the cloudless sky swallows pitch and swoop. Haizum is loping lazily in front of me, panting heavily with his tongue lolling out of the side of his mouth. The first on my rounds are Charity and Edwin Guntrip, who are buried together halfway up the hill next to a beautifully scented rose bush that today fills the warm air with its voluptuous perfume. Its branches are bowed with velvet blooms and I can't resist stealing one for a friend. Charity and Edwin won't mind. The couple were devoted to one another and the inscription on their simple grey headstone tells me that they died within six months of each other in 1953, aged 69 and 71 respectively. They grew flowers and fruit in their garden; soft, deep pink raspberries climbing up rows of soldier-straight canes; rich purple blackcurrants, tart little redcurrants and fat bristly green gooseberries. At their allotment they grew cabbages, onions, carrots, runner beans and a few new potatoes. Charity would boil the kettle on a little camping stove in their shed and make a pot of tea, whilst Edwin picked any of the vegetables that were ready, and after their tea they would wheel them home in a wheelbarrow. Edwin laughed when Charity had made curtains for the shed window out of some scraps of blue flowery material, but she said they made the place look homely, and secretly Edwin agreed. They had a budgerigar called Churchill. Their grave was completely neglected when I first came upon it, but it is now in perfect order and planted with some cheerful marigolds and fluttery petunias that I hope meet with

Charity's and Edwin's approval. I sometimes have a little chat with them about my garden. I tell them what Haizum has been digging up, whether or not the russet apple tree is bearing any fruit (it's rather temperamental – sometimes it will, other years not a single apple) and ask for their advice about the black spots on the roses. And no, they never give any, but I like to make them feel involved. Today I report that my gooseberry bush has sawfly, and leave them to ponder on it.

Next I visit Ezra Maltravers because I don't think anyone else would – even if anyone who knew him were still alive. Ezra was a con artist, an inveterate gambler and an incorrigible ladies' man. He had a rakish moustache, and wore a trilby that was just a little too shiny for my liking. His eyes were too narrow to be those of a gentleman, and his lips were too wet. Lady T provides a list of behaviours under the heading 'Conduct which is incorrect', and included on this list is 'to indulge in any unpleasant personal tricks'. Ezra almost certainly did. He died penniless and alone. I visit him because he may have repented on his deathbed, but no one was there to hear it. I visit him because none of us is perfect and because he has a great name. I really hope he doesn't turn out to have been a travelling salesman with a grey comb-over, a Pac-a-Mac and a thermos flask. You may wonder how I know all these details about my Family on the Other Side, and the simple truth is that I don't. So what I don't know I make up, although I'm not sure if that would be allowed if I ever get to be a proper cemetery guide.

My last call today is Rose. Today is Rose's birthday, and so I have brought her a small glass paperweight that contains a perfect pale pink rosebud. The rose in the paperweight is the Rose Hannah I imagine her to have been, never having had the chance to bloom. Maybe she has found little Marie and they are trampolining together with the angels. Rose Hannah Shakespeare, 'Doll', died in 1899, aged 4 – 'Tragically drowned'.

Is there any other way? In many countries, even today, drowning is one of the leading causes of infant death. It only takes a few centimetres of water. Children can drown in baths, buckets and even toilets.

Rose's headstone was thickly shrouded in ivy and home to more than thirty snails when I found it. Ten minutes of stripping and snail relocation revealed a beautiful white marble gravestone inlaid with lead strips, forming panels decorated with carvings of doves and roses and inscribed with the words 'Our precious daughter "Doll" – cruelly missed but fondly remembered'.

Edward and I have a favourite seat for our lunches. It is at the top of the slope on which the cemetery is built, and has magnificent views of the park, the town and the countryside beyond. The graves here are widely spaced and some of the oldest in the cemetery. The inscriptions on many of the headstones are now impossible to read, and some of the stones list forwards, backwards or sideways rather drunkenly and so we affectionately call this area the 'Field of Inebriation'. I sometimes wonder whether its inhabitants are lying at similarly precarious angles and are now clinging to the edge of their coffins – for grim death or dear life, I can never decide which.

Edward is already seated and basking in the sunshine as we walk across the grass to meet him. He is looking very smart in a raspberry waistcoat and an immaculate panama. Haizum is delighted to see Lord Byron, and almost pulls me over in his enthusiasm to greet him. Edward smiles at me and briefly takes my hand as I sit down next to him, and I hand him the rose that I have stolen. He has prepared egg mayonnaise sandwiches for us, and cold roast chicken (organic, free-range and raised in an environment approved by the

RSPCA and the chicken) for Haizum and Lord Byron. I pass him a napkin; a proper starched white linen napkin, ever mindful of the standards set by Lady T, who would most certainly not approve of paper serviettes.

'I have two favours to ask you.'

Edward looks unusually serious, and I feel a chill as though the sun has gone behind a cloud. But the flash of mischief quickly returns to his cool green eyes and I am reassured.

'Well, come on then, out with it. But I warn you now that I don't sleep with gay men, and I'm not lending you any of my frocks.'

Edward raises one eyebrow disdainfully as he takes another bite of his sandwich, and shakes his head ever so slightly. I so wish I could do the disdainful eyebrow as proficiently as he does. I have practised in the mirror, but he's still miles better at it than me.

'You flatter yourself on both counts.'

I attempt disdainful eyebrow but achieve only a fit of the giggles with a mouth full of egg sandwich. Not elegant, and not recommended by Lady T.

'I should like you to accompany me to an astoundingly appalling production of *The Mikado*.'

'Why? I mean, one, why are you going if it's astoundingly appalling? And two, why do you wish to inflict it on me?'

'I am going to support a good friend who is playing the role of the Lord High Executioner. He says it's the worst production ever, and that rotten eggs and fruit are sure to be thrown. He is desperate to see a friendly face in the audience. In turn, I need a good friend to support me through what is destined to be a torturous experience and, if necessary, resuscitate me at the end of it.'

'I should be delighted.'

I am tempted to ask who the friend is, but I know Edward

better than that. If he doesn't volunteer information, there is usually a good reason. In any case I shall find out soon enough.

'Shall I wear my best kimono?'

I may not be able to ask him about his friend, but I can't resist a little gentle teasing. Edward does the eyebrow again, but can't keep the hint of a smile from his suntanned face.

Chapter Twenty-Four

~

The soaring notes of Mozart's 'Lacrimosa' are a rather curious greeting as I push open the front door of the clinic and walk Haizum straight through to my room. I have no clients this morning and Haizum's sorrowful stares have persuaded me to let him keep me company whilst I catch up on some tedious but essential paperwork.

I leave Haizum reorganising the cushions on the sofa, and return to the waiting room to see Helen. I already know from her choice of music that she will not be alone. An unpleasant woman called Mrs Sweetie is sitting in the waiting room. She is anything but. Barely civil to 'the receptionist', she always sits bolt upright, looking as though she can smell a fish-guts-scented fart. She has an unfortunate face, unimproved by cold eyes and thin lips that are constantly pursed in preparation to criticise someone or something. She is one of Fennel's patients, and Fennel is welcome to her. The reason for 'Lacrimosa' is Mrs Sweetie's fur hat. Real dead-murdered-animal fur. She wears it all year round. In autumn and winter she teams it with a camel-coloured long wool coat with a fur collar. In spring and summer she wears it with beautifully cut glazed cotton dresses that she somehow contrives to make look ill-fitting and ugly. I expect she even wears it with her bathing suit when lounging on the terrace of her newly purchased villa in the south of France. She told a suitably deferential Fennel all about it, who in turn told us. We were not anything like as impressed as we were supposed to be.

Helen believes that the penalty for those wearing real fur should include being caged, scalped and forced to eat a smorgasbord of assorted excrement. However, in the absence of appropriate punitive legislation, we subject Mrs Sweetie to musical torture, although I suspect the irony of this specific piece will be lost on her. Helen turns up the volume. Fennel follows me into the waiting room and ushers Mrs Sweetie away like an anxious collie herding a wayward sheep. Helen changes the music.

'She was twenty minutes early today, so I just kept pressing the repeat button on the CD player. Do you think she noticed?'

'Hard to tell. She didn't look very chirpy, but then she always looks like she's been sucking a wasp to me.'

I tell Helen about my lunch with Edward, and our forthcoming theatre date.

'So who is this mysterious friend?'

Before I can answer, the phone rings and Helen spends the next ten minutes trying to book an appointment for a new patient. The longer it takes to settle on an appropriate day and time, the more clipped Helen's tone becomes. After eight minutes her jaw is clenched and she has broken the lead in two pencils. Finally, she delivers her coup de grâce.

'Perhaps we might make better progress if you were to ask your husband to contact us himself. That way we stand a fighting chance of booking an appointment that he will be able to attend. Presumably he has mastered the rudiments of operating a telephone unassisted, and has at least one fully functioning digit?'

Helen cuts the caller off after the first sentence, but I wonder if one day her mental or manual dexterity will fail her and some unsuspecting patient will experience the unexpurgated wrath of her tongue. She looks at me expectantly and raises her eyebrows.

'Well?'

'I really don't know. And you know what Edward's like. He had that "don't ask" look on his face. But I definitely got the impression that this is more important to him than he's letting on. Frankly I'm intrigued and I can't wait for the big night.'

Helen is sharpening the pencils she broke.

'Well, I shall want to hear all about it.'

Georgina strides into the waiting room and picks up the pile of patient notes that Helen has prepared for her. She flicks through them, her expression changing as she registers each one and what she is treating them for.

'Not too bad today. Only one really smelly one, and one poor old boy whose meat and two veg always drop out of the side of his boxer shorts on the treatment couch. Good grief, he's in his eight-ies and really ought to be in long johns by now.'

At the sound of Georgina's voice Haizum slinks into the wait-ing room to greet her. He is fully aware that the waiting room is out of bounds to him, but he is quite unable to resist the tempta-tion of a woman who always has bits of broken biscuit in her pockets and is therefore utterly adorable. The biscuits are for Mori-arty, but Haizum usually manages to scrounge a few by turning the full beam of his soulful eyes onto Georgina, and wagging his tail in a feeble but thoroughly winsome manner.

'Good morning, you magnificent creature.'

Georgina bends down and gives him an affectionate bear hug (or should that be dog hug?) and rewards his efforts with several large pieces of digestive biscuit.

'By the bye, Marion's made a run for it again, so keep an eye out. And,' turning to Haizum, 'if you find her, don't eat her. She won't be nice.'

I'm not brilliant with spiders any bigger than a raisin, and retreat to my room with Haizum leaving Helen to search for hairy Marion, the escapee, armed with a dustpan and brush.

Chapter Twenty-Five

The sound of Haizum's snoring is loud enough to wake the dead and I am suddenly aware that my room is very quiet. I have been pretending to deal with essential paperwork for the last hour, but actually reading a glorious little book about the history of cemeteries in Britain, and occasionally pausing to create a mental guest list for my fantasy weekend party at a stately home in the country. This is a new fantasy, still in its very early stages and I'm just debating the inclusion of Jeremy Paxman – frisky intellect but a bit smug – when I register the silence. Haizum's guttural gymnastics have been the soundtrack to my musings all morning, and now there is a definite lull. And I have a horrible feeling that it could be *the* lull.

It is.

One ear-splitting shriek from Helen followed by muffled barking and the demented skittering of claws across the tiled floor in the corridor outside confirm it beyond doubt. I join Helen in pursuit of a wildly excited Haizum who is racing circuits, amain (word of the day – *at full speed*), round the entire ground floor with something grey and furry in his mouth.

'I think the great daft bugger has caught a squirrel!' Helen gasps. 'It must have fallen down the chimney.'

I'm not convinced by Helen's Santa-Claus-impersonating squirrel theory. We corner Haizum in the waiting room. His jaws are firmly clamped around his furry trophy and his eyes are full excitement. He is contemplating his next move.

'Haizum! Drop, leave and sit the bloody hell down!'

I could have been a regimental sergeant major. I swear Helen nearly sat as well. Haizum, recognising the tone of my voice as being the one I use to tell cold-calling, personal protection insurance claims negotiators to 'bugger off', does as he is told. Unfortunately, his antics interrupted Helen just as she was feeding the fish. The lid is still off the aquarium and Haizum drops Mrs Sweetie's hat into the water. Within thirty seconds Haizum has, in Helen's estimation, transformed from zero to hero – from ruthless squirrel murderer to anti-fur protester. Helen and I are as pathetic with laughter as a pair of teenage girls poring over an Instagram they have posted of their dad wearing only his pants. Mrs Sweetie's hat is now floating in the aquarium like some sort of hideous, mutant sea anemone, and Haizum is sitting beside it looking as smug as Jeremy Paxman.

'Come on, Helen, get a grip! We need to get it out before it upsets the fish.'

More helpless, hysterical laughter follows. The kind that dislocates all your limbs, stops you breathing and makes you cry until every part of your body hurts. After several false starts we manage to compose ourselves sufficiently to hook the hat out of the water with Helen's ruler. The hat now looks like a drowned rat.

'Right, we've got twenty minutes before her treatment ends. Does Georgina have a hairdryer?'

Helen looks at me disbelievingly.

'Does the Queen have a balcony bra? Don't be ridiculous.

Does Georgina's hair ever, ever look like she owns a brush, let alone a hairdryer?'

'Well, the Queen definitely has a balcony . . . but fair enough.'

I send Helen to the house next door to try to borrow a hairdryer, and set about removing the excess water from the hat by alternately wringing it out in the sink and swinging it round and round my head. Much like drying lettuce in a tea towel if you haven't got one of those plastic twirly salad spinner thingies. Helen arrives back with a rather ancient-looking pink hairdryer – the colour of children's National Health glasses frames in the 1960s – courtesy of our octogenarian neighbour. It sends out a shower of sparks from the socket when plugged in and the jet of air it produces is no more powerful than the last gasp of a dying man, and smells just as bad. But eventually the drowned rat is reconstituted into a slightly damp fur hat, and we replace it on the coat stand in the hall with only seconds to spare. There is a rather distinctive aroma wafting around the whole ground floor that is a curious blend of wet fur, fish and burning, but we have no time to do anything about it other than to pretend it isn't there.

'There's rather an odd smell in here.'

Mrs Sweetie marches into the waiting room to be greeted for once (and I suspect it will only ever be this once) by a beaming smile from Helen, who takes her money and books her next appointment with eerie politeness. Helen and I peer through the open door of the waiting room to see Mrs Sweetie collecting her hat from the stand and adjusting it on her head in front of the mirror. She keeps sniffing the air, puzzling over the strange smell that seems to be stronger in the hall, but other than this she appears to be none the wiser. We exchange a conspiratorial expression of triumph, stifle a giggle and head off to the kitchen for a cup of tea. Just as I switch on the kettle, there is a glass-shattering scream from the hallway.

Mrs Sweetie has found Marion on one of the maiden aunts. Hurrah!

Chapter Twenty-Six

The fragile scrap of flesh and feathers cradled in my hands is still warm. But the body is limp and there is not the faintest tremor of life.

I had been crossing the park towards the café when I saw a horribly familiar group heading in my direction. Haizum was not with me today to act as bodyguard and it was obvious that Deliverance Boy had something to say. I kept my eyes on his, trying to control the anger that was welling up inside me like bile in my throat. The sight of his dead-fish eyes and arrogant grin as he swaggered across the grass were reason enough to make me want to punch him.

I kept my hands pushed deeply into my pockets.

Until he gave me the dead duckling.

'I've got something for you. It belongs to your friend – that fucking retard who feeds the birds. Thought you could give it back to her.'

It took me by surprise. A split second before my brain kicked in, my hand reached out. At the first brush of feathers on my skin I knew exactly what he had done, and exactly what was in my hand. His rabble of defective delinquents jeered and laughed, but Deliverance Boy was silent and grinning like Jack Nicholson in *The Shining*. In that moment he was a vessel for everything I hate.

I didn't touch him. I said nothing. But I drew so close to him that I could feel the warmth of his breath on my face. Close enough to register just a flicker of apprehension in those cadaverous eyes. I truly wanted to kill him, but instead, I spat in his face and walked away.

I have brought the duckling to the cemetery, but now I don't know what to do. I sit on a bench staring at the tiny corpse nestled in my palm, sobbing hot, angry, embarrassing tears. The wound that has never properly healed is torn a little further open. I could not save the duckling any more than I could save my Gabriel. I cry until my face is red and ugly, and my nose is sore and my head hurts. And then I stop and yell 'Fuck!' at the top of my voice until I feel a bit better (and one of the cemetery workers has heard me and is beginning to look worried). Eventually I take the duckling to the special angel and place it in her hands. I know that it will be eaten by a fox tonight, or even by the crows, but I am doing it for me; it's somehow kinder and more respectful than leaving it on the ground or putting it in a rubbish bin. The cemetery is almost deserted and two squirrels are chasing each other round the gravestones near the iron gate. Their fat bushy tails are twitching with excitement and one of them darts up a tree and the other follows. Their claws scratch across the bark as they helter-skelter up and down; racing and jumping and swinging; just for fun, just because they can.

As I cross the park towards home, Sally's crows are gathering on the grass in anticipation of their tea and suddenly I have a desperate need to see her. Even if, today, she is incoherent, I want to stand beside her. I want to bask in the reassurance that her corporeal presence brings. Haizum and I may have rescued her from Deliverance Boy, but she is certainly not one of life's victims. I have a feeling that she has fought far more formidable demons single-handedly and triumphs over them daily. I know nothing about her, but I know how she makes me feel. Safe. But at the same time strangely daring. It's as though, somehow, she gives me strength.

I hear her before I see her. She is singing 'Amazing Grace'. The crows jump and jostle at my feet as they watch her approach. It is too warm for her capacious coat, and today she is wearing a striped blazer over a blue velvet dress and her customary red shoes. She smiles when she sees me and hands me the bag of bread.

'You feed the buggers while I finish songing my sing,' she says. And so the crows and I are serenaded, while I scatter bread onto the grass. Sally doesn't sing quietly, to herself, or even just to me and her crows. She sings out to the world – or at least the park – launching the music into the air with unashamed pleasure and no trace of coyness. People stare as they pass us by and some even point and snigger, but Sally doesn't care. And neither do I. I'm not even angry with them. I feel sorry for them that they see a weirdo where I can see a wonder woman. And I'm proud and grateful that I'm with her.

Chapter
Twenty-Seven

~

Alice

Alice resisted the temptation to pick up the radio and hurl it across the room. But only just. The sound of it smashing against the hard floor and the sight of it fracturing and haemorrhaging its tinny innards would have been momentarily very satisfying, but she barely had the strength to lift it. That perky little theme tune that introduced *The Archers* had today become as intensely irritating as a persistent car alarm. She was trying to cook Mattie's tea, but it seemed a gargantuan task simply to pierce the plastic lid and place it in the microwave. The cardboard box said that it was tuna and tomato pasta bake, but the contents looked more like vomit. And she ought to know, she thought ruefully. She'd seen enough of it recently. She stared at the cooking instructions printed on the side of the box in tiny white letters. 'Cooking' was a rather overblown description for what was essentially simply 'making hot', she thought, wandering mentally away from the task in hand as she so often did these days.

A hungry Mattie came into the kitchen to find her stranded in the middle of the room, staring at the cardboard box. His stomach heaved with something other than hunger. Fear?

She hadn't even bothered to dress that day and was still wearing her pyjamas and an old cardigan.

'Mum?'

She looked at him with a mildly puzzled expression, as though she recognised his face but couldn't put a name to it.

'Are you okay, Mum?'

The sound of his voice seemingly jolted her back into their common reality. Back into their kitchen where tea was late again.

'Of course I am,' she snapped guiltily, as though she had been caught doing something she shouldn't.

'Shall I lay the table?'

Mattie's voice was quiet and deliberately patient; a treading-on-eggshells voice.

Alice nodded as she closed the microwave door and jabbed at the timer buttons with her finger. Exhausted by this simple task, she collapsed into the nearest chair and watched as Mattie set out plates and cutlery. Alice had no intention of eating anything, but she couldn't face Mattie's protests if she admitted it. He was watching the microwave and his mother as though they were both grenades that had lost their pins. The food had been in the microwave far longer than it should have been and Alice appeared to have forgotten it completely. The ping of the timer jogged her memory and she struggled to her feet.

'Sit down then, love,' she said to Mattie with a weary smile. 'Your tea's ready.'

But as Alice opened the microwave door a billow of smoke belched into the kitchen, setting off the alarm on the ceiling. The congealed contents of the carton were topped with a brittle, bubbled, inedible crust. She pulled at the hot plastic with her bare fingers, but, unable to hold it, sent it flying onto the kitchen floor where the plastic split and its contents oozed out into a puddle on the grubby lino. Alice howled, and kicked the remains of the carton, splattering globules of fish and tomato onto the nearby surfaces, and then sank to the floor where, hugging her knees, she began to rock and weep.

Half an hour later Mattie had cleaned up the mess, made his own meal and settled Alice in front of the television with a mug of peppermint tea. He sat down next to her with a tray, and as he tucked into beans on toast, he nudged her gently with his elbow and when she turned to him he grinned.

'Never mind, Mum. I didn't fancy that tuna thing anyway. It looked a bit like sick to me.'

Chapter
Twenty-Eight

Masha

Elvis is sitting in the front row wearing a white tuxedo jacket, a pink silk scarf, his usual hat and, unless I'm very much mistaken, a sweep of sparkly eyeshadow. The big night has finally arrived, and Edward and I are sitting several rows behind Elvis and slightly to his right in the rather uncomfortable wooden seats of our local theatre. The building is stuffy in the summer and draughty in winter. The parking is dreadful and the bar is tiny, but nonetheless we love it, and we also know that in this age where television is God and monstrous flatscreens rule, provincial theatres are closing as regularly as village post offices, and we are bloody lucky to have it.

According to the programme, which I made Edward buy, the role of Ko-Ko, Lord High Executioner of Titipu, is to be played by Marcus McMinn. So – this is Edward's 'good friend'. I am genuinely excited. This is a strictly amateur production and *The Mikado* is the perfect vehicle for every kind of glorious catastrophe that amateur dramatics can produce. I am intensely curious about the mysterious Marcus, and mildly intrigued as to what exactly Elvis is doing here. I didn't have him down as a Gilbert and Sullivan fan. Edward, who is looking particularly handsome tonight, is also looking a little nervous. I take his hand and squeeze it and he gives me a grateful smile. I have no idea what is going on here, but, as ever, when in doubt I think of Lady T and decide upon the all-round discretion and graciousness option for tonight, so I smile and don't ask any questions. Whatever it is, it is important to Edward, and Edward is important to me.

The lights go down and there is an expectant hush in the audience, punctuated by a couple of nervous giggles. The orchestra starts up – a couple of dodgy violins, a clarinet, a piano, some drums, a triangle, and wonderfully, unbelievably but unmistakably, a didgeridoo. If I start giggling now I shall have lost control of my bladder before the end of act one, so I dig my nails into my arm, bite my lip and stare straight ahead. I think 'graciousness' may have been setting the bar too high. Right now I'd settle for not embarrassing myself completely. The lights come up to reveal what looks like a reception area in a Chinese restaurant. There is a plain backdrop with a wooden screen on either side painted with rather odd-shaped pagodas, and men and women wearing coolie hats and waving chopsticks.

Two middle-aged Japanese ladies with very black slanted eyes and very red rosebud lips shuffle onto the stage in shoes that look like wooden platform flip-flops. They are wearing voluminous kimonos made of cheap, chintzy curtain material and black wigs that look like hats made of hair. They carry various items of scenery and props onto the stage, including a tree, a bush and a seat, and as they set each one down, they face the audience and motion to the item with both hands in the manner of a magician's assistant. I keep expecting them to exclaim, 'Ta-dah!' The director obviously thought that this was a clever theatrical device for setting the scene. In reality it just looks like someone forgot to put the scenery and props out before the audience arrived, and this is a last-minute solution.

Finally the stage is set and the Gentlemen's Chorus enters. These men are wearing brightly coloured nylon dressing gowns holding enough static to power the national grid, Smurf hats and Velcro-strapped sandals. They perform what looks like a clog dance (but without the clogs, obviously) and have a bit of a sing, but I hardly dare look as I am already struggling not to laugh. Some can apparently only sing or dance at one time, so the performance is a little disjointed. Edward is faring slightly better on the self-control front, but I can see the corners of his mouth beginning to twitch, and his hands are gripping the arms of his seat so tightly that his knuckles are turning white.

At the end of their song and dance routine, the audience applauds rather over-enthusiastically. In her guidance for appropriate conduct at the theatre, Lady T advises that 'indiscriminate hand-clapping is not only annoying but is a sign that the offender has poor judgement'; however, I suspect many members of this audience have been desperately suppressing hysterical laughter, and are taking the opportunity to release the tension and gird their loins for the next scene. I am now praying that for Edward's sake – and for mine, my graciousness hanging by a thread – his friend makes a better fist of Ko-Ko than the performances we have seen so far. The arrival on stage of the chorus of School-Girls certainly does nothing to restore my composure. The ages of these 'girls' range from post-menopausal to one poor old dear who's almost post-mortem. She needs to be discreetly helped around the stage by two more sprightly members of the chorus. These ladies are also wearing chintzy curtain-material kimonos, hair hats and platform flip-flops (except the really old one who is wearing tartan slippers). There is one 'girl' who is wearing slightly more lipstick than the others and whose kimono has a rather raunchy side split. She seems to be taking every opportunity to sashay and shimmy at Elvis in the front row. It's the scintillating sex-siren from the corner shop, and by the look of things, she and Elvis are now an item.

Chapter
Twenty-Nine

～

'Never mind Yum Yum, looks more like Big Bum to me.'

We are drinking wine in the courtyard outside the theatre during the interval, and reviewing the performance so far. Edward is clearly enjoying himself.

'Now, Edward, I think you're being a tad uncharitable. All the kimonos have got some sort of bustle affair at the back.'

'More like the back end of a bus in her case, don't you think?'

I can't help laughing. The production has been highly entertaining so far, for all the wrong reasons: the home-made costumes, created by a retired needlework teacher with a surplus of curtain material and a Smurf fetish; the wonderfully strange orchestra, and, most memorably, Elvis's latest flame. I have checked the programme for the names of those in the School-Girls' chorus. There is only one possibility. She has to be Kitty Muriel Peachey.

'Ko-Ko's rather good. Quite dishy, too.'

'Mmm . . .'

Edward seems to be occupied with fixing a cigarette into his holder, and is blushing ever so slightly. Ko-Ko has in fact been a revelation. Not only is he very handsome, but as a performer he is both talented and charismatic. He is certainly carrying this production virtually single-handed (with a little help from Kitty). Edward lights his cigarette and inhales deeply. He blows two perfect smoke rings and then smiles, and as I look into his sparkling eyes, the penny – in fact the whole purse of loose change – drops. Edward is in love.

Suddenly I feel rather hot and then, embarrassingly, my eyes fill with tears, so I pretend to look for something in my handbag. It's sheer relief that makes me want to cry, and as it hits me in a second wave I hiccup with the strain of trying to keep my emotions under control. I take a gulp of wine and blame Edward's cigarette smoke. He looks at me quizzically but says nothing.

I have always worried that Gabriel may have been the initial crack in Rupert's relationship with Edward. Not the sole cause of his flight to Hay-on-Wye with the reiki rake but the catalyst that precipitated its eventuality. Edward so adored Gabriel, but Rupert didn't share his enthusiasm. I think he may have been jealous. Even after Gabriel died. Since Rupert, Edward has had no significant other, which adds to my already considerable tally of things that I feel responsible for and therefore guilty about. But recently he has seemed more skittish. I thought he might be overdoing the espressos, but now it seems that Edward has been rejuvenated by romance and I couldn't be happier for him.

In the second half, the Mikado himself arrives, played by a rather handsome and imposing-looking man with all the stage presence of a brick. But on the positive side, he can walk unaided, sing almost in tune, and remembers most of his lines. Kitty Muriel continues to flirt outrageously with Elvis whenever she's on stage. And Edward is besotted. Each time Ko-Ko appears (tall, slim, dark hair and liquid brown eyes) Edward is transfixed. He is of course pretending not to be, and when he catches me watching him, he does the eyebrow thing and then points out something funny to distract me. But I can tell.

The performance ends with a rousing chorus including the

shuffling School-Girls (the really old one is now using a Zimmer frame), the clog-dancing Smurfs, and a final drone of the didgeridoo. The audience forces the cast to take several curtain calls with its enthusiastic clapping and cheering. Lady T is of the opinion that 'the stamping of feet, whistling or noisy acclamation of any kind is bad form'; however I'm pretty sure she never saw the like of this astonishing version of *The Mikado*, and Edward and I indulge in all three rapturously and in genuine appreciation of the entertainment that has been afforded, despite the fact that most of it was unintentional. I have tears of laughter running down my face, and my cheeks ache. And after two hours on a hard wooden seat, so does my bum; apologies, Lady T – *bottom*.

We retire to the pub where we are soon joined by Marcus, who in real life is an art curator from New York rather than a terminator from Titipu. He is every bit as charming, funny and kind as he looks. Well, as far as I can tell after five minutes in his company. I finish my drink, make my excuses and say my goodbyes. I recognise the role of first gooseberry on the left when I see it, and it's not one I'm going to play. Edward may just have found his leading man.

Chapter Thirty

⤿

On 13 January 1884 Dr William Price set fire to baby Jesus on a hill in Glamorgan. William was a Druid, a vegetarian, a believer in free love and an opponent of vivisection. He sounds like an interesting man. At the age of eighty-three he fathered a love child with his housekeeper and they called him Jesus Christ. Sadly, Jesus only lived for a few months, and William, reluctant to release the remains of his precious boy to the care of strangers and keen to honour his Druid beliefs, decided on the do-it-yourself funeral option, including a rather homespun cremation that was only partially successful. William's chapel-going neighbours were dreadfully put out (they perhaps had clean washing on the line that ended up smelling of bonfire) and insisted that his paediatric pyrotechnics be punished. However, Sir James Stephen of the Cardiff assizes judged that cremation was not an offence provided no nuisance was caused thereby to others. Sir James was a very forward-thinking man who clearly did not do his own laundry.

This is all true. I haven't made up a word of it, and I think it might be an original way to start the commentary when conducting my tour through the area of the cemetery where cremation ashes are buried. I'm really working hard on my material now, and I'm sure the injection of a touch of respectful humour wouldn't go amiss. It is a flat stretch of land over the top of the hill, shaded by ancient evergreens and bordered in places by miniature box hedges. On a hot day like today it provides a verdant sanctuary of sepulchral coolness, and is also the site of the 'dwarves' graveyard'. I wouldn't call it that out loud and certainly not on my tour, but that's how I think of it in my head. Rows of small headstones are laid out as though each marks the grave of a very small person. This is where I visit Ruby Ivy, Nellie Nora and Elsie Betty, who wore floral-patterned wraparound pinafores over their shelf-like bosoms, rollers under their headscarves, and all the proof of a lifetime's hard work etched onto their hands and faces. They were incorrigible quidnuncs (word of the day – *gossips*), and loved a night at the pictures, a glass of stout and their families; and the tea they brewed was strong enough to make you wince. Ruby Ivy swore like a navvy, Nellie Nora smoked roll-ups and Elsie Betty had a third nipple. They were neighbours in life, and remain so in death, and these ladies are my Guatemalan worry dolls.

Original worry dolls are tiny dolls dressed in brightly coloured scraps of woven material, who live in a little bag. Before you go to bed you take them out of their bag and tell them all your troubles, and then place them under your pillow. While you are sleeping, the dolls spend the night addressing your problems like nocturnal agony aunts, then in the morning you wake up with the solutions to all your problems present and correct inside your head. I haven't got any genuine Guatemalan worry dolls – and even if I had, Haizum would probably eat them – but I find Ruby Ivy, Nellie Nora and Elsie Betty do very nicely. I talked to them about my beloved boy. Admittedly that wasn't a problem they could solve, but I was at least able to share it with them. They are very good listeners. When Gabriel died, Edward sat and walked in the cemetery with me for hours in total silence, holding my hand and kindly pretending not to notice when I wept. I returned the favour. I knew that Edward was weeping too, and that his grief was almost as great as mine, but we simply couldn't talk about it. So I told the worry dolls. Sometimes it just helps to say the actual words out loud in a safe place and for me that means where nobody else can hear. Well, nobody still alive, that is. Today, I want to tell them about the duckling.

The air is hot and sticky with no whisper of a breeze, and the distant sky glowers with the promise of a thunderstorm. The silent shade of the dwarves' graveyard is a welcome relief after trudging up the hill, and I sit down on the cool grass in front of Ruby Ivy's headstone that is the middle one of the three. My back is facing Doris Priscilla, whose lips are no doubt pursed in sourfaced disapproval. Doris Priscilla lived in the same street as the others, but always considered herself to be somewhat above them. She never swore or wore her rollers in public, never took strong drink except at Christmas (and then only a small sherry), and never hung her underwear on the washing line 'for all and sundry to gawp at'. She thought smoking was only 'for men and chimneys', and never left the house without a brooch pinned to the lapel of her coat and a film of face powder on her turned-up nose. Elsie Betty felt a bit sorry for her and thought she needed to 'loosen her stays a bit', but Ruby Ivy said she was a stuck-up old cow and quite possibly a mucky sort on the quiet who didn't wear any underwear. I never talk to Doris.

After twenty minutes, I've got a numb bum and I've been bitten on my arm by a midge, but overall I'm feeling a bit better. And I'm considering raising another topic with my worry dolls.

'Ladies, what do you think about the idea of me possibly giving dating another go?'

The silence invites me to continue. I know that the ladies will be agog.

'It's not that I've met anyone in particular . . .'

'And I'm the bleedin' Queen of Sheba!' Ruby Ivy was never one to beat about the bush. 'Who's the lucky bloke, then?'

Well, it's not as though they're going to tell anyone.

'There's a man at the pool where I swim . . .'

I can hear Elsie Betty giggling. 'So, you've already seen him without his clothes on, then?'

'I haven't even spoken to him yet! But he seems nice, and yes, okay, he's also rather attractive. But I don't even know if he's single.'

'Well, I suggest you get a bloody move on then, and find out!' Ruby Ivy again. 'Because if he is, and he's as sexy as you say, he won't stay that way for long!'

'I didn't say he was sexy!'

'Bleedin' Ada! We weren't born yesterday, you know!' Ruby Ivy's on a roll now. 'You didn't need to spell it out – you're blushing!'

I am. But I think it's just the heat.

'And don't you go blaming the weather. You've definitely got the hots for this bloke.'

There's no fooling Ruby Ivy.

'Even if I have, and I'm not saying I have, it's been so long since I went out with anyone. Let's face it – I'm not much of a catch. Eccentric spinster with large dog, strange friends and an obsession with cemeteries and drowning, who talks to dead people and drives a 2CV.'

'It's no good fishing for bleedin' compliments. There's nothing wrong with you that a decent frock, a hairbrush and a bit of lipstick won't fix. Just break him in gently when it comes to the weird stuff. Wait 'til he's got his feet under your table, or better still, his toothbrush in your bathroom.'

Thanks, Ruby Ivy. Sound advice, but a bit premature.

'Well I reckon you should give him a go.' Nellie Nora always was the quietest of the three, but that somehow gave her words more weight. 'Give him the eye, and flirt with him a bit. See what happens. What have you got to lose?'

Good point. Nothing except my pride.

'And shift your bloomin' arse about it while you've still got your figure and your own teeth!' Ruby Ivy always has to have the last word.

I thank the ladies for their help and unfold my legs to stand up. I've got pins and needles from sitting so long, and I stamp about a bit until the fuzzy feeling disappears. As I'm leaving the dwarves' graveyard I say a quick hello to Percy Honey and Madge Jessop. Percy was a quiet, careful man who was very proud of his lawn and kept his garden tools immaculate. His dahlias won prizes. He never knew Madge in his lifetime, but was more than happy to be her neighbour after it. Madge Jessop had red hair, red nails and red lipstick, and she knew how to make a man happy.

I have no clients to see this afternoon, and I'm in no hurry to be anywhere so I take the winding path across the top of the hill towards the Field of Inebriation. From the path I can see the town and the countryside beyond, shimmering in the hazy heat of the afternoon sun. As I reach the highest part of the cemetery, a feeble breeze barely stirs the tall grasses and wild flowers. Here, inaccessible to the men and their mowers, the grass is left to grow as a meadow, and here, amongst the poppies, daisies and buttercups, lying on her back and sleeping peacefully, is Sally. Her hair, long and loose, fans out on the grass beneath her head and she is, unfathomably, wearing a beautiful, green tulle evening dress.

This unexpected sight reminds me of that famous painting that hangs in the Tate – Ophelia with her flowing hair and dress, singing as she drowns against a backdrop of jewel-hued flowers – the very same painting I'm intending to reference as part of my tour commentary to help illustrate the difficulties that were faced by those attempting to introduce cremation in this country in the late nineteenth century. I'm trying to develop my own style, and I'm going for a blend of history and humour. (I have now actually joined the 'Friends of the Cemetery', and paid my annual subscription, but I haven't volunteered for anything yet.)

Ophelia was painted by the very gifted Pre-Raphaelite artist John Everett Millais, and I'm rather surprised it didn't come back and bite him on the bum. The painting is exquisite, but not at all a suitable subject for a founder member of The Cremation Society of England such as Mr Millais. The Cremation Society of Great Britain was founded in 1874 by Sir Henry Thompson, who was a surgeon. He was also a stickler for hygiene and this was his principal argument in favour of cremation. It would therefore have been entirely inappropriate for Mr Millais to paint such a romanticised picture of a woman drowning. A woman who, in reality, would have quickly turned into a blotchy and bloated corpse and contaminated the water system with a variety of unpleasant bodily exudations. The very sort of pollution that pro-cremationists were seeking to eliminate. Perhaps Mr Millais was forced to release a press statement lamenting the shocking disregard for environmental issues shown in his early works, blaming his youth and an excess of romantic poetry.

As Sally sleeps I fidget awkwardly, torn between staying and walking on. If I stay I might be an unwelcome intrusion, but I am captivated. The breeze drops and the stillness intensifies. The air is thick and heavy, but I can smell the rain coming. The first growl of thunder is barely audible and the hairs on the back of my neck prickle. I love a good thunderstorm. Sally opens her eyes and looks up at me smiling as though I am exactly the sight she expected to see when she woke up.

'Fuck off,' she says cheerfully.

'It's going to rain.' I offer her my hand and help her to her feet.

'Lovely. Let's go up there and watch.'

From Sally's vague gesture, I gather that 'up there' appears to be the chapel. She takes my hand and sets off at a brisk pace, clearly fizzing with excitement. It thunders again, much louder this time, vibrating inside my ribs and almost rattling my teeth. When I was a little girl my well-meaning grandmother used to tell me that these heavenly rumblings were only the sound of God moving his furniture about. Frankly, I found the prospect of a giant sideboard crashing down to Earth and squashing me into a pile of blood and bones far more terrifying than a mere meteorological phenomenon. Big fat splashy raindrops begin to splatter down, and Sally claps with delight, sticking her tongue out to catch them. She tilts her head up to feel the cool rivulets running down her face, completely unconcerned that her dress is getting soaked. We pass beneath the canopy of a giant conifer that would serve as a splendid umbrella for both of us to shelter under, but Sally drags me on.

'Never stand under a bugger during a storm,' she instructs me seriously as the thunder cracks again and lightning catapults across the sky. I'm pretty sure she means 'tree', and once again, this is something I remember hearing from supposedly well-informed adults as a child, but I'm still not convinced. If the tree purportedly attracts lightning and you are standing under it, then I admit that if it is struck and falls, you may be crushed underneath and killed. But you may just be horribly maimed or even escape with minor scrapes and singes. If, on the other hand, you shun the shelter of the tree and stand about in the open, the lightning will surely be attracted to you as a primary target, and a direct hit is more likely to be fatal than a glancing blow from a falling tree. I always felt that if there were no nearby buildings in which to shelter, the best course of action to take would be to run like hell in a zigzagging, lightning-avoiding fashion. After all, a fast-moving target is surely harder to hit? We tumble into the porch of the chapel just as the storm is picking up pace. Sally's excitement is contagious, and with each clap of thunder and crackle of lightning, we squeal with delight and clutch one another like children watching a firework display. As the storm soars to its crescendo and the sky is ripped by another slash of light, Sally turns to me and winks.

'It's the same feeling as love with the right man. It fizzes your head, wobbles your legs and shakes, rattles and rolls your innards!'

As Sally thumps her chest to emphasise her point, I notice for the first time a small but exquisite diamond and opal engagement ring on the third finger of her left hand. It had never occurred to me that Sally might have a man, a lover or perhaps even a fiancé, but before I can ask her about the ring she draws back her shoulders, throws her arms open wide and begins to sing. Thunder and lightning are a perfect accompaniment to her rousing rendition of 'O Fortuna' from *Carmina Burana*, and once again I am astonished and delighted simply being in the company of this extraordinary woman. The rain is running in torrents down the paths from the chapel, and pooling in muddy puddles on the grass for the blackbirds to bathe in once the storm has passed over. Gradually the thunder rumbles away, and the lightning fizzles out like a spent sparkler. Sally's performance has also ended and she bows deeply in her drenched dress to the sound of my enthusiastic applause. She picks up the old canvas bag she has with her.

'Time to go and bollock the black birds.'

It's still raining hard.

'You'll drown!'

Sally turns to me and gives me a hug; brief, but a bear hug hard enough to squeeze my breath out. 'It's only water!' she replies.

As I watch her walk away towards the park, it occurs to me that if what she said is true, then I've never been with a 'right' man. My relationships have, at best, been passing squalls, and the only time my legs have turned to jelly and my innards have pitched and rolled was when I had morning sickness. It might be quite something to be swept away in a thunderstorm of passion. And now I'm thinking about the Olympian again! Sally is a distant figure, wandering unhurried and enjoying the rain, the hem of her dress dragging through the puddles. The hot humid air has been washed away, and the freshly drenched grass and leaves smell bright and clean. By the time she reaches the gate, my Ophelia too is drenched. Drenched, but definitely not drowning.

As for Mr John Everett Millais and his Ophelia, he must have been an undecided sort of chap. When he died in 1896 of throat cancer, he was buried in St Paul's Cathedral.

Chapter Thirty-One

Alice and Mattie

She couldn't sleep. It was pointless trying. The night stretched ahead of her like the infinite horizon of a desert, bleak and burning. Her skin had grown too small for her; it shrink-wrapped her flesh and bones. She wanted to rip it open before it burst. It was getting tighter and tighter and her flesh was boiling from the inside out. She felt as though she was being microwaved. She crawled out from beneath the bedcovers and as she crossed the room, bent and buckled with exhaustion, she caught sight of herself in the dressing-table mirror. The reflection both fascinated and repulsed her. The woman she saw was a grotesque stranger. At her bedroom window she gazed up at the flawless full moon, hung high in an inky sky glittering with raindrops. She had to go outside. She crept downstairs, every step a torturous effort of will, and eventually staggered out into the garden. Naked on the soaked grass, she raised her arms towards the moon and let the rain fall over her burning body. She felt each drop splash cold and hard on her bare head and, unimpeded by eyebrows or eyelashes, run down her face and into her eyes and mouth. The drugs had given her brain-fizz. A billion thoughts were growing and popping like bubbles inside her head.

Mattie heard the back door open. He jumped out of bed and peered cautiously into the garden from behind the curtain. The sight of his mother, naked and wet and baying at the moon was at once terrifying and heartbreaking. He couldn't bear to watch and he couldn't bear for her to know that he had seen her. She looked like Gollum. He threw himself back into bed and dragged the covers over his head.

Alice crumpled onto her knees. Her body was cold and exhausted, but her mind had bolted like a runaway horse. She just wanted to sleep.

Chapter Thirty-Two

⌒

Masha

Today's pool temperature is 15.2 and I am the only person in the water. I was here as soon as the lido opened, and there are others in the changing rooms, so my solitude won't last for long, but while it does it's blissful. The only sounds are my steady breathing and the water slapping against my body. Swimming has become my therapy and I haven't practised drowning for weeks now. The methodical repetition of movement, limb following limb, is strangely comforting and brings a peace I can't find anywhere else, even in the cemetery. It is the ultimate irony. Even when the pool is busy, swimming is a solitary exercise. I don't have to engage with anyone, it's just me and the water, and after a swim my mind feels clean.

By the time I start my twentieth length, there are a dozen others in the water, but the Olympian is not one of them. I don't like to admit it, but I'm more than a little disappointed. He is the one person I should like to engage with. My worry dolls would be disappointed that I haven't spoken to him yet, but when he's here, there's always a chance that I might. I've even practised in my head a couple of lines I might try, should the opportunity arise. It's Edward's fault. He's seeing Marcus – seeing as in *seeing* – and he seems so happy. It's made me think that it might be quite nice to have a man again. To permit the possibility of not growing old alone. It's only been – what? – four years since my last brief fling, so I hardly think I'm rushing things. My relationship with Gabriel's father ended as soon as he found out that I was pregnant. He wanted me to have a termination and when I refused, he terminated our relationship. I can't say I was sorry. By then I had seen what kind of man he really was, and he wasn't the father I wanted for my child. However, when Gabriel was born curiosity got the better of him and every now and then he made fleeting intrusions into our lives, bearing expensive gifts and empty promises. When Gabriel died, he blamed me. Simply because I was there. Since then I've found it hard to trust anyone except my closest friends, and my relationship history has been a barren wasteland punctuated by a paltry scattering of bad (single) dates and one affair that lasted a whole three weeks. Haizum didn't like him, and, come to think to of it, neither did I. He called Haizum a mutt. It was never going to work. But now I want to feel the thunderstorm inside me that Sally described. I wonder if the Olympian likes dogs.

I climb out of the pool just as the pedalo is getting in. She smiles at me as she lowers herself into the water and inexplicably I actually smile back. One small muscle movement for her, one giant social interaction for me. I never smile at people I don't know. As I peel off my wet costume in the changing room and rub myself dry, I catch sight of Masha in the mirror. I look as though I have shed a skin. I stare at my reflection in genuine amazement. My eyes sparkle and my cheeks are rosy. My once skinny arms and legs are toned and strong. I am growing stronger. Swimming is making me stronger. I am a very different woman now from the spectre I saw in Epiphany's bathroom mirror just a few months ago.

In the café, much to Flo's astonishment, I order a flat white and a full vegetarian breakfast.

'Stone the crows!' she exclaims as she takes my money. 'What's got into you?'

I smile (again!). 'I've just swum forty lengths and I'm bloody starving.'

* * *

After a busy day at work with three new clients (including a coulrophobic – coincidentally, word of the day, meaning someone with an unreasonable fear of clowns) I am looking forward to a stroll with Haizum followed by a fish and chip supper and a chilled glass of wine, but as I search for my key at the front door I can hear the phone ringing. Once inside, I dump my bag and fight my way past an excited Haizum to snatch the receiver.

'Your father's been arrested.'

It's Mum. This is startling news, but she doesn't seem unduly alarmed.

'What for?'

'Something to do with attacking someone in the park. Anyway, he wants you to go and pick him up from the police station.'

Mum doesn't drive, but I gather from her dissociative description of him as 'your father' rather than 'George' or even 'Dad', that she would be reluctant to fetch him even if she did. After years of marriage she is resigned to his resolutely confrontational approach to everything, but on occasion his bloody-mindedness wearies her. His angry letters to local councillors about the state of the roads and the pavements; his campaign for the reinstatement of corporal punishment in schools; his petition against the closure of the local library; his numerous visits to the local MP's surgery to complain about anti-social behaviour and to offer suggestions for improvements to local community services have all but driven Mum to an isolated cottage on the edge of Dartmoor. I may not always agree with his methods, but I admire his intentions and his enthusiasm. He is incapable of apathy, a trait that is as rare nowadays as it is laudable. He is essentially an honourable if rather old-fashioned man, which sometimes renders him a little naive and therefore vulnerable in a society where watching your own back is more common than looking out for your neighbours.

My dad can also be an awkward, cantankerous, bigoted and foul-mouthed old bugger, so it is with some trepidation that I pick up my car keys from the dresser in the hall. Haizum is not at all impressed. Having only just arrived home, the fact that I am clearly going out again without him is, in his eyes, indefensible. He heaves a heavy sigh of disgust, and returns to the sofa.

On the way to the squat, concrete 1960s block that serves as our local cop shop, I run through a few placatory niceties in my head that I feel sure I shall have to trot out to the pissed-off young police constable who will be babysitting my enraged father until a responsible adult arrives to pick him up. Having eventually found a parking space, I push through the grimy glass doors into the crowded reception area of the police station. Places like this make me want to run away. There is some sort of bizarre ticket system in operation, rather like the ones used on supermarket delicatessen counters. A pick and mix assortment of citizens sit clutching their pink scraps of paper, waiting for their numbers to be called. They include a drunk man propped in the corner shouting and trying to take his shoes off 'because they're full of fucking maggots' (judging from the smell in here, it could be true), a couple of skinny youths wearing gold chains that look heavier than their combined body weight, whispering to each other and texting on their mobile phones, and an anxious, middle-aged woman trying desperately to ignore the rantings of the man in the corner and clutching her handbag as though it might attempt to leap from her lap at any moment.

I am not going to queue for my father as though he is a ready-roasted chicken. I go straight to the desk, which is screened by protective glass, causing tuts and mutterings from those already waiting, and tell the duty officer that I am here to collect my wayward parent. A few minutes later a young and unexpectedly cheerful-looking police officer comes to collect me. On the way to the room where Dad is waiting he explains that Dad has been charged with assault on a minor. He doesn't go into details, but implies that they were reluctant to charge him but had no choice.

'I hope he hasn't been too difficult.'

'He was a bit upset when he came in, but he's calmed down since then.'

'You mean he was shouting and swearing and threatening you with his MP, but he's had a cup of tea and a chance to tell you his side of the story.'

'He's a lively old chap for his age, your dad, I'll say that much.'

The police officer smiles ruefully at me as he opens the door to the room where Dad is sitting. As soon as I see him, any irritation I might have felt vanishes. He looks physically smaller and frailer than the man I think of as my father, and just a little too relieved to see me. Once out of the building, however, he quickly regains his customary vigour and indignation, and gives a detailed account of his 'offence' in his usual colourful language accompanied by energetic arm-waving and head-shaking, so peculiarly European in such a British man.

Dad belongs to a community gardening group that looks after some small flower beds and a herb garden in the park, and he had volunteered to donate a few bedding plants and do a bit of weeding (which was rather a shock to Mum as he has staunchly shown a complete aversion to any activity in their own garden other than lying in the hammock). He was keen to go after it had rained, as he said the wet soil made it easier to pull up the weeds. As he arrived, he saw a young boy of about fourteen take the life belt from its wooden housing next to the lake and chuck it into the water. The boy then defaced the empty wooden case with a can of spray paint – a single word followed by a smiley face. 'Drown!' Even when he saw Dad approaching, the boy didn't stop. Dad yelled at him and was told to 'Fuck off! You stupid old wanker!' and hit on the forehead by the can of spray paint that was thrown at him. Dad tried to grab him but the boy jumped on his bike and, in exasperation, Dad threw the hand trowel he was holding at the boy. It missed him but caught in the spokes of his front wheel and he was thrown over the handlebars. Apparently, Dad was intending to make a citizen's arrest but 'the little shit' ran off before he had the chance. Dad washed the cut on his head in the public toilets and started doing the weeding. He was, he says, going to report it to the police when he got home, but events rather overtook him. About twenty minutes later the little shit reappeared with daddy shit, and two police officers who promptly arrested Dad for assault.

'But why didn't you tell them that he threw the can at you first?'

'I'm not an imbecile, my girl. I did. And showed them the cut. But that lying little toe-rag claims that the can flew out of his hand as he fell off the bike, and it hit me by accident.'

'What about the life belt and the graffiti?'

'He denied it. No one else saw him do it, so it's his word against mine.'

'But what about the can of paint?'

'Circumstantial, my dear Watson.'

The boy also claimed that Dad had stolen his bike and threatened to kill him.

'I didn't steal his bike, but I did threaten to kill the cheeky little bastard. They should bring back the rod if you ask m—'

'You may not want to share that view too widely when the police interview you again.'

I drive him home and stop beside his neatly mown grass verge. He doesn't look at me, but places his hand over mine.

'My grandson would never have behaved like that.'

And so it is that all roads lead us back to this same place. Gabriel's grave. And it is my fault. My grief has been the magnet that pulls everyone back.

It has to stop.

He kisses my cheek and gets out of the car.

'Make sure you put some antiseptic on that cut, and tell Mum I'll ring her later.'

'I wish I'd been holding the hoe. I might have actually hit the little sod then.'

Chapter Thirty-Three

Here comes the bride.
All dressed in . . . brown bombazine

Not exactly every girl's romantic dream. But for a Victorian bride who had the misfortune to find herself mourning a close relative inconsiderate enough to die close to her wedding day, a frock horror reality. This is going to be the fashion feature in my cemetery tour commentary. Pongee, bombazine, crape and barathea may sound like the names of canine characters in *The Hundred and One Dalmatians*, but they were actually fabrics unattractive enough to be appropriate for the fashioning of ladies' mourning outfits in the nineteenth century. Mourning was a complicated, expensive and miserable business, especially for women. In fact, it was a pile of crape. An astonishing variety of crape was available, to suit every style of mourning. Norwich crape was hard and very crimped; Canton crape was softer; Crape Anglaise was embossed, and bombazine was a cheaper crape substitute, coarse and scratchy. Women had to demonstrate their mourning proficiency by wearing dull black frocks trimmed with yards of crepitating (word of the day – *making a crackling sound*) crape, rough, black undergarments and matt black accessories, whilst staying at home and weaving miniature works of art using the hair from the deceased (head hair, I'm hoping), to be framed, or inserted into pieces of memorial jewellery.

Historical commentators have tried to argue that this enforced fashion moratorium was beneficial to women because mourning clothes identified the wearer as recently bereaved, and therefore attracted support and sympathy. I used to think that they were once again talking crape. Given the choice between a new frock, a pair of red shoes with killer heels and the chance to dance in them until you have blisters, and staying at home trussed up in a scratchy, black, ugly dress plaiting dead man's hair trinkets and embroidering black-edged, mourning antimacassars, I'm reasonably confident that most women would choose the former to lift their spirits, if only temporarily. But then it didn't work for me, did it – my freestyle mourning? Perhaps if I'd had a set of rules to follow I'd have done my time and got on with living my life years ago.

I haven't spotted bombazine blouses or crape coats on any members of the funeral party today. It is bright and sunny but very windy, and the trees in the cemetery are swishing and swaying against the bright blue sky. Haizum's tail is also swishing and swaying with excitement. The wind always makes him skittish. I keep my distance from the group that is now gathered around the freshly dug grave, and take the path up towards the chapel. Parked outside are the shiny black hearse and two more slinky black limousines. The drivers in their frock coats, top hats and gloves are chatting and laughing quietly, and enjoying a crafty cigarette between them in the sunshine. One of them seems vaguely familiar. They nod at us in friendly acknowledgement as we pass and one of them smiles and says, 'Good Afternoon.' It's Elvis.

Men, of course, were not expected to spend too much of their valuable time and effort mourning. After a few weeks wearing dark suits and abstaining from any big nights out, they were good to go. Indeed, a widower could even remarry as soon as he liked, if he could find a woman desperate enough to have him. And desperate she would have to be, for although her new husband could swan about in canary yellow waistcoats, or peacock blue gloves if he so wished, she would be expected to take up mourning for her predecessor, which wasn't much of an inducement to marry.

I climb further up the hill, past the chapel towards the dwarves' graveyard, and cut across the grass to a wooden bench where I sit down and survey the scene before me. From here I can see the mourners returning to the cars, and none of them is wearing black. There is green and brown and blue, and even red. But no black. It was probably stipulated in the funeral notice – 'No black'. No bombazine. It seems to be more usual nowadays for bright colours to be worn to 'celebrate the life of the deceased'. Lady T must be turning in her grave. Her advice on this matter is unequivocal: 'Vivid colours, either on a man or a woman, show a disregard for the feeling of the mourners, a lack of respect for oneself, and a distinct ignorance of the laws of good conduct.'

She would undoubtedly feel that brightly dressed funeral guests were not taking the matter seriously, but I should prefer people at my funeral to be seriously stylish in scarlet, rather than bleak and boring in black.

The doors of the limousines are closed with a soft clunk by the undertakers; serious and dignified now in their tall hats. The cars snake slowly down the hill, under the arch of the lodge building and out of the iron gates. As the cortège disappears back into the land of the living, I wonder if the grieving family cocooned inside the long black cars are looking out at the bustling streets where daily life continues, callously regardless of their loss. I wonder if any of them is thinking, as I have done, 'How can the rest of the world be so completely unaffected by this death? How can everything else be so normal?' But death *is* normal. We just can't admit it any more.

There was no funeral for Gabriel. His body was never found. No body, no funeral; that's the rule. And so there was a memorial service with music by Puccini and Postman Pat, readings from A. A. Milne and Dr. Seuss and white roses everywhere. It was beautiful. And it was the worst day of my life. But the rest of the world just carried on as normal.

I know what you're thinking. If a body was never found, then how did I know that Gabriel was dead? The police assured me that there was no other possibility. And besides, what good would hope have done? It would simply have been the exchange of one sort of pain for another; the pain of loss and guilt for the pain of fear and uncertainty. Where is he? Who is he with and what are they doing to him? At least the first kind of pain is constant and predictable, rather like an unexciting but dependable lover. The second flashes and fades, and then flares again like the fickle attentions of a cruel libertine, but still leaves you desolate, wasted and alone.

I am curious about the new arrival in the cemetery. I suspect Lady T would consider it rather bad form to nosey round a new grave so soon after it has been occupied, but there is nobody about, and I could just take a look in passing.

Instead of following the path we wander across the grass, skirting the dwarves' graveyard and passing the honey pots. The honey pots contain the ashes of those who did not wish to be buried underground. The structure is made up of hexagonal plaques that are screwed on to the front of individual compartments in which the urns are stored, creating a collection of honeycomb cupboards that I have christened 'the honey pots'. They are home to Bert and Effie Perkins who were ballroom-dancing enthusiasts, and amateur champions. They spent most weekends travelling the country taking part in competitions, and at least three evenings a week practising. Every Friday at 4.30 p.m., Effie would leave the optician's where she worked as a receptionist, and visit her local hairdressing salon to have her platinum-blonde locks teased and twisted into a spectacular high-rise coiffure robust enough to withstand a gale-force wind on the pier at Blackpool and emerge unscathed, which was just as well as it often had to. The Tower Ballroom at Blackpool was one of their favourite places to dance. Bert was the assistant manager in a hardware store, and all his hair needed was a fortnightly trim at the barber's and a generous slick of Brylcreem. At the age of sixty-eight, Bert's gout got the better of him, and his twinkle toes were unable to tango any more. The couple continued to follow their hobby as enthusiastic spectators until Bert died six years later. Effie lived on for another ten years, eight of them cruelly confused by Alzheimer's. She would dance around the ward of the mental hospital that was her last home, with her head high and one hand holding out the long skirt of her imaginary dress, until someone gave her another one of the pills that switched off the music that played in her head.

As we approach the Field of Inebriation I release Haizum from his lead with strict instructions not to cock his leg against anything he shouldn't. One of the few headstones here with a still-legible inscription is that of Raphael Chevalier, surgeon and doctor of medicine, who died in 1886 aged eighty-two, which was a jolly good innings for a man of his times. He never married, but was a beloved uncle to his sister's seven children, and lived alone in a large house facing the park, cared for by his irascible but devoted housekeeper, Mrs Bray. He was clearly a fine advertisement for his own profession by living such a long and healthy life (or perhaps a fine advertisement for not marrying, having no children, and paying someone else to do the cleaning). I'm always slightly worried that Raphael's grave is within sight of the bench where Edward and I have lunch, when lunch is accompanied by wine. I worry that Raphael may be totting up the units of alcohol consumed and raising his eyebrows in quiet disapproval.

Haizum is loping through the long grass, pausing now and then to enjoy a particularly pungent smell, or cock his leg up a tree to create one for fellow canines to appreciate. As I weave my way through the higgledy-piggledy headstones, I can hear snatches of a conversation carried by the wind. I look down the hill, and on the path below I can see Kitty Muriel – in a bright red dress and peep-toe, patent mules – walking arm in arm with Sally. Sally sees me and calls out. At the sound of her voice, Haizum gallops down to meet her. He associates her with food, which takes precedence over just about everything else, and he greets her with rambunctious enthusiasm. Sally bends down to hug him, but his participation in this display of affection is merely a ruse to allow him to shove his nose into her pocket and search for anything edible.

'What a splendid hound!' Kitty Muriel enthuses.

I have reluctantly followed Haizum down to the path. Why is it that on the one day I get up and drag on whatever clothes are to hand, eschew even a cursory trace of make-up, and leave my unruly hair to its own devices, I bump into one of the most glamorous women I know? Even Sally's attire has an air of rakish eccentricity – no evening dress today, but a wonderful wide-brimmed hat with orange flowers and bright pink wellingtons. I used to have what Edward called my own 'individual' style. It might not have been to everyone's taste, but my fashion fusion of vintage and whatever else took my fancy was always memorable. When Gabriel died, no one forced me to wear crape or bombazine, but bothering about what I wore seemed somehow frivolous; ridiculous even. The flamboyance may have faded away, but I normally look presentable. Boring, perhaps – but presentable nonetheless. Today I just look slovenly and unkempt. I am in no fit state to be seen by these two women, whose opinion of me has inexplicably begun to matter so much. But Kitty Muriel's joie de vivre is hard to resist.

'Did you see the funeral?' she asks proudly.

'Yes, I did.'

'Then you must have seen my gorgeous man. He was the tall, dark, utterly handsome one driving the hearse. I love to see him at work. He looks so capable and dignified. And let's face it, incredibly sexy. Of course, I never let him see I'm here. I should hate him to be distracted. It would be unforgivably improper of me.'

The wind whips her scarlet dress around her still shapely legs, and buffets her hair which is precariously twisted into her customary chignon, but she is clearly untroubled by the ravages of nature. Rather, I should say she is the type of woman who revels in them. This woman exudes old-school glamour and unashamed joy. If they bottled it, I'd be first in the queue to buy it. Small wonder Elvis is besotted. And so is Haizum, which is most unusual because she doesn't appear to be concealing anything edible about her person. Nonetheless, he is gazing up at her adoringly as she fondles his ears.

'Let's go and visit the new arrival.' Sally takes my arm and the four of us set off in the direction of the newly occupied grave. We leave the path and wander through the windswept Field of Inebriation. How Kitty Muriel manages such precarious terrain in her high heels is a mystery, but she is as surefooted as Sally is in her wellingtons.

'I saw you in *The Mikado*,' I tell her. 'You were marvellous!'

Kitty Muriel laughs out loud. 'Thank you, my dear, but I was also a shameless show-off. You see, my lovely man came to watch, and I was worried that the production was a little *sedentary*. I didn't want him to fall asleep.'

'Well, I'm sure there was no danger of that!' I reassure her.

'They're nice enough people, the Dam Rams, as I call them, but they are awfully conservative. We really need some more new blood like the gorgeous Marcus, who's recently joined us. He was the Lord High Executioner. He's very talented, and such a lovely man, too.'

I'm very pleased to hear it, for Edward's sake. 'I've met him. He's a friend of a friend.'

'Well then, you'll know just how lovely he is.'

For some reason, I'm reassured on Edward's behalf that Kitty Muriel thinks highly of his new beau.

After walking for a few minutes we see the new grave covered in flowers, directly below us. It is in the old part of the cemetery, and therefore must be a double plot where someone has been reunited with their partner or another member of their family. I reattach Haizum to his lead. I can't risk him weeing over the fresh flowers. He looks at me with the sulky expression of a small boy who has been called in for his tea before his game of football has finished. The grave is already occupied by Stanley Mortimer Graves (I kid you not), loved and missed by his wife, Sheila, and children, Robert and Tracy. So I'm guessing the new arrival is Sheila, judging by the rather horrid floral tributes spelling 'Nana' and 'Mum' in unnaturally coloured chrysanthemums. Dad says he wants one placed on the top of his coffin that says 'Dead'. I think it's a fabulous idea, but I'm rather afraid that the humour might be lost on some of our relatives, who will just think it's a spelling mistake.

Kitty Muriel is reading the cards attached to the wreaths and sprays.

'I always think it's rather a shame that so many flowers are left to die in a heap on top of the grave,' she says, cradling a pale pink rose from one of the more tasteful arrangements in the palm of her hand. 'It's not as though poor Sheila can even see them.'

'But they're not really for Sheila, are they?' Sally pokes gently at one of the flower words with the tip of her wellington boot. 'They're for her family and friends to show everyone how much they loved her.'

Kitty Muriel stands up and takes Sally's arm again.

'Well, when I die I want you to raise a toast to me over my grave with a bottle of champagne! Flowers will not be necessary.'

Sally smiles. 'It's a deal! And if I go first, I want the same.'

A little later, walking home with Haizum, I think about what Sally said. I took all the flowers from Gabriel's memorial service home with me and kept them until the blooms shattered and dropped petals everywhere, and the water they stood in turned green and rank. Perhaps now, after all these years, I can stop holding on to his death and drink to his life with champagne.

Chapter Thirty-Four

Alice and Mattie

'Incy wincy spider climbed up the water spout . . .'

It was the first song Mattie had learned at nursery. The veins in Alice's arms looked like spiders' legs; black and gnarled and spindly. And they throbbed and ached, weary of the poison pumped through them time and again. But today was a good day. She would take no drugs today. Outside the sun was shining. A spring sun, brittle and bright, but not yet ripe enough to bring any real warmth. Alice was still in her nightdress and her feet were bare as she wandered around the garden trying to remember why she was there. A spider's web caught in the rosemary bush trembled in the morning breeze. Alice crushed some of the eau de nil leaves between her fingers and breathed in their pungent aroma. She would cook something nice for Mattie's tea as a surprise. He had football this afternoon (at least, she thought it was this afternoon) and would come home ravenous. The spider was frantically repairing the tear in its web that Alice had made when she had plucked the leaves.

'Incy, wincy spider climbed up the water spout . . .'

Alice couldn't remember the rest.

Mattie was trying to make the walk home from the bus stop take as long as possible, but he knew that he was only postponing the inevitable. It was like eating all the things you enjoy first from your Christmas dinner; you'd still be left with the Brussels sprouts to eat at the end. He didn't want to go home at all. It didn't feel like home any more. He never knew which Alice was going to be waiting when he got there. Some days it was almost like it used to be. His mum would have showered and got dressed properly, and even made some dinner. She would ask him how school had been and then after he'd done his homework they might watch something on TV together. But on other days she seemed almost surprised to see him, as though she'd forgotten she even had a son. The house would be a mess and Mattie would have to get his own tea while his mum lay on the sofa still in her dressing gown, drifting in and out of sleep. In spite of all his teenage bravado with his friends at school, he felt too young to be dealing with this alone.

He didn't know what to do – whether to do anything. There were no grandparents or aunties and uncles that he could ask. He had almost told his teacher at school. His grades were suffering; nothing too disastrous, but a noticeable decline from last year, and Mrs Jackson had asked him if everything was all right at home. She was about the same age as his mum, but that was all that they had in common. Mrs Jackson was a brisk and confident woman who took no prisoners if anyone crossed her in the classroom. But she also had a genuine vocation for teaching and the welfare of her pupils was as much her concern as their academic achievements. It had been a carefully casual question, tossed into the conversation when she was going over some classwork with him at her desk, and he had been sorely tempted to confide in her. It would have been such a relief to admit that he was scared.

Scared of going home, scared of what he might find, and sometimes even scared of his own mum.

Mattie had told Mrs Jackson that everything was fine. To have said anything else would have felt like a betrayal.

His sports bag was heavy and digging into the scant flesh on his shoulder, but at least today his team had won and he had scored two goals. He wondered if his mum would even remember that he was playing. He pushed open the garden gate, dawdled reluctantly up the path and dumped his bags on the ground to fish his key out of his pocket. As soon as the door was opened, Mattie caught the delicious scent of something cooking and his heart sang. Shepherd's pie!

Chapter Thirty-Five

～

Masha

The snow is falling softly over Paris. The Eiffel Tower is veiled by a cascade of feathery snowflakes, and the va-va-vroom of the city's traffic is muffled by a sparkling blanket of white. The voices I can hear are muffled too, but I am no longer in Paris. I am in a plastic chair in an overheated, airless room, with green, white and orange wallpaper and a ferociously patterned carpet. I screw my eyes tight shut and try to re-evoke Paris, but the City of Light has vanished into the darkness. I am seated at a blue Formica-topped table, and in front of me is a powder blue plastic plate bearing a pink fondant fancy.

'She's not getting down until she's eaten it.'

It sounds as though the speaker is underwater. I form my mouth into a shape ready for speaking but no words come out. Something is missing. The familiar landscape inside my mouth is flattened, softened, useless. I have no teeth. My gums gibber fruitlessly. I can only manage a few pathetic sucks and gurgles. I make the Elephant Man sound as crisp as a Radio 4 news presenter. I kick the table leg in frustration, and am instantly rewarded with a rap over my bony knuckles with a wooden spoon (the pain of which is slightly tempered by the fact that I notice at this point that I am wearing a pair of bright red patent tango shoes). I pick up the fondant fancy and hold it reverentially in the palm of my hand, studying it closely as though it is a precious treasure, before slowly closing my hand and squeezing tightly until it oozes out between my fingers, a sticky mess of cream and sponge and icing. Once my hand is fully closed, I flick it open, flinging out my arm and sweeping it in a semicircle; a defiant flourish that pebble-dashes the walls and furniture with squished cake.

There is a poor soul whose scrawny limbs are folded up into a stained and musty armchair in the corner. He is so decrepit and desiccated by extreme old age that he looks more like a giant grasshopper with dentures than a human specimen. He was doing a convincing impression of a mummified corpse until a splat of cake hit him in the face. His tongue crawls out of his mouth and wriggles down his chin, searching for the cake, like a blind pink slug searching for a succulent lettuce leaf. A trickle of saliva bubbles out of the cracked corner of his mouth and his bony knees begin to jiggle with excitement. On the far side of the room, a fat old woman in a bright blue flowery dress, whose flesh is the colour and consistency of a strawberry blancmange, is sucking splodges of fondant fancy off the wall.

The underwater voice commands the blancmange to stop licking the wallpaper, and as I turn to face the speaker, the woman I see is clearly the less compassionate sister of Nurse Ratched. She lunges down towards me, gripping my frail thighs between her steely fingers and snarls, 'Bring me the beige tartan slippers!'

I would rather die than surrender my red patent shoes to this execrable nurse. I grab a dessert fork from the table, and with all the strength my rage can muster (which is a fair bit, surprisingly) I plunge it into her sinewy forearm. Now, I appreciate that this would definitely qualify as one of Lady T's 'ugly tricks at meals', but frankly, on this particular occasion, I couldn't give a flying fork. Her face contorts with shock and pain, and her response is a gratifying, 'I'm dying . . .' but the voice is different; sharper, clearer, closer, and the sentence is not finished: 'of boredom in my own little purgatory of domestic tedium.'

The Happy Endings home disappears like spit down a dentist's suction tube. I am in my consulting room holding my snow globe, and the dreadful thing is that I have obviously fallen asleep whilst with one of my clients. But the dreadful thing is offset by three splendid other things: 1) I've woken up and it was all a ghastly nightmare; 2) The client hasn't noticed; and 3) She's my least favourite client, so I wouldn't have minded much if she had.

Mrs Celine Hazel Bray (aka Saline Nasal Spray) is a slim, blonde, thirty-something with expensive caramel lowlights, a gym-toned body and perfectly veneered teeth. She has a generous and loving husband who works long hours as a neurosurgeon in a city hospital, two perfectly nice little girls in private prep school, a cleaner, an au pair, a gardener, a personal trainer, and far too much time on her perfectly manicured never-seen-a-day's-work-in-their-lives hands. She also has a psychotherapist. Me. She doesn't need a psychotherapist. She needs a swift kick up her taut little backside, and today might just be the very day she gets it.

Saline only came to me in the first place because one of the people in her book club had been to see a psychologist and had found it 'so empowering!' Saline wanted to combine the drama queen kudos of being 'in therapy', with what she perceived to be a trendy new addition to the plethora of requirements essential for her personal maintenance. I think she sees me as some sort of psychological personal stylist, although she completely ignores me, and continues to live her life in her own selfish and superficial fashion. She doesn't need me, she needs a proper life, with hopes and disappointments, fear and excitement, failures and successes. She needs rough and smooth, ups and downs, light and shade. Instead she is cocooned in safe, expensive, plush, predictable, 'dry clean only' taupe. She is not a bad woman, merely a rather self-centred and shallow one who has no idea how lucky she is. She needs to be a proper mother to her little girls instead of hiring an au pair she doesn't need. Their childhood is more precious than she realises and she is missing most of it.

I put the snow globe down carefully on my desk, turn my chair to face her (it had been sideways on, which may have helped hide the fact that I had dropped off) and surreptitiously wipe my hand across my mouth in case I have dribbled in my sleep. I look her straight in the eyes, and take a deep breath. I probably should have told her this a long time ago, but didn't have the courage. Now it seems I can't stop myself.

'Yes, Celine, you are dying. We are all dying. We shall all end up completely, utterly and absolutely dead. As doornails. But we are not dead yet. Your problem is that you are too lazy, too scared or too stupid to spend the time leading up to your death living. Really living. Do something! Instead of spending every day having your hair done, your nails painted, your teeth fixed, your body trained or your colon irrigated, for heaven's sake do something. Preferably for someone else – for your lovely little girls, your exhausted husband, the little old lady down the road, or some charity. The clock is ticking, Saline [oops!], and I'm sure you'll feel so much better when you die – and perhaps, if you're lucky, even before that – if you haven't wasted your life being a vain and useless ninny whose sole contribution was to keep handbag designers in Botox and foreign holidays.'

I feel much better already, having got that off my chest. I'm not so sure about Saline though. She is staring at me in amazement.

'Don't worry,' I hear myself say, 'there's no charge for today's session. Although it's probably the most valuable advice I've ever given you.'

Without a word, she picks up her ridiculous but very expensive snakeskin tote bag (that boasts more brass furniture than our front door) and clip-clops out of the room with sparks of indignation flying from her Manolos. Several minutes later there is a tap on the door, and Helen appears with a tray bearing a cup and saucer of steaming brown tea and a plate of rich tea biscuits. She sets the tray down on my desk as best she can amongst the piles of papers, and looks at me quizzically.

'I thought you might need this.'

'You're an angel.'

'You know perfectly well that I am no such thing. And neither are you, judging by the mood Saline left in. What on earth did you do to her?'

'I gave her a swift kick up her personally trained, taut little tush.'

'Oh well, that's all right then.'

Helen leaves me to my tea and biscuits. Lady T offers no specific advice about the dunking of biscuits in tea, which I have interpreted as tacit approval. However, I'm not too sure that she would be impressed by my technique. The timing with rich tea biscuits is crucial, and after years of practice I still finish up with half a biscuit sloshing around in the bottom of my cup, which then has to be fished out with a teaspoon.

The intercom on my desk buzzes and Helen's voice announces the arrival of my next client. A tall, attractive man in his late forties comes in and sets down his bulging black briefcase on the floor. He is slightly overweight, with the dark, glossy eyes of a Labrador, and curly brown hair, neatly cut and greying at the sides. He is immaculately dressed in a dark suit, striped shirt and highly polished black lace-up brogues, and he smells of expensive aftershave and mints. He takes off his jacket and sits down on the squishy sofa. There is a knock at the door and Helen comes in carrying another tray with a large mug of tea and another plate of biscuits. She sets it down on the side table next to the sofa, and the man thanks her in a deep voice that is a potent blend of kind and sexy. Helen flashes him her best smile and closes the door behind her. The man leans forward and undoes the briefcase, from which he removes a rather battered-looking hardback book. He settles back into the sofa, takes a sip of tea and then opens his book and begins to read *The House at Pooh Corner* by A. A. Milne.

Mr John Paddington is a high-profile barrister whose ruthlessness and proficiency, both in and out of the courtroom, are feared and respected in equal measure by all who know him. He commutes to London every day and works punishingly long hours at a job he loves and takes enormous pride in. He comes home to a delightful wife, four boisterous young sons and a cherished baby daughter, all of whom he adores unconditionally, and spends every minute of each precious weekend being a good father and husband. And that is why, once a week, for one hour only, Mr John Paddington comes to see me. This is his one self-indulgence; his oasis of peace and quiet. He asks nothing more of me than my silent company, and the use of my comfortable room (the tea and biscuits are Helen's treat, because she has a bit of a crush on him) where he can sit and read Winnie-the-Pooh without fear of intrusion or ridicule.

When he first came to me with his rather strange request, I was a little hesitant. 'Why not go to the library?' I asked. He explained that he wanted somewhere more cosy and homelike, and company, but not too much of it. He did not require interaction, only physical companionship. I asked him why he had chosen me, and he replied that I was in the business of helping people to live their lives in the best way possible for them. This one hour a week does exactly that for him. It is his safety valve. It dissipates the stress and pressure he accumulates, and enables him to live the life he chooses without burning out. It's a service that I am more than happy to provide, and more reciprocal than I care to admit. Sometimes, as he reads, I watch his handsome features slowly relax. The frown lines on his brow grow smooth, and the outer corners of his eyes crinkle as the beginnings of a smile softly steal across his face. Sometimes he catches me watching him and smiles at me before returning to his book. By the time he leaves he always looks much younger; more like the boy who first read about the bear of very little brain.

A little before his hour is up, Mr John Paddington checks his watch and reluctantly closes his book. He replaces it carefully in his briefcase, and struggles to escape the warm embrace of the squishy sofa. He puts on his jacket and, without a word, takes my hand and kisses it with tenderness and gratitude. And then he leaves. Each visit is the same. He is my favourite client.

Chapter Thirty-Six

The owner of the second-hand bookshop is a very kind man. Either that, or he believes that I am a madwoman whom it is safest to humour. When I took him two carrier bags full of books about death this morning, he behaved as though it was the most normal thing in the world. I am making room in my life for living and so I have been clearing out my books about death. Some of them came from his shop in the first place. But I do remember one that even he was unable to procure. *The Rule and Exercises of Holy Dying* by Bishop Jeremy Taylor (first published in 1651) was probably one of the earliest self-help books. These days we can buy books to help us do pretty much everything. You name it and someone somewhere will have written a book about it. There are even books about how to write self-help books. But in 1651 you could buy a book that taught you how to die properly – or rather how to die in a proper manner. Bishop Taylor was a sort of Lady Troubridge of death. His book was one of a particular genre of contemporary literature known as *ars moriendi* – the art of dying.

Back then a sudden death was unfortunate for the deceased in more ways than the obvious. Preparation for death was paramount and so a protracted demise was infinitely preferable because it gave one time for all the essential preliminaries. The deathbed was no place for slackers and its occupant was encouraged to pray, atone for past misdeeds, issue sage advice to kith and kin, pose for a final portrait and make his or her fond farewells. Of course, nowadays you'd probably be able to get a deathbed planner to do most of it for you. The planner could issue printed farewells and poignant advice to friends and family on tastefully designed mourning stationery, organise a personal shopper for your death-bed outfit, post your final selfie on social media and email a selection of contrite prayers to the god of your choice. You would simply have to turn up on the day looking fabulous, and die gracefully.

The approach to the entrance of my cemetery is a steep slope that becomes an unnerving hazard to hearse drivers in icy weather and is a strenuous walk in today's bright sunshine. The wrought-iron gates form the centrepiece of the redbrick gatehouse whose arch proclaims, in carved stone, that the cemetery was opened in 1855. As I pass beneath the cool shade of the arch, my footsteps echo through the silence. Even though the cemetery was built more than two hundred years after Bishop Taylor's book was first published, the Victorians buried here would still have made use of it as a handy reference on death etiquette and I'm hoping to weave all this fascinating information into my cemetery tour commentary. I've spoken to the person who is responsible for organising the tours. Brenda Smiley is the chairperson of the Friends of the Cemetery General Committee, and she isn't. Smiley. She's a stern-faced woman who wears cord trousers, a wax jacket and an habitual scowl. She didn't seem very pleased when I offered my services. She told me that being a tour guide was a very sought-after position, and one was usually only entrusted with such a hallowed responsibility (my sarcasm, not hers) after earning one's stripes litter-picking and weeding. I get the impression she doesn't like me much. One of the other committee members told me that they are in fact crying out for tour guides, but no one likes to contradict Brenda. We'll see. She doesn't scare me.

The sun is warm on my back and as I stand, debating which way to go, I remember Sally lying asleep on the grass and wonder if I will see her today. I hope I shall. I was so struck by her uncomplicated capacity for happiness that day that I bought a print of Millais's *Ophelia* and hung it in my office to remind me. The original model for *Ophelia* was the young Elizabeth Siddal, whom Millais required to pose lying in a bath of water in his converted greenhouse studio. The water was heated, not very efficiently, by oil lamps and candles placed under the bath. Mr Millais, untroubled in those days by health and safety regulations and an employer's 'duty of care', continued painting, day after day, well into the winter, oblivious to the fact that Miss Siddal's goosebumps had goosebumps, and her complexion had taken on an alarming blue tinge. One day the lamps and candles went out, and Mr Millais, in his artistic fervour, did not notice. Miss Siddal, in her stoic professionalism (or perhaps because her lips were frozen together) did not complain. Unsurprisingly, she contracted pneumonia, and her father successfully sued Mr Millais for the alleged sum of fifty pounds. She subsequently suffered from poor health until her early death aged just thirty-two. Historians attribute her demise to a variety of causes, including a then-fashionable addiction to laudanum. But some allege she suffered from tuberculosis, which Mr Millais could undoubtedly claim some credit for after the freezing-bath-in-the-greenhouse affair. Tuberculosis was the perfect prescription if a lengthy deathbed was required, and therefore Mr Millais could conceivably be accredited with at least compensating his model for her devotion to duty by providing her with the opportunity to die 'a good death'. I doubt she saw it that way, however.

I wonder if Lily Phyllis Phoebe died a good death. Today, bathed in dazzling sunshine, the white marble of her headstone glints in the light, and a bunch of lavender laid beside it is pungent in the heat. Lily was the first member of my Family on the Other Side. According to her memorial stone she had a long life and died an old lady, having been widowed twenty years earlier. Lily has an angel standing at the head of her grave with folded wings and one arm raised towards the sky. In her other arm she holds a bunch of lilies. Her nose has been smashed by vandals and she has several fingers missing but she still looks heavenly.

The Victorians believed that the state of the individual's soul at the exact moment of death was crucial – the heaven or hell moment when a snap decision about one's afterlife destination was made. But it does seem horribly unfair. Imagine if, having struggled through all the praying, apologising, farewells and giving wise advice to your family and friends, despite the fact that you're dying and would rather just have a lie-down and a nice cup of tea, at the very moment of death you have a saucy thought about George Clooney. There's nothing you can do about it. It simply pops into your head just before you pop your clogs. That's it – you're off to hell in a handcart.

The cemetery is full of life today. Squirrels are chasing up and down the trees, blackbirds are rooting in the grass for worms to feed their hungry chicks, and the crows are loitering aimlessly. Hidden songbirds chirrup and whistle, and magpies cackle in the tall pines. Seated on a bench near the chapel I see a familiar figure. Sally is enjoying the view and basking in the warmth of a late-summer afternoon. She waves and beckons for me to join her. She is looking well. Her cheeks are rosy and her face is tanned and sprinkled with freckles. Her speech is coherent, but we sit in companionable silence. A fat, black crow with something in his mouth is sitting on a headstone a few yards away, watching us. His feathers are somewhat dishevelled, a little dull, and here and there flecked with grey. He, like the summer, has lost the freshness of youth and is looking a little tired and raggedy around the edges. The grass in the cemetery is mottled with sunburnt rusty patches, and the air smells like hay. The leaves on the trees are still green and hanging on, but with less conviction, as though the anticipation of autumn has weakened their grip. The scent of lavender, baked by the sun, is carried on the breeze from the purple bushes tinged with brown that are scattered down the hill. The change of season is waiting in the wings.

Sally reaches into her frayed canvas bag and pulls out a couple of crusts that she tosses to the scraggly crow. He hops off the gravestone and swaggers jauntily across the grass. Almost at Sally's feet he drops what he has been carrying in his mouth and snatches one of the crusts. Sally picks up the object and turns it over in her palm. It is a brass button.

'Thank you, kind sir!' she says to the crow, and throws him another piece of bread.

She turns to me and smiles. 'It's a gift,' she says. 'People think it's just magpies that like little treasures, but crows do too. They often bring me things; buttons, bits of ribbon, bottle tops. I think it's to thank me for the bread.'

I tip my head back and watch the huge, fluffy clouds sailing across the flat, blue sky like cotton-wool galleons. There is no hope of a storm today.

After a while I feel, somehow, that I am being scrutinised. As I look up, I realise that Sally is studying my face intently.

'You have lost your joy.'

She says it matter-of-factly as though it were a glove or some other everyday item, but immediately I feel the tears pricking the back of my eyes. I am trying so hard to change; to let go of the grief that hobbles me. And sometimes I can. But grief is not a linear thing. It re-boots unexpectedly at a certain smell or sight or sound, and some days I still feel as though my world is like a patchwork quilt that's coming unstitched. But how can she know that? How can she tell that some nights I wake in a cold sweat because I can still feel the brush of feathers in my hands and the fury that I could do nothing and no one will be punished; that I am terrified of growing old alone and at the mercy of strangers? Can she see that despite all my efforts to change, I'm afraid I might not be strong enough? That eventually my son's death may defeat my life? I have a feeling that Sally can see a good many things that other people miss. She is waiting for my answer, but I have no words. I nod.

Still, Sally waits. Her silence invites explanation, but I don't know how much I can give. I am looking into the abyss.

'My little boy, Gabriel. He drowned. He died.'

She sits quietly for a moment, giving my words the respect that they command, and then she replies with infinite tenderness, 'But *you* didn't.'

'And I feel so bloody guilty for still being alive!' I blurt out angrily. The long unspoken truth that is the foundation of my perpetual mourning and the anchor that keeps me chained to my grief. 'Why the hell do I deserve to be happy when I let him die?'

Sally takes my hand. 'Was Gabriel a happy boy?'

I remember his ready smile and his constant laughter.

'Would he want you to be sad?'

He hated it when I cried. If I cried, he cried too.

'Did he love you?'

I remember all the hugs and cuddles, and the sloppy kisses he used to plant on my cheek.

'What would Gabriel want you to do?'

The answer comes immediately and from nowhere.

'He would want me to dance.' I can't quite believe that I've said such a ridiculous thing out loud, but Sally simply smiles and nods. And then I think of all those times when he jiggled around on his unsteady, chubby little legs, squealing with laughter and clapping his hands. Whenever he heard music he liked he would dance, but the thing he loved best was for me to dance with him.

'Mama dance!' he would command, holding his arms up towards me. Perhaps it's not so ridiculous after all. It's almost as though Sally has asked the questions because she already knows the answers. After a moment or two she stands up and starts singing a tune that is vaguely familiar. And then she begins to dance. I don't know whether to laugh or cry when she reaches for my hands and pulls me up to dance with her. Me and a bag lady waltzing round a cemetery to 'La Vie en Rose'. Sally looks at me and smiles.

'When the music ends for someone you love you don't stop dancing. You dance for them as well.'

We sit back down on the bench, Sally a little breathless from her exertions. She reaches into her pocket and pulls out a handkerchief, which she carefully unwraps. Contained in its crumpled folds is a small, delicate gold ring engraved with flowers and some initials that are too small for me to see. She hands it to me.

'It was my mother's and I want you to have it, because you helped me and you didn't have to. I've been looking for it for ages, and finally I found it. I've been keeping it in my pocket until I saw you again.'

'Thank you.'

I slip the ring onto my little finger. Whether it's the dancing, the ring, the company or all three I don't know, but I'm feeling lighter.

'I should be getting back. Haizum will be ready for his walk.'

'Your dog. The grand, big, hairy fucker.'

'That's the one.'

We wander down the hill together, passing little Marie on the way. As we turn to walk through the gate, I stop to pick up a tiny white feather that is lying on the grass. I do it without thinking. I once read somewhere that a white feather is the sign of an angel. It's ridiculous, of course, but I still pick them up. As did Gabriel.

'It's an angel,' I say to Sally, who is watching me curiously. 'I've got a pocketful of them.'

Sally shakes her head at me and laughs.

'You can't keep angels in your pocket. You have to let them fly.'

Chapter Thirty-Seven

⌒

Alice

Consider the full consequences of even one mortal sin. By it you lose the grace of God. You destroy peace of conscience; you forfeit the felicity of heaven, for which you were created and redeemed, and you prepare for yourself eternal punishment.

'Bless me, Father, for I have sinned. It has been twelve years since my last confession . . .'

The words chased round and round in Alice's head, but she couldn't bring herself to say them out loud. It had been too long, and perhaps her sin was too great. But if, as she feared, she was dying, atonement was her only hope of salvation.

The harbingers of doom had been the boxes of tissues and the pair of nurses. Sitting in the waiting room for over an hour, she had had plenty of time to work out which was the good room and which the bad. The first contained a lone consultant whose patients filed briskly in and out at fifteen-minute intervals. The woman who had gone into the second room hadn't come out yet. But one of the nurses had, to fetch a plastic beaker of water, and Alice had seen the boxes of tissues on the table through the open door. When she was finally called in (after the previous patient had left with a blotched face wet with tears, and a nurse at each elbow), she was greeting by a smiling Asian doctor who shook her hand and invited her to sit down. She half expected to see his black hooded cloak hanging on the coat stand and his scythe propped up against the wall. The nurses quickly rejoined them and the doctor consulted the file spread open on the desk in front of him. His words fluttered round the space above her head like windblown sparrows, before they settled inside it in a sensible order with a plain meaning.

'I'm afraid you have cancer.'

Alice didn't know why he was afraid. She was the one who had it, not him. And she'd known in her heart for weeks – from the moment she'd first discovered that small, hard lump. But still she'd ignored it, hoping it would go away of its own accord and terrified to admit to herself what might happen if it didn't. The nurses watched her, anxious at first and then puzzled. She didn't cry. The tissues poking out of their boxes like meringue peaks were redundant. The tumour was fast growing; a grade 3 (like a music examination, Alice thought). She would need surgery, che-motherapy and radiotherapy. And then they would see. The nurses, and even Alice, waited for tears, but still they did not come. The nurses looked worried; as if they thought that she was not taking it seriously enough. They needed tears for proof, but none came.

There had been plenty since. But they had not been for herself but for Mattie, and the terrifying realisation of the truth. Finally. If she died what would happen to him? The chemotherapy drugs sucked the life from her, poisoned her in the hope of returning her life to her, clean and polished and cancer free. But it seemed so unlikely. The weariness left her on the brink of comatose, but rarely brought the blessing of peaceful sleep. She kept her eyes closed to save herself the effort of blinking. But the burden of Mattie's fate made all that she was going through seem like fluff and air. She had known for some time now that she must tell him the truth. But how could she find the words? And what would happen to her most precious son? She gripped the wine-coloured prayer book between cold, bone white fingers. It had once been her Netty's. On the flyleaf she had written:

Alice,
Never be afraid to pray.
God will always listen,
Even if he doesn't answer straight away.
Love,
Netty x

But Alice needed an answer pretty quickly. She had to try something, something to help her find the courage to do what she knew she must, while she still had the strength. She sat up in bed and squeezed her eyes more tightly shut until silver stars burst across the blackness.

'*O my good Angel, whom God, by His divine mercy, hath appointed to be my guardian, enlighten and protect me, direct and govern me this night.*

'Amen.'

It was a start. Alice slumped back into the crushed and rumpled pillows. She would speak to God himself tomorrow. And the warm ooze of sleep seeped through her body, finally bringing rest.

Chapter Thirty-Eight

~

Masha

Elvis and Kitty Muriel are betrothed. They are standing in the queue ahead of me in the shop. Kitty Muriel is wearing a tight halter-neck top that is perfectly designed to display her formidable décolletage to its best advantage. Her bosoms look like a pair of ripe peaches nestling in a crisp white hammock. She is also wearing a very sparkly engagement ring. Elvis is looking very Errol Flynn in a white frilly pirate shirt, black skinny jeans and red winkle-pickers. And a diamanté hoop earring. When I joined the queue behind them I couldn't decide whether or not to speak. And I still can't. I have encountered Kitty Muriel on three previous occasions, very briefly, and each time I grow more and more star-struck. She, however, is completely at ease with herself – her own best friend.

My encounter with Sally in the cemetery yesterday has unsettled me. I'm not claiming to have had another 'road to Damascus' moment, but Sally has stirred my curiosity, like swirling a stick in a stagnant pool. She has tempted me with possibilities that make me uncomfortable, or perhaps excited (I'm not sure, at the moment, that I can tell the difference). And now I am confronted with the very woman I would give almost anything to become. I really want to speak to her, but I have no idea what to say and would be mortified if I said something stupid, which is quite likely because I'm trying far too hard to think of something appropriate. I am glad to be going to lunch with Edward and Marcus, where I can be distracted by their blossoming romance.

The queue has descended into torpor. The man at the till is waiting for the price of an item without a barcode. The woman attempting to purchase it is convinced that the item is on special offer. The item in question is a packet of winged panty-liners, and the supervisor has been summoned to deliver a definitive answer on the correct price. I'm certain Lady T would not approve of the rather public bandying about of such objects of intimate feminine hygiene; the man at the till is waving them aloft for all to see. But the would-be purchaser is completely unabashed. The rest of the queue languishes behind her, too lethargic even to shuffle or fidget. As I study their profiles (or the backs of their heads, depending on how they are standing) it strikes me that none of them looks very happy. None of them, that is, except Elvis and Kitty Muriel. Elvis has a protective arm around Kitty's waist, and her hand is resting cheekily on his buttock. It is her left hand, and her engagement ring is clearly visible. Elvis is in love. He's all shook up. So much so that as Kitty squeezes just a bit too hard, he drops the plastic bottle of fizzy drink he's holding and its contents spurt out all over the floor, which rather neatly solves my problem of how to start a conversation. I am drenched. Lady T is of the opinion that 'to some fortunate persons, charming manners are a gift of birth' and Kitty is clearly one of those persons. She apologises profusely to everyone in the queue, particularly me. She hugs me like a long-lost friend and proffers a minuscule lacy hanky that is about as much help as a sandbag in a tsunami.

'I'm so dreadfully sorry!' She sounds genuinely concerned. 'I do hope it doesn't stain and I insist you let me pay your dry-cleaning bill.'

I am wearing a 1930s silk tea dress for my lunch date. It's an old favourite and it always used to make me feel a little bit special when I wore it, but it hasn't seen the light of day for quite a while. Today, when I saw it skulking forlornly at the back of my wardrobe, I suddenly thought 'why not?' This beautiful dress now has vibrant orange splashes on its skirt, but I couldn't be more delighted. My normal response to an event of this nature would be an overwhelming desire to yell rudely at the person responsible, and flounce off in a huff, while in reality accepting their apologies with a red face and gritted teeth. Despite my admiration for Lady Troubridge, I have no innate talent for graciousness. My attempts at social niceties are often hampered by the brusqueness that is a cover for my insecurities. But Kitty Muriel's formidable charm rides roughshod over my reticence.

'Oh no, it's fine [clearly it isn't]. I'm sure it will wash out easily [any fool can see these are permanent stains]. You can hardly see it [if you're standing several streets away and have severe visual impairment].'

I'm even smiling at her. I offer her the hanky back, although it is now wringing wet and bright orange.

'You keep it, my dear. I'm only sorry it isn't larger. It would be such a pity if your lovely dress were to be ruined. It's silk, isn't it? 1930s? I still have some of Mother's at home in a trunk. There's even a ballgown somewhere. It's such an awful shame that they languish in tissue paper when they should be out and about, going to lunches, dinners and balls.'

My admiration for Kitty Muriel is further inflamed when I hear her talking about vintage clothes in such imaginative terms, attributing them with lives and social calendars of their own and recognising their magical attractions.

'I don't suppose you'd be interested in them, would you? It would give me enormous pleasure to find them a good home, where they will be wined and dined and generally shown a good time. I shall never wear them. Mother was rather less voluptuous than me so they don't really fit, and my adorable fiancé prefers me in something a little more modern.'

I now have a serious crush. And speaking of the 'adorable fiancé', Elvis finally returns with a replacement bottle of drink and a beaming smile for his beloved Kitty Muriel. She takes his hand and kisses it tenderly as though they have been parted for several weeks and although Elvis's method of selection when shopping is unarguably rather time-consuming, he has only been gone for five minutes or so. I'm not even embarrassed. Outside the shop Elvis places their shopping in the basket of his bicycle. Kitty Muriel hands me a small pink card with her name, address and telephone number on it, and I promise to call her.

I go home to get changed. My dress is ruined. But then perhaps I have made a new friend.

Chapter Thirty-Nine

'I told her it was a representation of the negative space between two jars of pickled wieners.'

Marcus has Edward and me in stitches. By the time I have been home and changed out of my orange-splattered frock, Haizum and I are late for Edward's birthday lunch but our hosts are very forgiving. Edward is delighted with his gift – a 1908 edition of *A Midsummer Night's Dream* with illustrations by Arthur Rackham – which I bought from the very kind man in the second-hand bookshop, and we are now drinking cocktails in the garden while Marcus entertains us with tales of his working life as the manager of a small but very fashionable art gallery in London.

'She's an awful woman anyway, with more money than she can count and no taste whatsoever. She even wears that ridiculous fur hat of hers in the summer. She said she was looking for "pieces" to decorate her villa in the south of France.'

I stare at Marcus in disbelief. This woman sounds horribly familiar and when questioned Marcus confirms that the customer he is describing is indeed Fennel's own dear Mrs Sweetie. I am then, of course, obliged to relate the episode of Haizum, the hat and the aquarium. Edward is clearly enjoying his birthday. He is wiping tears of laughter from his face by the end of my confession. I cannot remember the last time I saw him so happy and relaxed.

'So, was it really a representation of the negative space between two jars of pickled wieners?' I ask, as Edward refills my glass.

'I have absolutely no idea. It had only come in that day, and I hadn't had time to read the accompanying description. But the artist's a great guy who works really hard and has sold quite a bit of his stuff. He certainly doesn't deserve to be patronised in any sense of the word by that ghastly woman. So, when she asked me what it was "supposed to be", I said the first thing that came into my head. Obviously it's not "supposed to be" anything. It is something. I just didn't quite know what.'

Over lunch we discuss the next production that Marcus's amateur dramatic group will be performing.

'Edward and I so enjoyed the last one that everyone else has promised to come this time.'

Marcus wags an admonishing finger at me and laughs.

'Seriously, Marcus, it was hilarious, and you were really good. And the rest of the cast were . . . well, they were very entertaining.'

'Lehár will no doubt be spinning in his grave, but I'm pretty sure they've settled on *The Merry Widow*, and Kitty Muriel is straining at the leash to play the lead.'

Now that I have to see.

'How's horrid Hugo?' Edward asks, feeding Haizum and Lord Byron scraps of garlic bread. He knows that I spoke to Epiphany yesterday and is eager for gossip.

Hugo is now, apparently, Roni's ex-beloved.

'Hugo has been "let go" by his employers under suspicion of inappropriate conduct during business hours. He was apparently keen to go before said conduct was proven and made public and is currently selling retirement flats in Frinton.'

'Best place for him,' declares Edward.

Roni is training to be a belly-dancing teacher.

Much later, after tea and chocolate birthday cake (and tea and digestive biscuits for Lord Byron and Haizum), Edward is once again walking me home. Haizum strolls contentedly by my side and Marcus is ahead of us with Lord Byron, trying, with scant effect, to persuade the dignified little dog to walk briskly in order to work off the garlic bread and biscuits. Edward keeps glancing at me with a quizzical expression on his face.

'Something has happened to you, hasn't it?' he asks.

'What do you mean?'

'It's as though someone has lit a lamp in the window so that the old you can finally find her way back home.'

'I could say exactly the same about you.'

He smiles. 'Marcus.'

'I know. And I'm so pleased for you.'

'So, what happened to you?'

'An old lady in a cemetery taught me how to dance again.'

Edward shakes his head. 'Of course. I might have known with you it was hardly going to be anything as mundane as Prozac. But I was rather hoping that there might be some gorgeous man who has piqued your interest and perhaps stirred your slumbering libido!'

Well, there might be. But I don't want to give Edward false hope. After all, I still haven't spoken to *him* yet. But I'm working up to it.

Marcus is having a little more success with Lord Byron now, who has broken into a slow trot. I am grateful for the loan of Marcus's jacket, which is draped round my shoulders. The evenings are growing chillier, and flannel pyjamas and fluffy bed socks will soon replace summer's silken flimsies.

Suddenly I remember something that I've been meaning to ask Edward.

'The last time we had lunch in the cemetery, you said that you had two favours to ask me. But you only asked one. What was the other?'

Edward pauses to light a cigarette. He even manages to make smoking in the street look elegant.

'I was going to ask you to stop.' He pauses for a moment and takes a deep drag on his cigarette. He is obviously uncomfortable, but determined to finish saying what he has started. 'It's time to let Gabriel go and get on with your life.' He puts his hand up to touch my face and I see that there are tears in his eyes. 'I miss him too. More than I can say. But you didn't die with him, you know, and I can never be truly happy unless I know that you are too.'

Once again I am saddened and shamed by the burden my grief has obviously been to the people I love most.

I smile at him. It's not the response he was expecting.

'You're the second person who has said that to me this week.'

'And?'

'You're both right.'

Edward raises jazz hands to the sky.

Marcus glances back at us, and then turns back to chivvying Lord Byron. I have a feeling he knows what's going on.

'So, who was the other person?' Edward asks.

'Sally. The lady who feeds the crows in the park and dances in the cemetery.'

'Well, she's got more chutzpah than me. I chickened out the first time. But I was going to ask you tonight anyway.'

'Better late than never.'

'I think that's my line to you!'

Chapter Forty

꙳

Mattie

Mattie stroked the soft white fur and gently caressed the long ears. The rabbit's nose twitched contentedly, and it seemed unperturbed by the tears that were falling on its back like fat raindrops. Mattie was sitting on the grass with the rabbit in his lap. He had his back to the house. He didn't want his mum to see him crying. He had to be strong for her sake, but it was so hard. And she had made him promise not to tell anyone, so he had nobody to confide in or ask for help. The rabbit had grown bored of his attentions and hopped out of his lap, but it stayed close to him, nibbling the grass and occasionally kicking out its back legs. Mattie scrubbed the tears from his face with the sleeve of his top and sniffed loudly.

He was terrified that his mum was going to die and that he would be left alone.

He picked a daisy from the lawn and ripped the petals from its head one by one.

'She will die, she won't die. She will die, she won't die,' he chanted quietly to himself, but then stopped before all the petals were gone. He didn't want to know. Mattie lay back on the grass and stared up at the sky where a distant plane was scratching a thin white line onto the bright blue. He wished he was on that plane. He wished he was going on holiday to America; to Florida, or California maybe. A family holiday. He wished he was going with a proper family, his family; a mum, a dad and maybe even a brother or sister. If he had a family he wouldn't mind settling for Cornwall or even the Norfolk Broads. Mattie longed to be normal, more like the other kids in school. There were plenty who came from single-parent homes, but they usually knew who the absentees were. Mattie knew nothing about his father. He had asked his mum many times, but all she would say was that they were never married and that Mattie's dad had left her when he found out that she was pregnant.

'We're better off without him,' was how the conversation always ended. But Mattie didn't feel better off. There had been many times in his short life when he would have welcomed a dad; to teach him how to ride a bike, to mend a puncture and fix a broken chain. To fish, build a den and cook things on a bonfire. More recently he would have liked some advice on how to shave and maybe even about girls. His mum did her best, but there were some things he couldn't ask her. And he couldn't help but wonder who his dad was and where he might be living. Perhaps he was married now and had more children? Perhaps Mattie did in fact have a brother or sister – or both?

Soft whiskers brushed his hand and he sat up to find the rabbit stretching itself out alongside him on the grass. It was pointless dreaming about the things he didn't have. He had to concentrate on the things that he *did* have. He had his rabbits, and he had his mum.

And his mum had cancer.

Chapter Forty-One

❧

Masha

Today's pool temperature is 22 degrees and once again I am drowning in the deep end. Not because I want to, or even because I need to. I'm not that Masha any more. Today I'm drowning only because of the Australian.

That bloody woman is in the pool and she has been watching me like a not-very-undercover cop since I got into the water. She even waved at me! And so I have no choice. I have to practise drowning in order to maintain the whole singing subterfuge. The only problem is that I'm not very good at it any more. I'm out of practice. The best I can manage is just over a minute, and as I break the surface of the water gasping for air, I can feel the glare of her sceptical surveillance from the other end of the pool. I don't even have the singing book with me to flaunt in the café. I really want to swim now, but that means I'll have to swim towards her, and when I reach her, she'll probably talk to me. And that wouldn't be a good idea. Because what I want to say to her is, 'I lied. I don't sing, except in the shower. I used to force myself to stay underwater because my little boy drowned and I needed to know what that felt like. I also did it to punish myself because, whatever anyone told me, I still thought that it was my fault. But now I'm trying to stop. Now I want to swim. And by the way, none of this is any of your business and I really wish that you wouldn't ask me questions, or even talk to me at all.' But, of course, I don't say any of that. I get out of the pool.

Dried and dressed, I make my way to the café. Today is Flo's birthday and I have made her a cake. It's not an exemplar of its type, but then it was always a risk to attempt a lemon drizzle, of which Flo is an accomplished exponent. The cake in the tin I am holding is a little burnt around the edges and its rise is undulatory rather than uniform. I used both lemons and limes, and I can't guarantee absolutely that it won't contain one of Haizum's hairs. But it was made with another key ingredient – genuine affection for its intended recipient. A few weeks ago while she was preparing my order, Flo was chatting to me, and I remarked that she must get fed up with cake, working with it all day as she does. But she told me that she loves it and that lemon drizzle is her favourite, and what she would really like is for someone to make it for her. Nobody ever does, because it is her signature cake (she is an avid *The Great British Bake Off* fan), but what she longs for is one that she hasn't had to bake herself.

'And I don't mean a shop-bought lump of stodge, sweating in cellophane. I mean a proper, home-made job!'

And so that is what I have made for Flo. It even has a candle.

It's quiet in the café, and only a few of the tables are occupied. Flo is standing behind the counter, drying cups. She grins broadly when she sees me approaching and before she can say anything, I whip the lid from the tin.

'Happy birthday, Flo!'

It's the first time I've ever seen her blush. She looks genuinely astonished.

'It's probably not that good, and the edges are a bit burnt . . .'

Flo flaps away my reservations with a tea towel.

'Stone the bleedin' crows! It's the most beautiful cake I've ever seen!'

It absolutely is not, but I'm delighted that Flo is so pleased.

'And now, you have to sing,' she commands, nodding towards the candle. How can I refuse? Flo lights the candle. I take a deep breath and begin quietly, so as not to attract the attention of the other customers, and hoping that my rendition of 'Happy Birthday' is at least recognisable as such. As Flo blows out the flame with an enthusiastic puff, a cheery voice behind me pipes up with an unmistakable twang.

'Good to hear that all those breathing exercises are beginning to pay off.'

It is, of course, the Australian.

* * *

After a cup of coffee and a slice of cake with Flo (it was, surprisingly, quite nice, and there were no dog hairs in mine), I am now in the car park apologising to Edith Piaf. Lady T would not be impressed. I have said 'Fuck' twice and kicked Edith. I kicked her because she is refusing to start and I'm now going to be late for my visit to Kitty Muriel's. And what's worse, the Olympian pulled in to the car park just in time to see me do it. He even came over and asked me if everything was okay. Of course I said that everything was fine, but I know I was blushing like a teenager, and now he probably thinks I'm a complete madwoman. And, yes, that does matter, because yes, I do fancy him. And even though he's probably got a very lovely girlfriend called Annabel, who is annoyingly poised and elegant, doesn't swear and certainly doesn't kick cars, I still want him to like me. Or at least not think I'm a total head-case.

When I *was* a teenager, mooning over Scott Harvey, who dumped me at the school disco for a willowy Wendy with big boobs whose father drove a Mercedes (not sure the car influenced his decision, but pretty sure the cup size did), I consoled myself with the thought that when I was a grown woman I would be able to handle relationships so much more competently. I would be cool and sophisticated, and I would do the dumping, rather than be dumped. That hasn't quite gone to plan. I blame Edith for my latest embarrassment. She has a lot to answer for. She's recently been serviced. She has petrol in her tank, a newish battery and no excuse whatsoever for her obdurate inertia. But she is also a temperamental diva, and I really need her to start, so now I'm trying a different tack. I'm apologising. I promise her a new air freshener – her favourite, rose-scented – and turn the key in the ignition. She splutters, clears her throat and then her engine begins to sing. *Merci mille fois!*

Chapter Forty-Two

The black skirt of the nun's habit is slightly fuller than is customary, in order to accommodate the spare roll of lavatory paper upon which the nun is seated. The cloakroom in Kitty Muriel's flat has cream-coloured walls, black-painted skirting boards and, curiously incongruous with the nun, a splendid collection of erotic prints by Aubrey Beardsley. The hand basin is spotlessly white, the hand towel is soft and black, and the liquid soap smells of vetiver. As a notoriously reluctant user of other people's toilets, I am once again won over by the extraordinary charm of Kitty Muriel, which clearly extends to the decor of her home. The sitting room is a stylish confection of marshmallow pink walls and dark chocolate woodwork, comfortably furnished with a velvet-covered sofa and chairs and an art deco cocktail cabinet. A large rug in matching colours is a luscious island on the pale parquet floor. Above the 1930s fireplace hangs a large black and white lithograph of two rather earnest-looking young men, dressed in suits and ties, standing next to a wooden bench under a tree that is foaming with flowers. It is Gilbert and George by Gilbert and George, entitled *A Touch of Blossom*, and it is the perfect choice for this elegant room. I must admit that I'm intrigued by the contrast between Kitty Muriel's rather rococo sense of fashion and her still flamboyant,

but tastefully chic, interior design. I am even more intrigued by
the nun.

'Oh, that's Sister Mercy,' Kitty laughs, 'although I always
called her Sister Shona Mercy because she was such a cruel and
detestable shrew.'

It took a moment for the penny to drop, but I got there in the
end.

'Believe it or not,' Kitty continued, 'I was a convent girl.
Daddy was in the Army, and Mummy travelled with him, and so
did I until I was eleven, when they thought it would be better for
me to stop in one place for the sake of my education. I dare say
they felt they were doing the best thing for me, but the truth is I
was utterly miserable.'

Kitty pauses to pour tea into two pale pink and silver china
teacups from an elegant matching art deco teapot.

'I've never been someone who blends in particularly well.
Daddy always used to say that in a field of buttercups and daisies,
I'd be a gladiolus. It was never a conscious choice; it's just who
I am. But individuality in a convent is certainly not encouraged
and nor was it considered very seemly. To Sister Shona Mercy it
was a cardinal sin at least akin to attending Holy Communion
without wearing knickers and pouting at the priest as you received
the holy wafer.'

Kitty Muriel hands me a cup of tea, and offers me the milk
jug. Her engagement ring twinkles on her finger as she sets down
her own cup of tea in front of her and adds one lump of sugar
with a pair of silver tongs. Lady T would be delighted.

'The convent aimed to transform a pick and mix of little
schoolgirls into a homogeneous class of young women suitable for
marriage, childbearing, a good Catholic life and very little else.

Sister Shona took great pleasure in baiting me relentlessly about my perceived shortcomings: the waywardness of my hair (slovenly); my dancing in the corridors (provocative); and my inability to produce a satisfactory Victoria sponge cake ("you'll never find a husband, Kitty Muriel Emmanuel, if you can't even bake a simple cake"). She made everything I saw as sparkling and magical and precious seem tarnished and tawdry and cheap. Frankly, my dear, none of the men I've ever cared about has shown more than a passing interest in my cake-baking abilities, and as a punishment for her abominable cruelty, Sister Shona Mercy is relegated for eternity, symbolically at least, to a place where she must not only endure pictures of God's children engaging in what she would call "filty, dirty devil-riding", but also the sight of real, live bare derrieres and basic bodily functions. I feel I owe it to the little girl I was.'

Perhaps this is also the explanation I am seeking for the way she dresses – part fairy princess, part hooker. Perhaps she has spent her life railing against the strict convent regime that chafed her lively spirit until she could escape.

Kitty Muriel has invited me, as she promised she would, to look at her mother's dresses, and after we have finished our tea, she leads me through to her bedroom. This is a sumptuous boudoir of berry-coloured velvets, silver mirrors, silk negligees and frothy feather boas. Her dressing table is strung with pearls and beads, and on its polished surface stands an array of cut-glass perfume bottles and a little silver music box. There are also two photographs in ornately worked frames. One is of a dapper-looking man in his thirties, with dark eyes and a rather fetching moustache, wearing a smart suit and a trilby. He is looking straight at the camera and grinning broadly, full of life and confidence. The other shows a little girl about five years old. She is a picture-perfect combination of fair curls, peachy cheeks and a winsome smile. But her eyes have the promise of something altogether more extraordinary – more exciting, less safe. She is wearing a ballet outfit and was clearly dancing at the very moment that the camera's shutter snapped. Kitty Muriel has followed my gaze and senses my hesitation.

'It's perfectly fine for you to ask,' she says, except that now, obviously, there is no need.

'Valentine was my husband.'

Kitty picks up the photograph of the handsome young man. She sits down on the edge of the bed and pats the space beside her, indicating that I should join her, and as I do, I catch a whisper of her perfume – Joy by Jean Patou. She hands me the photograph.

'When I was nineteen Mummy and Daddy took me to Brighton for a summer holiday. I should have much preferred the south of France or Italy, but they were tired of travelling abroad, and Mummy had an inclination to see the Pavilion. We stayed at The Grand, and we walked along the promenade watching the sideshows and poking around in the little souvenir shops. Mummy wasn't over-keen. She tried to sustain a semblance of enjoyment because she knew that Daddy and I were having such fun, but after a few days she'd had enough. She said it was all too "tuppence ha'penny" for her, and she insisted that Daddy take her to visit some of the more refined attractions that Brighton had to offer. Fortunately, by this time I had made friends with a girl called Josie, who was also staying at The Grand with her family. She was a little older than me, and I was permitted to go for walks with her in the mornings, whilst Daddy sought to satisfy Mummy's yearning for "haute culture". Josie was nice enough at first, but it quickly became apparent that I was little more than her alibi. She was conducting a clandestine romance with a young man whom her family considered to be entirely inappropriate, and her walks with me were simply a ruse so she could meet him on the promenade, where they would stroll, arm in arm, talking and laughing and completely ignoring me. It was easy enough to persuade Josie to let me go off on my own and meet up again later, so that we could return to the hotel together.

'I had never had so much freedom and I took full advantage of it. I chatted to all the traders and stall keepers; ate fresh cockles and winkles from a cardboard punnet and dripped vinegar on my gloves and second-best frock; and took off my stockings and skipped and hopped across the grey pebbles to paddle in the breaking waves. One day, walking along the seafront, swinging my hat in my hand, I met Valentine, or rather "The Great Mercurio – Thaumaturge Extraordinaire". He was demonstrating magic tricks to entice people to come and see his show that played nightly on the West Pier, and he was the handsomest man I had ever seen. He called me over and took my hat, which he set down on an empty table, and when he lifted it seconds later a plump white dove was sitting underneath it. He was truly a magical man; larger than life and full of charm and excitement, and I fell completely under his spell. All of my qualities that Sister Shona had belittled, he cherished and encouraged. By the end of our three-week holiday we were secretly engaged to be married, and on the last evening we eloped.'

'Blimey! I bet your mother was less than delighted.'

'She was absolutely apoplectic. But to their eternal credit – or at least, to Daddy's – they made the best of it. They helped us find a flat in Brighton and even came to the show once. Daddy grew to like Valentine very much indeed once he knew him better, but

Mummy could never get past what he did, to see who he really was. You see, people are often so very much more than they seem to be.'

I hand the photograph back to Kitty, who smiles at the man in the frame before replacing him on her dressing table. Her hand hovers over the other photograph but instead of picking it up she turns to me and asks, 'Would you like a dry Martini, my dear?'

Kitty clearly would, and I get the impression that she would like me to join her. She has the look of someone steeling herself to plunge into water that she knows will be cold and dark and deep, and the fragile smile that plays on her lips is bittersweet.

'I'd love one.'

My mouth has gone dry in trepidation. I suspect that this story will not end in a Happy Ever After. Kitty returns with the drinks and hands me a glass. She sits down again and takes a sip from her Martini, gazing at the second photograph on her dressing table.

'The little girl is Joy, our daughter.'

Bugger. I had a feeling that this is where we were going.

'We called her Bunny Joy, because she was always hopping and skipping about. She loved to dance and I encouraged her. After all my years at that hateful convent I wanted her to feel free to dance whenever she liked. I had a silver music box with a dancing ballerina inside. It was the first gift Valentine gave me. It was Bunny's favourite thing, and she would always ask for it to be wound up and then waltz round the room to the music. She used to say that one day she would be like the dancing lady in the box. Valentine worshipped her. He always said she was the best magic trick that we had ever performed.'

She pauses and I wait. I don't need to ask what happened to her little girl, I just need to give her time to tell me. The hand that holds her glass trembles slightly as Kitty takes another sip and then she continues.

'It was a beautiful spring day, warm and sunny, and Valentine went to meet Bunny Joy from her ballet class. His act had become very successful and we had a little motor car by then, but because it was so lovely outside he decided to walk. Bunny Joy was bubbling with excitement because she had been chosen to dance in the end of term show. She was so thrilled that she insisted on walking home in her ballet outfit, although Valentine was able to persuade her to change her shoes. On the way home she chattered non-stop about the dance she would have to do, demonstrating her steps with skips and twirls, whilst holding on to her daddy's hand. A street vendor was selling balloons and, knowing how much she adored them, Valentine stopped to buy one for her. She wanted a red one. He took the balloon from the vendor and slipped his other hand free for a second to pull some change from his pocket. Free for a second, she danced off the kerb and straight into the road.'

Bugger.

'When I got to the hospital and found him sitting alone in an empty corridor, he was still holding the balloon.'

Kitty sips her Martini once again. 'He never came back. The man I met and married, so full of life and afraid of nothing, disappeared that day forever. He said that he made his living by sleight of hand, and lost his life by one slip of the hand. He just gave up. One year later to the day, he finished his show as usual, drank a bottle of whisky, and threw himself off the end of the pier.'

Double bugger. Now that one I didn't see coming. If I were at work I would be able to deal with this; I would find something neutral to say, and encourage my client to continue talking. But the off-duty Masha is utterly hopeless at knowing what to say to a person whose young daughter was tragically killed, and whose husband subsequently committed suicide. I know from personal experience the trite and sentimental sympathies that are normally trotted out on such occasions, and I know how hollow they sound when spoken aloud. I struggle to gather together some words that will show her how sorry I am, and that I understand what it's like to lose a child, but before they can get from my head to my mouth they slip away. It's like trying to win a prize on those wretched slot machines where you pick up a toy with a remote-controlled grabber, and then direct it to the chute. No matter how firm your grip on the prize appears to be, just as it reaches the chute the claws on the grabber inexplicably slacken and the prize is lost. The best I can manage is, 'Bugger.'

I fear at this point Lady T will have disowned me forever, but Kitty Muriel looks at me, amused in spite of everything.

'Yes, it was. An absolute 24-carat-gold bugger.'

'How on earth did you carry on?'

Kitty Muriel seems completely unfazed by my question. She puts down her glass, turns to face me and takes my hand in hers. I can feel my cheeks burning although I have no idea why. She knows nothing about Gabriel. Kitty looks me straight in the eyes and answers my question.

'Because I believed that one day, the joy of being alive would be brighter than the despair that my Joy was dead.'

'And were you right?'

'Yes, my dear, I was. It took a while, but yes, I was right.'

The tears that I have fought so desperately to keep pooled in my eyes spill down my cheeks, and a strangled sob catches in my throat. Once I've started I can't stop. After years of holding back, holding in and grinding on, the dam has finally burst. Kitty Muriel's story has taught me the lesson that I have so desperately needed to learn. The pernicious fear that if I live, fall in love and laugh again it will somehow dishonour the memory of my son and diminish his death, has been soundly debunked by Kitty Muriel's life. Unlike Valentine, she found the courage to carry on and has been following the advice that Sally gave me. She has been dancing for Joy ever since.

She pats my hand and waits. Her child is dead and so is mine, but she still loves her life and she doesn't need Lady T to tell her how to live it. I want that too. But there's something I need to do before I can truly let go of the past. So I do the thing that I haven't done for twelve years. I tell someone what happened. I say the words out loud to a living person instead of a dead one. And not just the broad facts, but every speckle, every semi-quaver, every comma, every full stop, every breath, every whisper. Every single detail that I can remember about that day that I can never, ever forget. I tell her that it was a glorious spring day, full of new life and fresh, green leaves. I tell her what a gorgeous boy my Gabriel was and how he loved to feed the ducks and snatch tiny white feathers from the air because I told him that they were angels. How, in the car that day, on the way to the river, we sang, and Gabriel did the actions to the song with his chubby pink hands and arms.

He was wearing his new blue sandals and he kept trying to pull them off, and laughing when I told him not to. As we walked down the lane to the riverbank, Gabriel clutched the bag of bread in one chubby pink fist and I held tightly on to his other hand. He almost tripped several times in his excitement to get to the ducks, and each time I caught him. But no one was there to catch me. As we clambered down the shallow slope to the riverbank I slipped and lost my footing. And then there was nothing. The next thing I remember was my head pounding, sticky and wet with blood, anxious voices somewhere very near, and someone touching my arm. I could smell damp earth and warm grass close to my face, and see a plane like a silver splinter slicing through the empty blue sky above. The first word I spoke was my son's name, but he was gone.

I had lost consciousness, but for how long I have no idea. I had hit my head on the only rock in the vicinity. A couple walking their dog found me and called for an ambulance, but they had no way of knowing that I had not been alone. The police found one of Gabriel's sandals, the left one, close to the water's edge, and the bag of bread floating just a few feet away. They dragged the murky water for two days, but Gabriel's grave refused to give him up. The divers weren't surprised. The river was too long, too wide, too deep, too fast; too full of twists and turns and secret crypts and tombs and catacombs of tangled weeds and knotted roots. He was gone forever. Now, after all these wasted, waiting years, I too must let him go.

Kitty Muriel squeezes my hand, but for a moment she says nothing. Then she looks straight at me with a gentle smile.

'Bugger.'

And that's it. She doesn't need to say anything else. She knows what I know. She produces another tiny hanky, with which I try to salvage my face, and fixes me another Martini.

'And now, what about those dresses?'

She lifts the lid of a beautiful wooden travelling trunk and pulls out a mouth-watering collection of dresses, one after another, like a magician pulling silk scarves from his sleeve. There are three floral tea dresses, a lavender chiffon evening gown with a beaded bodice, two day dresses in pistachio-coloured raw silk, and a black strapless taffeta ballgown. The next hour is spent with me flitting backwards and forwards behind a fabric-covered screen, trying on these stunning vintage creations whilst Kitty perches on the edge of the bed waving an ostrich-feather fan in approval. Each dress fits me perfectly, and Kitty is insistent that I take them all as her gift. I am thrilled, overwhelmed and embarrassed all at once, and begin to gabble my attempts at a thank you, but Kitty is as dismissive of my gratitude as she is generous with her mother's wardrobe.

'They look beautiful on you. You do them justice in a way that I never could. I think Mummy always wished that I was a little more Audrey Hepburn, and a little less Barbara Windsor. I sometimes felt she thought I was rather too "tuppence ha'penny" for her as well.'

'She was wrong.'

Perhaps it was not just the convent that had chafed at Kitty's lively spirit. We pack the dresses in tissue, and Kitty finds a suitcase for me to borrow.

'I really don't know how to thank you . . .' I begin again.

'Take me swimming in that wonderful outdoor pool that Marcus mentioned you frequent. That will be thanks enough.'

'I should love to. By the way, how is your gorgeous fiancé?'

'He reads me poetry in the bath, brings me flowers every week, holds my hand in the park, cooks a delicious Thai green curry, and always puts the lavatory seat down.'

'He sounds perfect.'

'He is to me.'

As I gather my things to leave, Kitty Muriel once again takes my hand.

'Gabriel would be very proud of you. To live through a child's death takes great courage and we had no choice, but it takes greater courage still to live on without them when we do.'

As I leave Kitty Muriel's flat carrying my suitcase full of beautiful dresses, I remember what she told me. People are often so very much more than they seem to be. Indeed they are.

Chapter Forty-Three

⌒

Today's pool temperature is 20.1 degrees. The sun is unseasonably hot for early September and Kitty Muriel is even hotter. The pool is crowded and people are sitting or lying on towels spread out on the grass and enjoying the sunshine. When Kitty Muriel emerges from the changing rooms, heads turn. She is wearing a scarlet halter-neck bathing suit that shows off her hour-glass figure to its best advantage. Her shapely legs are smooth and tanned, her matching red manicure and pedicure are immaculate and even the flower-covered swimming cap looks glamorous on her. She walks to the pool with her head held high, back straight and her hips gently swaying to a samba that only she can hear. I trot along behind, grateful to be in her slipstream. The wonderful thing about Kitty Muriel is that she is truly proud of the woman she is. Exactly as she is. Her age and its physical manifestations are wholly insignificant. She doesn't care. She doesn't need to. She's magnificent. As she climbs into the water I feel like the geeky girl in the playground who has, for some unfathomable reason, been blessed with the friendship of the coolest girl in school.

Kitty is, of course, a beautiful swimmer. She glides through the water slowly, with hardly a splash, keeping her face dry and smiling at everyone she passes. I don't want to swim. I just want to watch her. And watch everyone else watching her. But Kitty turns and calls to me, 'Come on in, my dear. The water's lovely!'

Kitty swims two lengths, and then has a break and then swims two more. As she approaches the deep end for her second break, the Olympian is just getting in. Bugger. I just keep swimming. No break for me this time. When I reach the other end of the pool, I turn to see Kitty happily engaged in conversation with him. When she sees me looking, she waves.

After our swim we go to the café for a cup of tea and a slice of Flo's famous lemon drizzle cake. I introduce Kitty Muriel to Flo and Flo is 'Charmed, I'm sure.'

It's the first time I've ever seen Flo almost lost for words. Kitty Muriel, gorgeous in a white and gold kaftan, sits down at a table close to the counter and I take our tea and cake over on a tray.

'Well,' says Kitty Muriel, spreading her paper napkin carefully onto her lap, 'that was wonderful. I haven't been swimming for ages, and now I've finally made it to this gorgeous pool I shall be swimming much more often. I might even persuade my fiancé to accompany me.'

Flo is shamelessly listening in.

'I noticed your ring. It's very sparkly.'

Kitty Muriel smiles at her and holds up her hand for Flo to take a proper look. It's all the excuse Flo needs to escape from behind the counter and come and have a chat. The café is cool and quiet, with most people preferring to take their refreshments outside in the sunshine. Flo takes Kitty's hand and inspects her ring carefully.

'That's a proper rock, and no mistake.'

Kitty retrieves her hand and breaks off a piece of cake.

'I know it's very lovely, but to be honest, if he'd given me a ring from Woolworths, I'd still have said yes.'

Flo looks suitably impressed. 'He must be really something then, your fella?'

Kitty Muriel winks at Flo. 'He's sex on legs!'

Flo laughs out loud and then asks, 'I don't suppose he's got a brother for me, has he?' And then, looking at me rather pointedly, 'Or a son for this one?'

Kitty Muriel takes a sip from her cup of tea and dabs her lips with her napkin.

'Actually,' she says, smiling across the table at me, 'I did meet a very nice man in the pool.'

I can feel the colour rising in my cheeks. Flo is desperate to know more, but two teenage girls have come into the café and are waiting at the counter to be served. She reluctantly leaves us to go and take their order. Kitty Muriel reaches across and pats my hand.

'Don't be embarrassed, my dear. I'm only teasing. But wouldn't you like to meet someone?'

Actually, yes. Actually, I've already met someone. The problem is he probably thinks I'm a complete basket case.

'Perhaps . . .' I mutter, toying with the remains of my cake.

The girls at the counter start giggling as two teenage boys wander in and stand behind them in the queue. A tall figure follows them in and comes over to our table.

'Would you ladies recommend the lemon drizzle cake?'

It is the Olympian.

Chapter Forty-Four

~

Alice

An Act of Contrition
*O My God! I am most heartily sorry for all my sins; and I
detest them above all things, because they displease Thee, Who
art infinitely good and amiable, and I firmly resolve, with the
help of Thy grace, to do penance for them and never more to
offend Thee.*

*Sprinkle me with Thy precious Blood, and I shall be whiter
than snow.*

The scarlet berries on the holly tree outside Alice's bedroom window looked like droplets of blood against the leaves and branches
lustrated by sparkling frost. Alice and God were on proper speaking terms again after all these years. Well, Alice was speaking and
she really hoped that God was listening. She couldn't have gone
to Father Peter at her local church. She had been going there with
Mattie, on and off, since he was born. But now she knew that all
that had been a lie. That had been the other Alice.

So she had spoken to Father Thomas, the priest at the hospital, before her most recent chemotherapy session. She hadn't gone into details; not even the bare bones. She just wanted to know if it was too late for atonement; too much to even hope for forgiveness. True confession was unavoidable now, but could God, could anyone, still love her after what she had done? Father Thomas's faith was like a favourite well-worn sweater; loose threads here and there, a little faded in places and patched at the elbows, but still the warmest and most comforting thing he had. He spent his days consoling the dying and those they left behind; trying to persuade them that life was a gift, no matter what. It was always harder for the ones left behind – it was sometimes a gift that they no longer wanted. Father Thomas used to tell them that God wasn't like Marks & Spencer; he didn't accept returns. But for some, there was no consolation to be had. They refused to live on, choosing instead to simply wait for death. These were the ones who made him the saddest of all. He had told Alice that it was never too late; that God always left the door ajar for even the worst of all sinners. Looking at the fragile woman in front of him, despite the lines and shadows that haunted her face, her eyes were those of a child. He couldn't imagine such a woman having even an overdue library book or parking ticket to her name. That she was capable of a mortal sin was virtually inconceivable. And yet her gratitude had been palpable. Almost desperate.

Alice was in bed, too frail to get up. She had been trying to read – *Hard Times* by Charles Dickens. It was an old favourite, but her unremitting exhaustion befogged the words on the page in front of her and made the familiar story incomprehensible. She felt like a phantom. What was left of her flesh and bones seemed as insubstantial and polluted as the factory smog that hung above Dickens's Coketown. With excruciating effort she propped herself up on the pillows so that she could see the whole garden that ran long and narrow at the back of the cottage, cutting a stripe through the fields to the woods beyond. A few bedraggled chrysanthemums still made splashes of colour in the flower beds, and Mattie's beloved pet rabbits, Bugs and Bunny, were hopping about in the large run attached to the wooden hutch where they slept at night. The last third of the garden was cut off by a sturdy fence. Alice had had it put up once Mattie was old enough to play in the garden alone. She had wanted to be able to see him from the kitchen window, and the bottom of the garden was too far away to be in plain sight.

But not from here. From her bedroom window Alice could see the wilderness that it had become, strangled and smothered in a shroud of vicious brambles, silvered into barbed wire by the frost. And right at the bottom, close to the woods, the dark mound that had once been a brick shed, but now resembled little more than an ivy-clad tumulus. The cold crept over Alice like the breath of a ghost and she slunk back down under the bedcovers and closed her eyes.

Chapter Forty-Five

～

Masha

The spinning glitter ball showers the dance floor with a blizzard of silver lights, and the pulsing disco music competes with the rhythmic rumble of wheels on wood. The Bee Gees are stayin' alive, and so am I. But only just. I've twice (narrowly) avoided falling over backwards and breaking my neck, and I can't remember the last time I laughed out loud so much. Kitty Muriel has brought me to the local sports hall for an evening of drinking, dancing and near-death experiences, otherwise known as a roller disco. When she picked me up in a cab earlier this evening, she wouldn't tell me where we were going, only that it was a surprise. She told me to put my best disco knickers on. Just as well. If I end up in an ambulance on my way to A&E, at least I'll have the consolation of knowing that my underwear won't embarrass me. Apparently, Kitty Muriel has been longing to come here, but couldn't find anyone daring or maybe daft enough to come with her. Until she met me.

I'm beginning to find my groove now. Well, I haven't nearly fallen over for at least five minutes and I've let go of the side barrier. Kitty is streaking ahead of me in a short, black skater skirt and silver leggings teamed with a pair of neon pink leg warmers. She is completely fearless, weaving in and out of the other skaters, occasionally glancing backwards to make sure that I'm still in one piece. She completes another lap at breathless speed and then swooshes to a halt beside me.

'I'm so sorry, my dear, to have left you to fend for yourself for a bit, but I had to get it out of my system. I've been dying to have a go at this for ages, and I can't quite believe that we're here. It's absolutely brilliant, isn't it? Shall we get a drink?'

We lean against the barrier sipping vodka and tonics and watching the other skaters roll past through a kaleidoscope of coloured lights. There are people of all ages, shapes and sizes on the dance floor, but the one thing they have in common is that they all seem to be enjoying themselves. Even the ones who end up with a thud on their bottoms or pitch forward and crash onto their knees. They just pick themselves up and carry on. This normally rather spartan and soulless sports hall has, for one evening, been transformed into a joyful cacophony of music and laughter. A teenage boy hurtles past at breakneck speed, hand in hand with his girlfriend. I assume she's his girlfriend because I saw them smooching at the bar when we came in, but who knows – they could have just met tonight. I wonder if Gabriel would have had a girlfriend by now. He would have been a bit younger than them, but then I had my first kiss at thirteen. I can't imagine what it would be like to be the mother of a teenage son. I'm not even sure I would have been any good at it. I always assume that Gabriel would have turned out to be a son I was proud of, but perhaps that's just complacency. How could I know? How could I know that he wouldn't have turned out like Deliverance Boy or one of his disciples?

'Penny for them.' Kitty Muriel interrupts my reverie.

'I was just wondering about Gabriel – whether he would have turned out the way I always imagine.'

Kitty Muriel sighs. 'We'll never know, my dear.'

I'm grateful for her honesty, untainted by any meaningless platitudes. But then she adds, with a wicked smile, 'I'm sure he would have been impressed with his mother's roller-disco dancing!'

I laugh. 'I'm absolutely certain he would have been mortified to see his aged parent in sequins and roller skates. But that, I'm afraid, would have just been his tough luck, because I'm loving it!'

A short, plump woman in a sequinned jumpsuit chugs past us, puffing and blowing like a steam engine. She is hand in hand with a tall, skinny man with flying dreadlocks and a satin shirt. As she draws level with us, she catches my eye and waves with her free hand. It is the pedalo from the pool.

Kitty drains her drink and grabs my arm.

'Come on. Let's boogie!'

As my favourite T. Rex track blasts from the speakers, Kitty glides and I thunder after her round the floor. The vodka has improved my balance and I'm skating faster and faster. Suddenly I'm swooped upon from both sides by two young women, each of whom grabs one of my hands and drags me along, shrieking and laughing. Unfortunately, whatever they've been drinking has had the opposite effect to my vodka, and as they grip onto me more tightly in a desperate attempt to stay upright we veer into the barrier and crash onto the floor in an inelegant heap. My companions barely pause for breath before their laughter continues, despite a bloodied knee for one of them and ripped tights for the other. Clutching onto the barrier, they haul themselves up by pushing down on my shoulders. I'm still sitting on my now sore backside, scrabbling to control my disobedient wheeled feet. It's a good job I did wear my disco knickers. I expect everyone has seen them now. As the two women teeter off to the bar, a hand reaches down and takes mine. I look up and see it belongs to the pedalo's dreadlocked companion. He has a lovely smile, and is stronger than he looks. He leaves me safely propped against the barrier with a solicitous Kitty Muriel before he rejoins the other skaters on the floor.

Kitty fetches me another drink. 'It's a double,' she tells me, 'for the shock.' And I am shocked. Not by the fall – but by my reaction to it. There are several reasons why I would normally be mightily pissed off by what has just happened. Firstly, my aversion to strangers – particularly those who physically touch me. Secondly, the public embarrassment of not being good at something. Kitty Muriel's skating skills have been a revelation, whereas I am as stable on my skates as a newborn giraffe on its spindly legs. And thirdly, the rudeness of being abandoned on my bottom, while my fleeting companions buggered off to the bar. But, actually, I'm fine. In fact, I'm grinning. And I'm pretty sure it's not just the vodka. Kitty Muriel, however, looks upset.

'I'm so sorry, my dear. It's completely my fault. I should never have dragged you here. I can be such a selfish old fool sometimes. Perhaps it's time I learned to behave with a little more decorum.'

This time it's me who downs my vodka, grabs Kitty and pulls her back onto the dance floor.

'You must be bloody joking! The night is young and . . .' At that moment, blasting from the speakers, Annie Lennox finishes my sentence for me: *sisters are doin' it for themselves!*

Chapter Forty-Six

Here comes the bride. All dressed in . . . swathes of sunshine-coloured chiffon, scattered with sequins over a silk moiré corseted sheath dress.

Still not exactly traditional, but a good deal more cheerful than the brown bombazine model.

There is a sudden hush from the assembled guests, and then a collective gasp. Kitty Muriel looks absolutely radiant as she waltzes down the aisle of the impressive Grand Hall in vertiginous diamanté-studded stilettos to the velvet tones of Elvis's 'The Wonder of You'. Kitty moves slowly, taking in every sight and sound of this precious day, smiling warmly at all the friends who have gathered here to share it. I know everyone says that the bride looks radiant; it's a matrimonial maxim like the 'Wedding March', or the big, white, exploding marshmallow frock. But today, for the first time ever, I'm witnessing an incandescent exemplification of the cliché. Elvis is waiting for her at the front of the room, handsome and distinguished in a double-breasted pinstriped suit, black and white brogues, and just a hint of eyeliner. Kitty is carrying a glamorous bouquet of darkest red Grand Prix roses, and Elvis has a single large rose pinned to his lapel. As he turns to watch his bride approach, I can see that his eyes are brimming with tears.

Bugger. I hope I've brought a tissue. I think I may have got an eyelash in my eye. The woman seated next to me notices my discomfort and offers me a tissue from the packet that she has very sensibly brought with her, and which I gratefully accept. In case of eyelashes. I was a little early and kicking my lovely patent heels for a while in the reception area of the town hall, where civil marriage ceremonies take place, dressed rather obviously for a wedding in one of Kitty Muriel's mother's tea dresses, when the same woman approached me and asked me if I was waiting for Kitty Muriel's wedding. She introduced herself as Rosie Bottoms, an ex-colleague and still friend of Kitty's. Rosie is an eminently sensible-looking woman with a broad smile, silver grey hair cut into a neat bob, a smart A-line skirt suit, and low-heeled court shoes. She looks like my old geography teacher.

'Kitty and I taught together at the same school.'

I learned a little more about Kitty's past from Rosie while we were waiting. After Valentine's death, Kitty went to college and trained to be a teacher of dance and drama. She and Rosie both started at the beginning of the same term at the local girls' school.

'Kitty was very kind to me, back then. I was a rather timid thing, a bit wet behind the ears, and of course my name didn't help. I have no clue what my parents were thinking, or indeed if they were thinking at all. The girls picked up on it straight away, and made my life hell for the first few weeks. But Kitty helped me tough it out. "Show no fear!" she used to say, and then take me out for a couple of gin and tonics after school. By the end of the first term I was more than a match for any of them. They may not all have liked me, but they certainly respected me, which was a good start.'

Rosie continued her story as the doors were opened to the ceremony room and we made our way in to find our seats.

'Of course, all the girls adored Kitty Muriel. She was glamorous, confident and charming, and a damn good teacher too. She knew exactly how to ignite their enthusiasm. Ruffled a few feathers amongst the rest of the staff though.'

'Why was that?' I had a pretty good idea, but I wanted to hear the details. Rosie sat down and placed her bag neatly on her lap before answering with a smile.

'She wasn't exactly what you would have called a conformist. Her outfits were responsible for raised eyebrows and coffee spluttering in the staff room; and her debut production of *Romeo and Juliet* with real boys and actual kissing resulted in an extraordinary meeting of the Parent Teacher Association. Only Kitty Muriel could have got away with it. She soothed away any objections with that seductive charm of hers, which is of course reinforced with formidable intelligence and determination.'

As Kitty Muriel joins Elvis in front of the registrar, she takes his hand and squeezes it tightly. The registrar welcomes us all, and the ceremony begins. Kitty and Elvis promise to love and care for one another forever and I know they will. There is a reading by one of Kitty Muriel's old pupils from *The Velveteen Rabbit* by Margery Williams about how you become 'real' when somebody loves you. Cole Porter's 'You Do Something to Me' is played and dedicated to Kitty Muriel by Elvis, and the newlyweds process joyfully out of the room, arm in arm, to the sound of Barry White's 'You're the First, the Last, My Everything'.

We follow Kitty and Elvis outside, into the unseasonably warm, bright sunshine of an early October day. A shiny black car is waiting outside to take them on to the reception. It is decorated with yellow ribbons, and yellow and white flowers, and a huge bunch of yellow and white balloons is tied to the gleaming chrome of the rear bumper. In amongst the yellow and white is a single red balloon. If anyone is in the least bit surprised that the car is Elvis's hearse, no one shows it. The reception party is being held, much to my delight, at The Cock and Curtain, which is only a ten-minute walk from the town hall. Rosie Bottoms and I stroll there together, with Rosie telling me more about their teaching days along the way. It seems that many of Kitty Muriel's old pupils have kept in touch, and several of them are here today.

'And are you still in contact with any of your old girls?'

Rosie smiles.

'Absolutely. Teaching eventually became my life. After a rather unprepossessing start, I did rather well at it. I finished up as head-mistress, and since I retired I've been secretary of the Staff and Old Girls' Association.'

When we reach The Cock and Curtain, Kitty and Elvis are there to greet us. Elvis introduces us to a sprightly old gentleman, smartly dressed in a suit, with a dark red satin waistcoat and matching tie, and a natty trilby. He has a silver pocket watch in his waistcoat and its fob chain sparkles as it stretches across his generously flesh-cushioned ribcage.

'This is my father.'

'You'd never believe that I'm ninety-two.'

We agree that indeed we wouldn't if it weren't for the fact that we'd heard it from his own lips. There is a pianist playing more Cole Porter songs on the old but well-tuned piano in the bar, and the whole pub is decked out in flowers, balloons and ribbons. Even the horrid Damien Hirst/Laura Ashley stuffed-birds-and-flowers monstrosity is sporting a jaunty crown of yellow and white chrysanthemums. There are speeches from Elvis and his father. Lady T advises that 'long speeches are always boring on social occasions' and she would therefore have been perfectly satisfied with the exemplary concision of Elvis senior and his son. One thanks us for being there, and Kitty Muriel for blessing him with more happiness than he had ever dreamed of. The other declares Elvis and Kitty to be a perfect match, like stew and dumplings; and we wouldn't hardly believe it, but he's ninety-two.

We are offered delicious little canapés and tiny crustless sandwiches to eat, accompanied by chunky chips, mini sausages and little punnets of cockles in vinegar. To drink there is a choice of champagne, snowballs and Guinness. After an unholy mixture of all three, I vaguely recall the Cole Porter segueing into 'Knees up Mother Brown', 'Underneath the Arches', and Madonna's 'Like a Prayer', which we all sang with commendable enthusiasm but questionable musicality, holding on to the piano for support. We serenaded the bride and groom with an emotional and enthusiastic reprise of Elvis Presley's 'The Wonder of You' as they left the pub for their honeymoon. My final and abiding memory of the evening was that of Rosie Bottoms singing '(Is This the Way to) Amarillo', wearing a chamber pot on her head and waving a yellow chrysanthemum, as I crawled into a taxi and went home to prepare myself for a stupendous hangover.

Chapter Forty-Seven

The rocking horse is a lonely plaything, in a cold and empty space. But now the time has come to make the space a proper room once more. I have ordered furniture. I push on the dapple-grey neck with my hand and set it rocking, making one of the floorboards beneath the motion creak. Once again it is *Día de los Angelitos*, but this year it will be different from all the other years. This year Edward and I will not be remembering Gabriel alone. It was Kitty Muriel's idea. 'Any excuse for a party is a good one' she joked, before gently telling me that sharing this day with my friends and family would be a gift to them and one that they might treasure. At first I wasn't so sure, but Kitty Muriel can be very persuasive and how will I know unless I try? This afternoon she and Edward are going to help me prepare for the party. Everyone coming tonight is bringing with them a photo or a keepsake to place on the *ofrenda* of someone they want to remember, and tonight we shall all remember – and most importantly celebrate together.

Looking out through the bedroom window, I am satisfied that all my hard work has paid off and, despite the time of year, the garden is looking presentable. A few bedraggled chrysanthemums still make splashes of colour in the flower beds, and I am glad that they are orange – the perfect colour for Day of the Dead. Luckily, it is a fine day – cold but bright with silvery sunshine – as there is a big bonfire waiting to be lit. It is fenced off with chicken wire to deter any wandering hedgehogs who might decide to make it their winter quarters. I certainly don't want it to become a funeral pyre, or for roast hedgehog to be on the menu tonight. What there will be is plenty of *pan de muerto* and sugar skulls that Edward and Kitty Muriel have agreed to make. They met quite recently through Marcus at one of the amateur dramatic society events and immediately bonded over Michael Bublé. I still can't say if I'm more surprised or delighted, but they are fast becoming firm friends.

I keep Gabriel's things in a suitcase on top of the wardrobe in my bedroom. Not the photographs, which are displayed all around the house, but the other things. As I leave the empty room to go and fetch it, I give the rocking horse a final push and suddenly I can hear Gabriel's laughter just as clearly as if he were here. He loved the horse. He would cling onto its neck with chubby little fingers as he rocked back and forth. The horse is Haizum's namesake. According to Islamic tradition, Haizum was the Archangel Gabriel's horse; a white, flaming steed with wings given to Gabriel by God as a reward for pleasing him. I christened the rocking horse Haizum, but Gabriel called him 'Azey'.

Gabriel's favourite rabbit toy is always on my bed, and despite his fondness for furry, fluffy things Haizum has never touched it. In the weeks that followed Gabriel's death I used to cuddle it close to my face when I went to sleep, and imagine that I could still smell the sweet, baby scent of Gabriel in its soft, white fur. It will be on the *ofrenda* as usual, but today I want to put something else on there as well, so I need to bring the suitcase down. It is covered in dust, which makes me sad, as though the memories it contains are just as neglected. But when I click open the metal lock, the lining of the case is bright and clean and my mementos of Gabriel are as fresh as if I had placed them there only yesterday. Haizum has followed me upstairs and is sniffing the suitcase with interest. I am looking for the blue sandal and Haizum helps by sticking his nose into the case and rummaging through its contents. Gabriel would have loved him. The sandal is carefully wrapped in pale blue tissue paper. It was found by the police on the riverbank, the day Gabriel drowned.

The Victorians often used a pair of small, empty shoes on gravestones and in pictures to signify a life cut short in childhood, and for me this single shoe is the last remaining link left in the loving chain that bound a mother to her son before it was so cruelly broken. It is his final relic and my most precious talisman, and it is, therefore, the thing that hurts me the most. It's so small. It fits into the palm of my hand, no bigger than the duckling that I cradled there. Dark polka dots splash onto the soft leather and I realise that I am crying. Without bothering to wipe my tears, I snap the suitcase shut and turn to pick up the photograph of Gabriel from my bedside table. Of all the many photographs I have of him, this is my favourite. He sits astride his beloved rocking horse and is not just smiling but laughing. Full of joy.

I am fortunate to have so many photographs. The families of the children that I visit in the cemetery may not have been so lucky. For them photographs were still an expensive luxury reserved for important milestones and special events. And death. So many children died before a photograph was warranted that the first picture made of them would also be the last. Post-mortem. The most important occasion of their short life was their death. But a photograph of your dead child was better than no photograph at all, because memories are not enough. The pictures in our heads are unreliable. They shift and fade and scatter like broken reflections on restless water, and one day they may disappear completely. A paper picture is insurance. I found some once, at a flea market, and of course I bought them. The stallholder was pleased to be rid of them.

'Horrible things they are,' he said with a theatrical shiver. 'Downright ghoulish!' But he gladly took my money. And he was wrong, because in a heartrending way they are very beautiful and were clearly made as an act of love. They have a quality of exquisite tenderness that makes the stallholder's revulsion seem both prudish and ignorant. Trying to get Gabriel to pose for a photograph was like chasing a butterfly. Almost all of the pictures I have of him are best described as 'action shots'. He was always on the move, impossible to capture. Which is why I love the one on the rocking horse. The Victorian photographers who specialised in post-mortem pictures had no such problems with their subjects. There was no fretting over best sides or blinking at the wrong moment. They simply had to prop their corpses up, plump a few pillows, and fold their hands in a peaceful position across the chest. Scatter a few flowers around the bed or coffin and the job was done. The children wouldn't fidget or whinge. They would simply recline peacefully, clutching a favourite toy, pretty as a picture. Sometimes the photographs would try to mimic life and disguise the dead as sleeping. A mother would hold her baby or small children would pose with a sibling. But you can always tell that one of them is dead, because no one is smiling.

I take the blue sandal and the photograph and go downstairs. As I reach the hall the doorbell rings and Haizum flings himself at the door, tail wagging frantically. Standing on the doorstep are a small dog and a man and woman laden with bags and smiling broadly. It is Lord Byron, Edward and Kitty Muriel.

* * *

'It's a wonderful party!' Edward gives me a delighted hug. We are sharing a cigarette, huddled up to the warmth of the dying bonfire. From here the *ofrenda* is a magical sight, illuminated with lanterns and fairy lights. This year it is much bigger, to accommodate everyone's memorials, and we set it up on the terrace close to the house. There are lights, too, in the pergola over the terrace, and we can see Elvis dancing a salsa with Epiphany, and Kitty Muriel sashaying seductively in the arms of a rather nervous-looking Albert. Mum is dancing with Marcus, and Dad, Stanley and Helen are watching the festivities from the open doors of the garden room, drinking tequila sunrises and feeding tidbits to Haizum and Lord Byron. Georgina was invited, but she is on an adventure weekend with her Brownies.

'And what about the Olympian?' Edward tosses the butt of the cigarette into the flames and raises his eyebrow questioningly in my direction.

I shrug my shoulders, desperately feigning innocence or ignorance. Or both.

Edward wags his finger at me.

'It's no good,' he says. 'Kitty M told me all about your paramour at the pool.'

'He's not my paramour!'

'But you like him?'

I sigh. 'Kitty wanted me to invite him tonight, but how could I? I barely know him. I've only spoken to him once.'

Edward takes my hand and gives it a squeeze. 'Well, get to know him, then! Trip over in front of him, or drop your glove or spill your tea over him.'

'I don't even know if he's single.'

'Well, I do.'

'How can you possibly know that?

Edward laughs. 'Because Kitty M asked him! Now, come and dance with me.'

We join the others on the terrace and the music changes. Michael Bublé invites us to *sway* . . . As Edward twirls me round in a carousel of lights and music, Sally's words whisper in my ears: 'When the music ends for someone you love you don't stop dancing. You dance for them as well.'

At last, I am dancing for Gabriel.

Chapter Forty-Eight

Today's pool temperature is 7.8 and I really enjoyed my swim this morning once it was over. Now I am skulking in the entrance hall pretending to read the noticeboard. I am dried and dressed and even sporting a touch of mascara. It's so embarrassing and I can't quite believe I'm doing this. I'm trying to 'bump into' the Olympian. I have taken Edward's and Kitty Muriel's advice, but now I'm beginning to feel foolish. What if I do bump into him? What exactly am I going to do or say? At least when I was fourteen the dating playing field was more or less level between the boys and the girls. We were all as embarrassed as each other; floundering through our fledgling relationships as best we could. All equally afflicted with the purgatory of puberty; the girls longing for breasts and periods, and the boys desperate for muscles, moustaches and more to their sex lives than wet dreams. I bet if I were to 'bump into' the Olympian now I would either say something stupid or fail to think of anything to say at all – but he, of course, would be as distinguished as Denzel Washington. It's a cruel irony that I can only channel my inner Audrey Hepburn when faced with a Jim Carrey. I last precisely two minutes before giving up and heading off to the café. As soon as she sees me, Flo starts grinning.

'You're looking very glamorous today. Are you going some-where nice?'

She starts making me a flat white, but she can barely contain herself.

'Or perhaps you're meeting someone,' she adds, just a little bit too loudly.

The café is already quite busy and as I scan the room for an empty table I spot the cause of Flo's amusement. The Olympian. For once he is having his coffee here instead of 'to go', and he is sitting alone at a table reading a newspaper. There are precious few empty seats left, and two of them are at his table. It is the perfect opportunity. I take my mug of coffee and go and sit at the one remaining seat at a table near the door. Flo looks aghast. Kitty Muriel will not be pleased and I can hear Ruby Ivy's string of expletives ringing in my ears. I wish I had a newspaper to hide behind, but I haven't even got a book today. I take out my phone and pretend to be checking something. If the coffee wasn't so hot I'd have swallowed it as fast as I could and beat a hasty, if cow-ardly, retreat. But the first sip scalds my lips. There is the sound of a chair scraping across the floor and I know that he is leaving. He gets up, tucks his paper under his arm and takes his empty cup back to the counter. Flo takes it from him with a beaming smile.

'Thanks, love. You have a good day.'

'You too.'

As he passes my table I force myself to look up. He looks straight at me and smiles.

'No cake today?' he asks.

'I had a biscuit.'

As lame lines go, it's right up there with Baby's line to Johnny Castle about carrying a watermelon in *Dirty Dancing*. And I can't think of a single other thing to say to prove to this gorgeous man that I'm so much better than that. I'm funny. I'm great with dogs. I'm going to be a tour guide at the cemetery. 'I had a biscuit' is my pathetic effort to beguile the Olympian. It's not even true. I didn't. Unsurprisingly unbeguiled, he nods and walks away. If it were possible to kick myself I would. I look across to Flo and she is shaking her head in disbelief. I bet she'll tell Kitty Muriel.

Outside in the crowded car park my day doesn't improve. Someone has backed into Edith Piaf and cracked one of her head-lamps. She looks strangely forlorn, and I'm pretty sure she'll make me pay for her injury by refusing to start or breaking down on a busy roundabout. At least the culprit has had the decency to leave a note on my windscreen. It is a brief apology, a name and a phone number. Gideon. It's very apt. It means 'destroyer'.

I put off calling the number until early evening. I almost don't bother. The damage looks minimal and probably not worth claiming on the insurance, but I suppose it would be better to get it checked. I punch the numbers into my mobile and listen to the ringing tone.

A male voice answers, and as I explain who I am and he responds, I realise why his voice is familiar. Gideon is the Olympian.

Chapter Forty-Nine

~

Alice

As the stars are known to the Night;
As the stars that shall be bright when we are dust,
Moving in marches upon the heavenly plain;
As the stars that are starry in the time of our darkness,
To the end, to the end, they remain.
From 'For the Fallen' – Laurence Binyon

So many dead babies. Another day had slipped away in a drug-dazed fog. Alice gazed out of the window at a starry night, much like the one Vincent van Gogh saw and painted from his room at the asylum in Saint-Rémy-de-Provence. It was her favourite painting. What if each star was the soul of a dead baby, like Netty had told her when she was a little girl? Well, she hadn't said 'dead', she had said 'babies who had gone to heaven'. But she had meant dead. Alice wondered if her babies could see her from so far away. She leaned forward and pressed her cheek against the freezing glass pane. There had been four before Mattie: one boy, a little girl and two other pitiful mites who were too young for anyone to say. 'Miscarriages', the doctors had called them, but to Alice they were all her babies, no matter how imperfect or unfinished the scraps of flesh and blood were when they had abandoned her wretched body. The little boy had been a maquette with insufficient detail to survive. She had had the briefest of glimpses before they had taken him away. Her daughter, Emily, had been a perfect miniature. When she was born, every detail had been present and correct. Except one: life.

Alice went to the wardrobe and steadied herself against the door before opening it and reaching up to the top shelf to take down a battered brown shoebox. She hugged it to herself and took it over to the bed. Inside, wrapped in yellowing tissue paper, were a tiny plastic hospital bracelet, a faded photograph and a set of doll's clothes. Alice held the soft, pink bonnet to her face and breathed in.

They had dressed Emily in the miniature clothes and given her to Alice to hold. They had even taken a Polaroid of Alice and her husband, Michael, and their dead baby daughter. But what happened after that she never knew. She left it all to Michael and lived inside her head for weeks, never leaving their bedroom. The doctor came to see her and gave her tablets, but she flushed them down the toilet. She re-emerged into the world only when the familiar obsession possessed her once more; the all-consuming physical ache of longing for a child, to the exclusion of everything and everyone else. But for Michael that dream had soured irrevocably into the worst nightmare and he wanted no more of it.

Alice took the photograph from the shoebox and stared at the image of her broken family through a mist of tears. She was cradling Emily in her arms and Michael sat next to her, wooden with grief. No one was smiling. As Alice returned the photograph to the box, the wedding ring that she had worn for all these years slipped off her finger and landed on top of it. The ring had been

part of the pretence that she had kept up for so very long, imply-
ing widowhood or perhaps divorce, evidence of a family life more
normal than the one that she and Mattie had actually lived.

They had married young; Alice was only eighteen and Michael
just two years older. His parents hadn't been pleased – they never
seemed to be quite at ease with Alice. Alice had no parents to
express an opinion either way. She had been born to a sixteen-
year-old girl, who would have been described at the time as 'back-
ward', and put up for adoption as soon as she was born. Her
adoptive parents were good people who made an honest and sus-
tained effort to love the little girl that they had taken into their
lives. But a bond between them was never forged, and their relationship with Alice was defined by a cool, well-meaning kindness
rather than warm and unconditional love. The closest thing to
family that Alice had was Netty, the old lady who lived next door
and told her stories and gave her sweets. Their adoration was
mutual and when Netty died, Alice, who was then still a little
girl, was inconsolable for weeks.

When Alice left the home of her adoptive parents at seven-
teen, neither party made much attempt to stay in touch and eventually even the perfunctory exchange of birthday and Christmas
cards fizzled out. She had met Michael when he came into the
sandwich bar where she was working and within six months they
were engaged. Michael had a good job working in a bank, and with
a little help from his parents they managed to rent a flat and set
up home together. When they married, they took it for granted
that a happy family would follow. Instead it had been a holocaust.
Each time a baby died, she begged and pleaded with him to try
again until she eventually drove him away. But they had had sex
just once more; for old times' sake – a farewell fuck. It had been
enough.

Alice replaced the lid on the shoebox and returned it to its shelf. She lifted a small, old-fashioned blue and white suitcase from the floor of the wardrobe and carried it back to the bed. She clicked open the two silver catches and the lid burst open, spilling out some of its contents onto the bed. Alice began searching through them, caressing each item with infinite tenderness. There was a photograph album, thick with images of Mattie, from a few minutes old in his proud mother's arms, to a smiling young man, tall and with the promise of a muscular frame, on his fourteenth birthday last year. Wrapped carefully in a muslin there was a breathsoft curl of baby hair and two tiny milk teeth. Other treasures included a cycling proficiency certificate and some Cub Scout badges sewn onto a scrap of felt.

When Alice had found out she was pregnant again she didn't tell Michael. She gathered her worldly goods and chattels and disappeared. This time it would be different. She would make it perfect all by herself; a new home and a fresh start. Because then he would live. And he had.

There was a soft knock on the bedroom door and Mattie's smiling face peered in.

'Like a cup of tea, Mum?'

She held her arms out and motioned for him to come and sit with her. She hugged his strong, young body to her bony frame and hoped that he couldn't smell the sickness on her, the way that she could.

'You know I love you more than anything in this world?'

Mattie rolled his eyes at her in good-natured embarrassment.

'Yes, Mum, I do. Now do you want tea or not?'

Chapter Fifty

~

Masha

They shall not grow old, as we that are left grow old:
Age shall not weary them, nor the years condemn.
At the going down of the sun and in the morning
We will remember them.

From 'For the Fallen' – Laurence Binyon

It is a perfect day for ghosts. The familiar contours of the cemetery are lost beneath a heavy pall of November's finest fog. Like wet smoke it swaddles the tombstones and angels exactly as it is supposed to, according to the best gothic ghost stories with which the Victorians loved to frighten themselves. The dripping trees are strung with delicate chandeliers of glistening spiders' threads, and the grass is silver stiff with frost. Haizum's panting breaths are swallowed into the churning mists, but his bark, at a solitary crow standing sentry on little Marie's grave, cuts through the thick silence and echoes around the damp stones. The prospect of Haizum's walk this morning was not an enticing one. But I couldn't afford to delay it for too long. I have a busy day ahead. Preparing for what might just be a date with the Olympian this evening.

I'm not afraid of ghosts – I find the living far more alarming. It seems strange that the Victorians, who celebrated death so splendidly, should be afraid of ghosts. I think they were more likely fascinated by the frisson of ghouls and spectres. The physical aspects of death were universally mundane, so perhaps the exploration of its spiritual mysteries injected some welcome excitement into what was otherwise commonplace. Diseases like scarlet fever could destroy an entire family in weeks, and children as well as adults were very familiar with death as a regular house guest. They knew only too well that if one of their brothers or sisters contracted the disease, it would often be fatal, and might well result in their own death to boot. There was no hiding place from one's own mortality and so protection from it was considered pointless. It was a perfectly acceptable topic in children's literature of the day, along with lovely fluffy kittens, jolly nice table manners and Lizzie's new bonnet.

But that didn't mean that it was any less painful for those left behind.

Of course, nowadays, people are rather uppity about the Victorians' approach to death, condemning it as excessive, sentimental and overly dramatic. But I'm not sure our attitude towards it is any better. Our considered approach to death is to try very hard to ignore it. We can't even say it. We say someone has 'passed away'. We talk about having 'lost' someone, or someone being 'late'. They are neither lost nor late. We know perfectly well where they are, and they're not late, they're just not coming. Nobody, apart from Edward, ever described Gabriel as dead. Well, certainly not to my face, at any rate. They hid behind polite euphemisms. We are so much more comfortable saying 'fuck' than 'dead'. We are happy to let children spend hours merrily slaughtering, maiming and motherfucking in front of their computer screens, and yet baulk at them attending the funeral of a dearly loved grandparent in case it upsets them. I think we are teaching them to be afraid of the wrong things.

If there are any ghosts in the cemetery today I won't be able to see them because the fog is too thick. But I can hear them, and they're playing bagpipes. Surely it must be ghosts, because no one in their right mind would be playing bagpipes in the middle of a cemetery, on a dank November morning in fog thick enough to choke your chanters. Unless it happens to be Remembrance Sunday. Today is the eleventh day of the eleventh month, and it is now the eleventh hour.

The bagpipes are for the men of the Royal Highlanders who were posted in the town during the war. There is a raised rectangle of grass bordered on three sides by a retaining wall of stone blocks about two thirds of the way up the hill. It contains a large white memorial cross engraved with military insignia, and twenty or so smaller stone crosses that mark the graves of the Scottish soldiers who died. I always stop by that of James McKilroy, who 'was killed accidentally aged eighteen years, his courage untried'. I beg to differ. Aged just eighteen years old, he volunteered to fight for his country, and die for it if necessary. I believe his courage was not in doubt, but am nonetheless eternally curious about how he was 'accidentally killed'. Each year a small group of friends, relatives and comrades makes the long journey from Scotland to remember their fallen men. Each year the group grows smaller. The pipes are silent now, and I can hear snatches of conversation drifting through the fog. Haizum lifts his head and, cocking it to one side, listens for a moment, clearly puzzled as to where the disembodied voices are coming from. He ignores the bagpipes completely. Once the small service of remembrance is finished, I hear muffled footsteps and the soft clunk of car doors.

As the last of the cars pulls away, the silence creeps back across the cemetery, as all-embracing as the fog, and the only sounds I can hear are my own footsteps and Haizum's panting. It's just as well that I know this place as well as the lines on my face, as I can hardly see more than a couple of feet in front of me. We are following the bottom path; well, I am at least – Haizum skips on and off as though he is playing a rather disorganised game of hopscotch, although he is clearly following his nose rather than a thrown pebble. As we pass the nursery of babies' graves, we turn to climb the narrower path up the hill. Many of these infants were 'born asleep'. And failed ever to wake.

I know that if we climb for about three minutes, we shall be just about level with the Scottish regiment. I am certain there are other visitors to the cemetery today. There is quite a collection of military graves scattered across these rambling acres, and many will be decorated with wreaths of scarlet poppies before the end of the day. But the fog has swallowed everyone and everything, and those who are here will be making their acts of remembrance alone.

I remember my little boy differently now. I can cherish his life without the memory being tainted by his death. I can see his beautiful, happy face without the picture being washed away by the cold and murky waters that enveloped him. I can even hear him laughing and playing games, instead of screaming and thrashing in fear as the river stole him away. My own bloody battle has come to an end, and my armistice is in sight.

I leave the path and cut across the grass until I can see the large white military cross looming up ahead of me. There are three crimson wreaths laid on its pedestal, and a large red poppy is fixed to each stone cross. Haizum is sniffing around the base of the pedestal with worrying interest, and just as I am preparing to

grab his collar to prevent him from relieving himself inappropriately, he snatches one of the wreaths and gambles off into the fog.
Lady T would be appalled, and frankly, so am I. By the time I
catch up with him, Haizum has tired of his new toy and drops it
at my feet. He looks up at me, panting, with some poppy petals
still caught in his teeth. We return the wreath to its proper place
and head off home through the park.

The fog is beginning to clear a little and I can see Sally in the
distance. My stomach lurches as I realise that she is being followed. I can't see their faces, but I'm pretty sure they're the morons
who attacked her before. There are only three of them this time,
but as I hurry across the grass with Haizum, I recognise Deliverance Boy. I'm about to send Haizum after them when an extraordinary thing happens. Sally stops and turns to face them. She
throws her arms up towards the cinereous (word of the day –
ashen, ash-coloured, greyish) sky, and one by one in accelerating
succession the crows abandon their treetop vigils and fly down to
her feet. Soon she is surrounded by a flapping, cawing circle of
shiny black feathers and beaks. But they are not facing Sally; they
are facing outwards and as the youths draw closer a few of the
crows break rank and lunge at their feet, pecking at their precious
trainers. The youths kick out at the birds and shout, but more
crows join the skirmish, their sharp beaks aiming higher at the
soft, exposed flesh of hands, necks and faces. Even the crows not
involved in the physical assault are noisily cawing their encouragement. The youths cut and run, and Sally rewards her bodyguard of crows with the contents of her bag. It looks as though
Sally was right. The birds are grateful for their daily bread and she
now has her very own 'murder' of guardian angels.

Chapter Fifty-One

~

Aretha Franklin's 'Who's Zoomin' Who?' is the soundtrack to the chaos in my bedroom. Marc Bolan has already ridden a white swan, got it on and loved to boogie, but still I am no further forward. This is my 'getting ready to go out' playlist, but it's not usually the cue for a pile of clothes on the bed that looks like an explosion in a launderette. Haizum is surveying the scene of sartorial pandemonium from the doorway with a bemused expression on his handsome face. The Kaiser Chiefs are now predicting a riot.

'Too late!' I say to Haizum, as I throw yet another rejected outfit onto the growing pile. 'Looks like it's already happened.' It's not that I'm nervous. Well, I am a little. But I'm more excited. I just want to get it right. Kitty Muriel's advice on what to wear was 'Knock him dead!' I bet she was probably thinking along the lines of Madonna's conical Jean Paul Gaultier bra, but that's more likely to take one of his eyes out. 'He' is the Olympian. Gideon. And 'he' has asked me out for a drink so that we can exchange insurance details. I do hope that's a euphemism. Edward's outfit advice was not to wear a dress just in case I come back from the loo with the skirt tucked into my knickers. But then he very kindly said that I always look 'original', whatever I wear. I'm pretty sure *that* was a euphemism. Bono is now reminding me that I still haven't found what I'm looking for. Well, quite. I just want to feel comfortable, look nice – well, 'hot' actually – and not get cold on the walk to the pub. Eventually I settle on a pair of black skinny jeans, a red silk kimono top (shades of *The Mikado*!) and a pair of scarlet biker boots. Eddi Reader and Fairground Attraction proclaim it to be perfect. Normally I would take Haizum with me. They know him in my local pub, and he's always made very welcome, but tonight is something of a reconnaissance date. If it is a date at all. The Olympian may not like dogs, and if he doesn't and it is a date then it will be our first and last. Finally dressed, I must now attempt to do something with my hair. Up or down or somewhere in between? After a couple of minutes wrestling with my unruly locks, I decide to simply let them be. As I check in the mirror for stray dog hairs on my jeans and lipstick on my teeth, Marvin Gaye promises sexual healing. Lady T would be aghast!

* * *

'So, tell me something about yourself that I wouldn't guess.'

The Olympian is sitting opposite me, leaning forward and awaiting my answer. It's very distracting to be this close to him in the flesh.

'I've got a very large dog.'

This is definitely progress for me. Until very recently, my response to a question like this, on a date, would have involved Gabriel. 'I had a son, but he died' or 'I used to be a mother'. I would never go into details, even if asked, but I couldn't separate myself from him. I didn't exist as an individual entity. It always felt disrespectful not to acknowledge him at the earliest opportunity. And besides, it's a hell of an icebreaker. But that was the old Masha.

The Olympian smiles.

'Ah, but I *do* know that.'

'How, exactly?' I'm thinking Kitty Muriel.

'Flo told me that she found a dog hair in her birthday cake.'

I'm mortified, and I can imagine Lady T covering her mouth with her hanky in revulsion. The Olympian sees the look of horror on my face and takes pity on me.

'I'm joking! Flo gave me a piece of that cake and it was delicious. Kitty Muriel told me about your dog. Haizum, isn't it?'

He was obviously paying close attention.

'And what else did she tell you?'

He leans back in his seat and grins. His teeth are astonishingly white.

'Not a lot. She told me that if I wanted to know any more, then I'd have to ask you myself.' He takes a sip from his wine glass. 'But she did tell me that you were single.'

I silently thank the Lord – and Kitty Muriel. But now it's my turn.

'And what about you? Tell me something about you that I wouldn't have guessed.'

He thinks for a moment and then replies, 'I used to be a lifeguard.'

I remember his strong, muscled arms and legs scything through the water and his Daniel Craig trunks.

'I *might* have guessed that. You're a very good swimmer.' I want to kiss you. Shit. I hope I didn't say that out loud.

'Well, I wasn't a lifeguard for long. It was a summer holiday job while I was at university. But it's always a good line to impress the ladies.'

'It'll take more than a fantastic front crawl to win me over.'

He laughs. 'I somehow thought it might.'

I'm really enjoying myself. He's easy company and the fact that he's ridiculously handsome hasn't tainted him with the arrogance that sometimes accompanies such dazzling physical perfection.

'So, come on. What else have you got to offer?' I tease him.

'Well, I'm a photographer, so I could take your picture.'

I pull a face that clearly conveys my lack of enthusiasm and he laughs.

'And I can do this.'

The movement of his hands and fingers is so fast I wonder if it's a tic. Maybe he has Tourette's. He repeats the actions more slowly this time.

'I can sign,' he explains. 'When I was a kid, I had trouble hearing. The doctors were worried that it might get worse and I'd end up completely deaf, so I was taught to sign.'

'But it didn't?'

He cups his ear and raises his eyebrows questioningly. I laugh dutifully and dig him in the ribs with my finger.

'No, it didn't. I'm still completely deaf in one ear, and I'd struggle to hold a conversation in here if it was busy, but otherwise it's fine.'

Strangely, I like him even more now he's turned out not to be so perfect. I really do want to kiss him. Lady T would definitely not approve. She advises that public displays of affection anywhere and at any time are beyond the pale. She also says staring is inappropriate. I fear I am both staring (at the Olympian) and – therefore – clearly behaving inappropriately. But I'm beginning to think that as role models go, Kitty Muriel might be a lot more fun than Lady T, and I'm seriously considering switching allegiance.

'So, I know it's really boring and everyone probably asks you the same question, but how do you sign my name?'

He grins and then with one hand mimes mashing potatoes.

Ha ha! I suppose I asked for that one. But there's one more question I really need to ask. It's the deal-breaker.

'Do you like dogs?'

*   *   *

As Gideon walks me home, I realise with a jolt that I've barely thought about Gabriel all evening and I haven't mentioned him once. Not yet. But I don't feel bad about it. For once I am just being Masha, the woman, instead of Gabriel's mum – Gabriel's mourner. And actually, it's okay. Gideon takes my hand. I'm tempted to take a circuitous route home, just to make this feeling last. This feeling of ridiculous excitement and the promise of all kinds of possibilities. Because when we get to my front door, he might just say 'Thanks' and 'I'll be in touch', and mean about Edith Piaf, and it won't have been a date at all. What would Kitty Muriel do? As we head up the garden path towards the door and Haizum begins to bark, I think I know the answer. I kiss him.

*   *   *

If you cry when you are lying on your back, the tears trickle down the sides of your face and into your ears. Which is why I'm awake in my bed, in the dark, with wet ears. I'm not sobbing – it's just that a few tears have escaped. I'm not even sure why. Relief that I still know how to be with a man in bed? Shock that there is a man in my bed? Or fear that now I've allowed this man into my bed, I'll never see him again. Nice girls never sleep with a man on a first date, let alone only a 'possible' date, and I daren't even begin to think about what Lady T would have to say about it. On the other hand, I'm fairly sure I know what Kitty Muriel would say, and I smile in spite of my tears. Now I have a runny nose and to avoid a snail trail, I either have to sniff – not very attractive – or get up and blow my nose and risk waking the man in my bed. Gideon. I fumble for the box of tissues on the bedside table and succeed in knocking the alarm clock onto the floor. Bugger.

'Hey,' a hand reaches across and touches me, 'are you trying to escape?'

'No.' And now I don't need a tissue because in the kerfuffle I've sniffed. I hope he didn't notice.

'Good,' Gideon replies, in a voice smoky with sleep or maybe (hopefully!) lust, as he winds his hard-muscled swimmer's arms around me and draws me close.

'I had a little boy. Gabriel. He died.' Excellent! Where the hell did that come from? I was doing so well. It's as though he squeezed the words out of me with his embrace. I hold my breath, waiting to see what effect my blurted confession will produce. His hold on me doesn't loosen. He nestles his face closer and kisses the nape of my neck.

'I know.'

How does he know?

'How do you know?'

'I used to work for a local newspaper. I'd just started there when Gabriel drowned. It was such a tragic story that I never forgot it. And I never forgot your face. It's my job, you see. It's all about faces.'

He kisses me again, very softly.

'The paper ran the story with a picture of you and Gabriel. It struck me at the time how alike you were; same eyes, same hair. I didn't recognise you at the pool. Your face seemed vaguely familiar, but I couldn't place you in any context. Then you told me your name on the phone and it sparked a memory. Your surname – it's quite unusual.'

I sense his hesitation, and wonder what's coming next.

'I'm afraid I Googled you,' he admits sheepishly. Thank God for that! He knows. And he still asked me out – I'm definitely counting it as a date now – and he's still here. It hasn't frightened him off like it has some of my previous would-be suitors.

'I didn't know what to do,' he continued, 'whether to say anything or not. In the end, I decided that if you wanted me to know, you'd tell me.' He squeezes me tightly. 'I'm glad you did.'

'I'll tell you all about him, one day. What he was really like. But not now.'

'Whenever you're ready,' he whispers, nuzzling the back of my neck. I'll never get to sleep now. I arch my newly toned body to press back against his naked skin, and although he can't see it, I'm smiling.

Chapter Fifty-Two

⟡

The circle of gigantic salmon pink cranes looks like a group of prehistoric creatures having a coffee morning. The glass gherkin glitters in the pale winter sunshine and the mud-coloured Thames crinkles beneath us as the train chunters slowly on through central London. Mum and I are on our way to Brighton. Haizum is staying with Edward and Lord Byron, and I'm taking her away for the weekend as a belated birthday present, and to escape from Dad for a couple of days. The prospect of his forthcoming court appearance is making him increasingly irascible, and even more difficult to live with than usual.

'Sixteen since the last station.'

Mum likes to count things. And people. She counts them in restaurants, the cinema, the theatre, in church – in fact just about anywhere where they keep still long enough to be counted (she should come to the cemetery – that would keep her occupied all day). It's a bit like trainspotting, I suppose, except that she's not at all interested in the make or model, just the quantity. I think perhaps it's a nervous habit. She does it when she's feeling anxious, which is a lot of the time. If her head is full of counting, it leaves no space for worrying thoughts to sneak in. Is this the right train? (She asked the guard and another passenger before we boarded.) What will happen if she loses her ticket? (I have it in my bag for safekeeping.) Will Dad remember to turn off the gas cooker? (Who knows?) Will anyone guess that she's wearing a wig? (I doubt it – it looks completely natural.) But we know for certain that there are sixteen people in our carriage.

It is early afternoon but already the late November sun is languishing, slipping down the grey mottled sky towards its twilight. A young woman gets up and heads off in the direction of the toilet. She is obviously blessed with a more robust constitution than I am. I'm not good with any kind of public lavatory. I have to spread at least four layers of toilet paper on the seat, and even then I try to avoid any actual physical contact with it by adopting the skiing position, which is great for the thigh muscles, but not a very relaxing way to spend a penny. Frequently the downward draught caused by the squatting motion will blow away the paper, and then I'm back to square one again. I usually wait until I get home.

'Fifteen.'

Mum will be fully occupied soon enough as the commuters begin their Friday exodus and the train fills with weary-looking souls clutching coats, laptops and hopes of a quiet weekend; the bright young things of the selfie generation armed with energy drinks and iPhones. One stop later and I am being squashed by a businessman doing the *Telegraph* quick crossword, although 'quick' is rather a misnomer in his case. I can tell because there are some really very easy clues that he hasn't solved yet. I can't help but see because he's taking up all the room; spreading himself out as far as possible, legs akimbo and elbows flapping. 'Look how important I am that I require all this space,' he is thinking. I am thinking that it is simply because he is rude and arrogant. I wish I'd brought a hat-pin to poke him with.

Mum is more fortunate. She is now sitting beside an elegant

elderly gentleman. He is very tall, and slim almost to the point of skeletal. His bony, hollow-cheeked face is illuminated by a pair of piercing, bright blue eyes behind gold-rimmed spectacles. He is wearing a striped shirt, a sleeveless cashmere sweater, and a beautifully cut sage green tweed jacket. He smiled charmingly at Mum when he asked if the seat next to her was taken, and was most solicitous about ensuring that he didn't disturb her in any way. He too is studying the *Telegraph* crossword, although I'd bet my hatpin (if I had it with me) that it's the cryptic option that is causing him so little difficulty. Within fifteen minutes his gold-nibbed fountain pen is returned to the top pocket of his jacket, and his long, slender fingers are quietly folded in his lap while he watches the landscape fly past the window. In the meantime the space-hogging businessman has only filled in nineteen across. I'm pretty sure it's wrong.

The train is lumbering through dark tunnels punctuated by brief shafts of daylight in the black, high-walled sidings. The walls are covered with graffiti art that looks like some sort of modernist cave painting. The tunnels, offices and blocks of flats eventually give way to the back gardens of terraced houses. Some have neat little squares of lawn, plastic tables and chairs, and the occasional flower bed, but more are filled with rubbish and broken furniture jettisoned through the back door – out of sight, out of mind. These gardens look like an extreme version of the cupboard that most houses have, where clutter is hastily hidden from the judgemental eyes of unexpected guests. But the inhabitants of these houses have forgotten about the people on the trains – the uninvited visitors who can see it all. Perhaps they are beyond caring. In some places there is a bordering strip of land between the bottom of the gardens and the railway track that has ended up as a dumping ground for every kind of commercial and domestic rubbish.

As we pass by one of these, I see a bedraggled pink teddy bear sitting in a muddy puddle. It looks unbearably forlorn.

The businessman gets off the train at Haywards Heath, jettisoning his copy of the *Telegraph* in his wake. The old gentleman remains seated and I really hope he is going all the way to Brighton. As the train pulls out of the station, I check. I knew it: nineteen across is wrong.

Chapter Fifty-Three

⁓

'That which we consider to be true art, is that which appears not to be art at all.'

Castiglione's words welcomed us to Brighton. They are written on the wall of Grand Central, one of the first buildings you see when leaving the train station. When we arrived, Mum was tired from the journey and the counting, so we are spending the evening at the hotel. While Mum unpacks her things and changes for dinner, I stand at the window of my room staring out at the fairground lights twinkling on the pier and wondering whether or not I should ring Gideon. We have been on five official dates now: twice out for dinner, once to the cinema and twice to the pub. And the sex is amazing. I know everyone says that at the start of a relationship, but I'm positive this is even more amazing than the usual start-of-a-relationship amazing sex. I can't believe I'm dithering over ringing him. I'm about to pull up his number on my phone when it rings. It's Gideon.

'Can you see the sea?' he asks.

'I'm gazing at it right now.'

'I wish I were there with you.'

By the time I have collected Mum from her room and we have made our way downstairs, she has rallied sufficiently to inform me that there were eleven people drinking in the bar where we enjoyed our pre-dinner Martinis, and forty-seven falling to thirty-two fellow diners in the restaurant during the course (or should that be courses?) of our spinach and ricotta cannelloni, and steamed chocolate sponge pudding with custard.

*   *   *

This morning is cold, clear and sparkling. Having eaten a variety of things for breakfast that we would never eat at home (in the company of twenty-three other guests) we are taking a bracing walk along the promenade. The waves are bubbling and frothing over the stones, and the wind is cold enough to make our faces sting. It is the kind of day to make your soul fly and your heart dance. But Mum is clearly anxious, as ever, about the effect of the wind on her hair, and keeps checking it with her hand.

'Perhaps I should have worn a hat,' she worries. I take her arm.

'It's fine, Mum. That wig wouldn't come off in a hurricane! Don't forget, the saleswoman told you that you could swim in it if you wanted to.'

The gratitude in her eyes is heartbreaking. Looking at the choppy sea she manages a fragile smile and even jokes, 'I don't think I'll be tempted to go for a dip this morning!'

Mum has alopecia – another legacy of Gabriel's death. It started on the day of his memorial service. She was getting ready and one brushstroke pulled out a handful of hair. By the end of the week she was completely bald. Endless treatments have proved futile and as Mum is definitely not the kind of woman who can rock a Sinead O'Connor coiffure with any confidence, wigs have been the only solution. The latest is a recent purchase named the 'Raquel', according to the saleswoman. It is a stylish, dark blonde creation and almost completely indistinguishable from the real thing. Mum looks lovely – I just wish I could get her to believe it.

The burnt-out West Pier is still visible above the sea, its scorched and twisted frame clinging on, like a desperate and exhausted swimmer battling to escape inevitable drowning. In the arches beneath the iron balustrades, the little shops and cafés are opening – the cafés first, to provide steaming cups of tea and coffee to the early-morning dog walkers and tourists. Madame Petulengra, the fortune teller, is not yet in residence, and the little art galleries are still shut up, but buckets of whirring windmills and postcard stands are beginning to appear as the small traders lift their shutters and unlock their tills. As we retrace the steps of the teenage Kitty Muriel, swinging her hat in her hand and con-templating abandoning her stockings for the deliciousness of an unseemly paddle, I stop for a moment and stare out at the glitter-ing, grey waves. I wonder if this could be the very place where Valentine, 'The Great Mercurio – Thaumaturge Extraordinaire', had set up his pitch, and charmed her with his magic.

Further on, the sky blue pillars that support the balustrades are framed by intricate iron crochet work, softening the right angles with arches of wrought-iron doily. The turquoise metal is beautifully mottled with deep orange rust, and the shadows it casts are a carpet of charcoal grey lace on the walkway below. The Palace Pier is waking up now. The siren slot machines are ready to gobble up the coins of those mesmerised by their flashing lights, music, bells and buzzers, and teetering piles of ten-pence pieces. Already the smell of frying onions and fresh crêpes is tainting the sea air. The carousel of galloping horses is my greatest delight. Gabriel would have loved it too, and it is just a single entry on the long and painful list of things that I never got to share with my son. But I shall ride for him. The dappled grey horse called Peter is my favourite, but his groom has not yet arrived, and so my ride will have to wait. We shuffle through the crowded Lanes with their dwindling number of antique dealers, and their increasing number of gift and novelty shops, but eventually tire of the constant jostling, noise and smell of fast food.

'Shall we go for a coffee?'

Mum likes coffee, but what she likes more is to 'go for a coffee'. That is, to find a café or bistro, be seated at a table and have someone ask you which kind of coffee you would like, and then bring it to you with froth and chocolate powder on the top. She always pretends to consider the choice, and then always has a cappuccino. She especially likes it if the sugar comes in several varieties packaged in little paper tubes. She always slips a couple into her bag to take home because 'they might come in handy'. Handy for what exactly, I don't know. I've seen piles of them in her pantry, and some of them have been there for years. We find a quiet little Italian place just off the main street. There are already quite a few people in here (I shall know exactly how many any minute now) as it is fast approaching lunchtime.

'Would you like anything to eat?'

'Are you having anything?'

She always does this. It is as though she needs to be in step with those around her. If I have a cake, she will. If I don't, she still will, but I shall have to persuade her first that it is okay for her to have one even if I don't. It seems she has spent her life trying to blend in, and I have spent mine doing the opposite. I order two cappuccinos and a sweet pastry for Mum, and slip off my long velvet coat. It feels very warm inside after the biting wind along the promenade, and our cheeks and noses are flushed a deep cherry red. I tell Mum that we look like a pair of ladies who enjoy their drink, and suggest that we order a bottle of wine as well. But she is only half listening as she has begun the serious business of counting.

I glance around the tables that are now almost all occupied. Sitting just a few yards away from us, two women are deeply engaged in conversation. Their heads are bent closely together and their intimacy is unmistakable. The woman facing me is disconcertingly familiar. She is small and trim, in her mid-fifties, and her dark brown hair is cut in a stiff, no-nonsense style. She is tastefully dressed in a navy suit and knee-length boots. Her companion looks to be a much larger woman, with a more flamboyant sense of style, judging from her boldly patterned satin blouse and dangling earrings. Our coffees arrive along with the pastry and a little bowl of assorted sugar tubes.

'Forty-nine. This pastry's delicious.'

Now it is my turn to be only half listening. The identity of the woman is really bugging me. I start listing all the compartments of my life in my head, and the people who live in them. She is a work person. I know her through work. But who the hell is she?

'I'm so pleased you've finally found a boyfriend.'

I almost spill my coffee in surprise. I haven't told her anything about Gideon. Mum has relaxed a little now, and is smiling at me knowingly.

'So, when were you going to tell me about him? And it's no good denying it, because I bumped into Epiphany and she told me that you were seeing someone.'

I can't help but laugh. I'm fairly certain that Gideon has been the only topic of conversation amongst my friends ever since they found out.

'Well, I was going to tell you. Soon. But we've only been out a couple of times and it might not be anything serious . . .'

'That's not what I've heard. Edward told Epiphany that he's very handsome, a lovely man and that the pair of you are a perfect match.'

Mum takes another bite of her pastry while she waits for me to answer. I have a feeling that she is enjoying this.

'Does he like Haizum?'

She knows me well. Finally, I surrender.

'Yes, he adores Haizum. And yes, he's gorgeous and lovely and I like him very much. There! Are you happy now?'

Mum reaches across and takes my hand. Her face is suddenly serious.

'More than you can imagine.' She pauses for just a moment before continuing, 'We all loved Gabriel, but you were – no, are – his mother. I can't imagine what it was like for you. But as well as losing my grandson, I have had to watch all these years while my only daughter muddles on with gritted teeth, as though her own life has become something simply to be endured. There have been so many times when I have wanted to say something, do something to shake you out of your misery.'

She takes a sip of her coffee, but doesn't let go of my hand.

'Do you remember when you were a little girl, that time we took you to visit that stately home? The one with the maze?'

I do. I was a wilful little tyke of about six and I pulled free of my mum's hand and ran off into the maze on my own. Needless to say, I got lost, and by the time Mum and Dad found me I was furious with frustration and sobbing with fear. I can still remember the panic at being surrounded by those tall, dark walls and the terror that I would never escape.

Mum puts down her cup. 'I used to have nightmares about that day for years afterwards. I could hear you screaming but I could never get to you. And that's how I've felt for all this time since Gabriel died. In the end, all I could do was trust that one day you would discover the strength and courage to find your own way out of the maze that mourning for Gabriel had trapped you in. And now, when I look at your face, I believe you have.'

My face now has tears running down it, and Mum hands me a paper napkin. This is the longest speech that she has ever made about our lives after Gabriel died. We have never been the kind of family that shares these sorts of emotions easily. These were always the kind of conversations that other people had. But now I am so glad that we finally got around to having one of our own. We finish our coffees and Mum slips off to 'spend a penny' while I settle the bill. When she returns, she tells me in the manner of a child sharing a naughty secret that the woman I think I know is holding hands with her 'friend'. As we are leaving, Mum's bag catches the taller woman's coat, which is hanging on the back of her chair. I bend to pick it up and as I stand up apologising, I find myself looking into the fully made-up face of the Deputy Chief Fire Officer.

'How lovely to see you. You're looking well. Are you enjoying Brighton?'

Lady T would have been proud of me. I don't miss a beat, and poor Bob is so flummoxed that all he can do is smile and grip the hand of his companion so tightly that her fingertips begin to turn white. And speaking of his companion, I'm on a roll now.

'And Mrs Lewis, how are you? Let me introduce you to my mother. Isn't the weather wonderful? Especially lucky for us as we're only here for the weekend.'

Mrs Rosamund Lewis: magistrate and member of the Police Committee, known for her strong views on traditional family values, and self-crowned queen of the moral high ground. Devoted wife to Howard and mother of two teenage boys. Long suspected in some circles of being a closet homophobe. Apparently residing in a different sort of closet altogether.

Once outside, Mum asks me how I know Bob.

'He's the Deputy Chief Fire Officer now, but I knew him as a station officer when I used to work for the council.'

She thinks about it for a moment.

'So, is he a lesbian then?'

I don't know, Mum. I really don't know.

Chapter Fifty-Four

Sally stole my funeral.

Except she wasn't Sally, she was Phoebe — after her mother, Lily Phyllis Phoebe, whose initials are on my ring. The last time I saw her was the week before I went to Brighton, in the park as usual, late one afternoon. It was drear and chilly and the sun had almost set, but Sally was rosy-cheeked and smiling. She greeted us with an enthusiastic wave when she saw us approaching, and threw Haizum a couple of pieces of bread. I stood with her while she finished feeding the crows, and then she took my arm and I walked with her to the café, now shut up for the winter, and down to the bandstand. Conversation was not possible as her scrambling switch was on, but neither was it necessary as we strolled in comfortable silence. When we reached the gate, she gave me an affectionate hug and told me to 'Fuck off and die'. And then she had.

Her obituary was in the local paper along with a short article about her life. It began, somewhat predictably, with 'Local eccentric', followed somewhat surprisingly by 'and former opera star dies peacefully in her sleep'. Sally, or Phoebe, as I should now call her, had apparently had a successful career performing as a soloist in operas all over the world in the late 1960s and 70s. She had sung the roles of Mimi at La Scala, and Violetta at the Royal Opera House. She had never married, but had had a long-term lover – which was pretty racy back then – who had died suddenly in an accident in 1979, leaving Phoebe heartbroken and quite suddenly afflicted with a mysterious condition that put an end to her singing career. The stark, black words on the page drew a picture of a sad, old woman, whose life, which had once glittered with promise, had been irrevocably tarnished by the tragic death of her lover, leaving her to withdraw from the world and skulk in the shadows of madness until she eventually died frail and alone. This was supposedly the story of my friend, whose life I knew virtually nothing about. It was a worthy plot for an opera, but did no justice to the Phoebe I had known.

Her funeral, however, did.

It was the first week in December and it was snowing. Not the wet, grey, half-hearted apology for snow that we usually get in this part of the country, the kind in which the promise of snow-men, sledging and Christmas-card scenes dissolve before it hits the ground. This was real, winter wonderland snow. Pure white-feather flakes floating down thick and fast, cloaking the grubby, grey mud and tarmac of the church's drive with a sparkling, soft white carpet ready for the arrival of the show's leading lady. Phoebe arrived in a gleaming, glass-sided hearse drawn by a pair of magnificent black horses crowned with ostrich plumes, who were prancing and puffing steam from their nostrils. Her small coffin was covered in white arum lilies and wreaths of holly, ivy and mistletoe. It was very quiet as the horses jostled to a halt outside the church. The snow had hushed life's everyday soundtrack, and all that could be heard were the horses snorting and champing on their bits, and the cackle of two crows who were observing the scene from their perch on top of the lych-gate. Phoebe would have been pleased that they were there to see her off.

The church was a monument to the glory of gothic architecture and the pews were filled with people. I was happy to see Kitty Muriel amongst them and sat down next to her. The pallbearers, wearing immaculate tailcoats and top hats, bore Phoebe to the altar while the sublime melody of 'Casta Diva' filled the church. (I noted that Phoebe showed sufficient restraint to forgo the Gaultier model in the sailor suit – or perhaps she simply didn't fancy him.) I had chosen my outfit carefully, and hoped that Phoebe would have approved; black velvet opera coat, deep-red silk rose corsage and, obviously, dark red satin tango shoes; not great for walking in the snow, but fabulous for dancing.

The vicar was certainly divine, and clearly one of God's finest men. He was tall, dark and dignified, with a voice like Irish coffee and a coffin-side manner that made me weak at the knees. He spoke of Phoebe's life as an opera singer; her rare talent and her love of music. He told of her beloved Charles who died when she was just thirty-nine, and how she became ill and hid away. But that was only half the story; only half a life. After several years lost in mourning for her love and her music, Phoebe built a way back into the world. She walked out of her front door and joined in again. In the community where Phoebe lived, everyone came to know her. She said 'Good Morning' and 'Good Afternoon' and 'Fuck Off' to everyone. She arranged the flowers in the church. She volunteered to help at the local old people's home, and continued to do so until she died, by which time several of the residents were younger than her. She provided entertainment with singing evenings; less 'O Mio Babbino Caro' and more 'I'm Forever Blowing Bubbles', but hugely popular nonetheless. If the lyrics were, on occasion, a little unusual, most of the residents were happy to put it down to a dodgy battery in their hearing aids. She gave dancing lessons: the waltz, the foxtrot and even the rumba for the more young-at-heart, slinky-hipped pensioners. She cooked hot suppers for neighbours when they were ill, fed pet rabbits when their owners were away on holiday, and took in parcels for people when they were at work. And every afternoon she took the bus to the park to feed the crows.

Far from being frail and lonely, she was a very lively and much-loved member of the community that she embraced and enriched with her enthusiasm, affection and expletives. She also threw water over any Jehovah's Witnesses who knocked at her door, picked flowers from other people's gardens, and let the air out of the tyres of any yellow cars parked in the street where she lived. But no one really minded (except perhaps the Jehovah's Witnesses), because on balance, Phoebe gave more than she took. All she asked was to be accepted for the woman she was, and allowed to live her way in her eccentric clothes and red shoes, dancing to her own tune. Lady T says that 'refinement lies in the heart and the spirit rather than in outward appearance, but it is by what we do and say that we prove that it exists within us'. It clearly existed in Phoebe. In spades.

Phoebe had made detailed arrangements for her funeral several years before she died. She had no family to second-guess her wishes and clearly wanted to make sure that her last show was to die for. We sang an emotional 'How Great Thou Art', an exuberant 'Bread of Heaven', and 'Non, Je Ne Regrette Rien' surprisingly well in French.

Phoebe had rekindled friendships with several of her colleagues from the world of opera, and one of them, a former tenor and more recently a musical director, gave an affectionate speech about Phoebe's more memorable performances both on and off the stage. It seems that as well as a beautiful voice, she had a prodigious talent for mimicry, and was forever using this particular skill to make mischief.

I learned far more about Phoebe's life at her funeral than I had ever discovered during my friendship with her, but all the additional details merely served to confirm and embellish what I already knew: that she was an exceptional individual who had lived life with gusto, courage and enormous generosity towards others. I was lucky to have had her as a friend.

The congregation rose to bid their last farewell as the coffin glided through the gold-fringed, purple damask curtains, and I knew with absolute certainty that the next music I should hear would be the song to which I had danced with Phoebe in the cemetery. As the final notes of 'La Vie en Rose' faded, everyone sat back down and gathered their handbags, gloves and glasses cases. But although Phoebe had taken her final curtain, the real show-stopper was yet to come. The sad, shuffling silence was suddenly exploded by the opening bars of a song that goes straight to every disco diva's feet. Soon the joyful chorus of Abba's 'Dancing Queen' filled every dark corner with life. The mourners were smiling as they left the church.

The divine vicar told us that Phoebe had made it clear that all those who attended her funeral should honour her wishes by moving on to a nearby hotel and toasting her life and memory with what she called 'after-show' drinks and nibbles. Everybody went and drank pink champagne, and ate tiny, crustless sandwiches filled with cucumber, salmon, egg and cress, potted shrimps, and cheese and pickle. As I was leaving, one of the waitresses handed me a large paper bag containing the crusts that had been removed from the sandwiches.

'I was asked to give you these for the crows.'

The paper bag was tied with a brown parcel label, upon which the following words were scratched in pencil: *ubi aves ibi angeli.*

Where there are birds, there are angels.

Chapter Fifty-Five

❧

Alice

Hail, Mary, full of grace, the Lord is with thee. Blessed art thou amongst women, and blessed is the fruit of thy womb, Jesus. Holy Mary, Mother of God, pray for us sinners now and at the hour of our death. Amen.

Alice felt poisonous; full to the brim with poison. She could taste it, smell it, even feel it seeping round her body just under her skin. She had been to confession, but it hadn't made her pure. In fact, she felt even more sullied, if that were possible. But then it wasn't *the* confession. It was a warm-up; a prelude to the main act for which she would need all her strength and courage. And she wasn't ready yet.

The chemotherapy unit was wearing its Christmas cheer, but it was a thin disguise and unconvincing; like a grave-digger in a clown's outfit. Mattie had gone to fetch a beaker of water. When she had finally told him about her cancer, he had begged to come with her. To be there for her. She had managed to pass off her initial surgery as a small, routine operation – nothing for him to worry about. She had only been in hospital for one day as an out-patient. But once her chemotherapy had begun, she had been unable to hide it from him for much longer. Alice shifted uncomfortably. Her wig was hot and scratchy. She detested what she thought of as her 'hair hat' and only wore it for Mattie's sake. She watched the bright red poison dripping into her weary black vein and fought the urge to rip the needle from her arm. How much would be enough? How much did it take to kill a woman who was already so toxic that she had given birth to death over and over again?

'Here you go, Mum.'

Mattie returned with the water and sat in the hard chair next to her huge, padded armchair. He had brought his iPod with him, but the earphones dangled out of his pocket unused.

'You always were such a good boy. That's why you had so many badges in the Cubs,' she teased.

'Yeah, like when I nicked the apples from old Jenkins's orchard, or threw blackberries at your nice clean washing.'

Mattie laughed, but the memory jolted the wiring in Alice's brain, threatening to make an unsettling connection.

'You always blamed your imaginary friend,' she said carefully.

Mattie laughed and pulled a mock scared face. '"*Help me! Help me! Help me!*" *he said,* "*Before the huntsman shoots me dead!*"'

He sang the words whisperingly, but threw his hands in the air dramatically for each 'Help me!'

Alice shushed him, trying to smile, but the connection was almost there. Mattie stretched out his long legs and tugged at his beanie.

'I always thought that the shed at the bottom of our garden was the cottage in the wood from the song. My friend was a little boy who lived in there with the rabbit and the little old man. He seemed real enough to me.'

Alice clutched at his wrist; her face suddenly grey.

'I think I'm going to be sick.'

Chapter Fifty-Six

⁓

Masha

It's Christmas Eve and the strawberry tree that is in a tucked-away corner right at the top of the cemetery is covered in red berries that look like clusters of tiny, frosted glass beads. Haizum is at home with Edward, Marcus and Lord Byron helping to make mince pies. I am hosting Christmas lunch, but Edward and Marcus are cooking it. Mum and Dad, Helen, Albert and Julia will also be joining us tomorrow.

And Gideon.

I have come to the cemetery to see my other family, and, in particular, Phoebe. The snow has gone, but there is a hard frost today and so the old part of the cemetery looks very seasonal in a Dickens *A Christmas Carol* way. For the last few years I have taken to hanging a few small decorations on the strawberry tree for my beloved boy and the others. The delicate glass reindeers and snowflakes look perfectly at home nestled in amongst the scarlet berries. I just hope the thrushes and blackbirds don't think they're edible.

In the new part of the cemetery, where the headstones are placed in long, straight lines, there are dozens of holly wreaths and some candles flickering in glass-sided lanterns. Here the dead still have families and friends to remember them, and miss them and bring flowers. But it is not so beautiful and I shan't be lingering too long here when I give my tours. (I've done two stints of litter-picking, and my knowledge of the cemetery and its history is pretty damn extensive now, so in the new year I'll be having a chat with Brenda the Brusque again, and this time I'm not taking 'no' for an answer.)

When the cemetery first opened, originality was the latest trend. As more people made money and climbed the social ladder on the broadening back of trade and industry, more people could afford to distinguish themselves from the masses and achieve the covetable status of an individual. This aspiration to stand out from the rabble applied equally in death as in life, and the Victorian inhabitants of the cemetery would have longed for a stonking great monument. They would have dreamed of classical sculptures and columns, towering obelisks, guardian angels and granite crosses. It was not enough for one's status and achievements to be recognised during life, and a glorious, handcrafted, designer tombstone with matching accessories was considered the perfect way to ensure that one's worth (in every sense of the word) would be appreciated in perpetuity. It also gave family and friends a pleasant spot to come and grieve and chat to their dear departed.

But we have gone full circle. Now the trend is for uniformity, ruthlessly driven by the financial implications of maintenance. In the newer part of the cemetery, the headstones must have the same dimensions and stand up nice and straight. The jaunty angles of the Field of Inebriation would not be tolerated here. The rows of graves must be easily accessible to the onslaught of the ride-on mowers and their cavalier coachmen. There is just enough sameness to make it dull, and just enough variation to make it look untidy. The headstones conform in principle, but rebel in detail. Some have little lanterns and others have integral vases. The overall impression is rather like a 1970s housing estate; each house built to the same rather uninspiring design, but over the years embellished with a porch, a bay window, a satellite dish, an extension – or, worst of all, stone cladding. In the end, it just looks a bit scruffy. For it to be beautiful the sameness must be absolute. In the American military cemetery at Madingley, just outside Cambridge, every monument is identical. Swathes of simple, pristine, white stone crosses sweep in ribbons across the neatly cut grass. The effect is poignant, pure and absolutely beautiful.

I assume that Phoebe will have joined her mother, but I am wrong. There are no wreaths of ivy and mistletoe on Lily Phyllis Phoebe's grave. Her angel stands sparkling with frost, and her lilies are the only flowers here. But there are flowers and wreaths on the grave next to hers. The headstone is flecked grey granite, with barley-sugar-twist columns on each side and an engraved starburst at the top of the stone. The inscription reads:

Charles Aubrey Crow
15 October 1934 – 25 June 1979

And underneath, a very recent addition:

Phoebe Jean Violet Porter
16 November 1940 – 23 November 2016
Ubi aves ibi angeli

I wish Phoebe/Sally, Charles and Lily a merry Christmas, and tell Sally that Kitty Muriel has not forgotten her promise to drink champagne at her graveside – we intend to do it together in the new year. I take the bottom path that winds beneath the dark, hushed canopy of some of the oldest conifers in the cemetery. The crows are gathering on the grass as I leave through the gate in the metal railings and cross into the park. It is already growing dark and the last few flecks and slivers of orange and raspberry sunset are melting into the steel blue sky. I can hear church bells calling children to fidget and wriggle their way excitedly through candlelit carol services. I have half a stale fruit cake as well as the usual bread for the crows, as a Christmas treat, and as I scatter their tea at my feet the individual birds become an undulating, pecking black carpet of feathers, beaks and bright elderberry eyes. They finish the final crumbs, and I scrunch the paper bag into a tight ball and shove it deep inside my pocket. I shrink into the depths of my huge tweed coat, hiding from the cold, and head for home.

I am being followed. I'm certain before my ears confirm the fact at the sound of soft but quickening footfalls on the frosty grass. I know it because the hairs on the back of my neck are prickling, and my heart is scudding inside my coat. I turn around and see a figure wearing a hoodie, jeans and trainers coming towards me. And suddenly I'm furious. It's Christmas Eve, for fuck's sake! I'm in the middle of a park, having just been to the cemetery, not a bloody cashpoint. What's he going to take? My coat? My empty paper bag? My Doctor Who scarf? He stops a few feet in front of me, and before he lays a hand on my knit-one, purl-one masterpiece, my fury explodes in his face.

'What?' I yell at him, flinging my hands towards the sky.

I know that my eyes are blazing rage and with my windswept hair, giant coat and flailing arms I probably look like a fearsome banshee, but I'm somewhat taken aback by his response.

'Sorry. Are you okay?'

He looks a bit nervous and genuinely concerned. I'm feeling a bit embarrassed and a bit ashamed of myself (although if he pulls a knife on me in the next thirty seconds, I shall die feeling completely vindicated).

'I just wanted to say something to you.'

He's looking really uncomfortable now, and, not for the first time in my life, I feel like I have woken up halfway through a film, and have no idea what's going on.

'You don't remember me, do you?'

'No. I'm afraid I don't.'

I have absolutely no idea who he is. For one completely surreal second, I even imagine that he's going to tell me that he's Gabriel; a grown-up ghost come back for Christmas. But then that's what comes from too much Dickens, and vodka and tonic at lunchtime.

'We pushed your friend. We were messing about and it got out of hand. You stopped him. You and your dog.'

I wasn't expecting that. I was expecting to be mugged, murdered or even haunted. But not that.

'He made her eat the bread, and she was crying . . .' and so is he now.

He is angrily scrubbing silent tears from his face with the back of his hand. I look at him properly for the first time and even in the dark and beneath the hood I can see how young he is; about the same age Gabriel would have been had he lived.

'He killed the baby duck. He's a total fuckhead. We told him not to, but we didn't make him stop. None of us made him stop, and we should have. I should have made him stop.'

I hand him a tatty tissue retrieved from the depths of my pocket, and he blots the tears angrily from his face. I say nothing because there is nothing for me to say. I can't tell him it's all right, because it isn't. I can't tell him that he isn't to blame, because he was there and has to share the responsibility. So I say nothing and wait.

'I've been watching for you, and I've seen you loads of times, but I always bottle it. I've been watching for your friend too, the old lady with the red shoes, but I don't want to speak to her in case I scare her. I haven't seen her for a while now.'

He's shivering now, but the tears have stopped.

'I wanted to say I'm sorry, because I am. Really. It was out of order and I keep thinking about it.'

And there it was. His Christmas present to me. Because I actually believe he means it.

'Will you tell your friend when you see her? Tell her I'm sorry?'

'Yes, I will.'

We walk through the trees to the main road and cross over.

'I go this way now,' he says, pointing in the opposite direction to my way home.

He smiles at me. A shy smile of youthful optimism and relief. I smile back. A smile of gratitude. I want to hug him, just for a moment; to touch him with love, because he has touched me with hope. But I can't. Instead, I briefly lay my hand on his arm, and he lets me, seemingly without embarrassment. I watch him striding away with his gangling legs, hands in the pockets of his hoodie, jeans hanging perilously off his nonexistent hips.

Just before he disappears out of sight, he turns and shouts, 'Happy Christmas!'

Chapter Fifty-Seven

❧

Alice

Prayer for a Happy Death
O God, Who hast doomed all men to die, but has concealed
from all the hour of their death, grant that I may pass my days
in the practice of holiness and justice, and that I may deserve to
quit this world in the peace of a good conscience, and in the
embraces of Thy love through the same Christ our Lord. Amen.

When Alice came to she was lying on the bathroom floor. She had thrown up so violently that she had hit her head on the cistern and knocked herself out. Now she was cold and shivering, with a throbbing bump on her forehead and vomit in her wig. Her first thought was Mattie. Thank God he wasn't here to see her in this state. He was still at school. She hauled herself onto her hands and knees and groped unsteadily for the edge of the bath. Eventually she managed to stand. Her face in the mirror was grey and haggard, and her skin was slick with the sweaty sheen of her sickness. But it was her eyes that gave her away. Calderas of despair haunted by a darkness far more terrible than her cancer and all its cohorts.

She splashed her face with cold water from the hand basin and rinsed the sick from the straggled ends of nylon hair. It had been the other woman's face that had brought her to this. She was shocked by how physically alike they were. The other woman was perhaps a little younger, but their colouring and features were almost similar enough for them to pass as sisters. It had taken the omnipotent Google just seconds to locate the woman that Alice was looking for; her name, address and profession. There were several local news items and one national. Of course, Alice knew what she was looking for; dates, times and places. The woman still lived in the nearest town, but it was big enough and far enough away to have kept them separated and safe for all this time. But as well as the facts and figures there had been a photograph. The face on the screen belonged to a real woman, and that face had, in a single moment, destroyed every last pretence that Alice had spent so many years constructing, protecting and eventually believing. It was the face of her judge and jury, and inevitably, ultimately, her executioner.

Alice really wanted to take a shower before Mattie got home, but she felt too unsteady to risk it. Instead, she changed her clothes and dabbed on a little make-up, but it was a thin disguise to hide the woman she really was. Downstairs Alice closed the file she had been compiling on her laptop. Now she had the information, she had to decide what to do with it; decide whether she had any choice but to desecrate the happy home that she had built for herself and, more importantly, for Mattie. When he had been very young, she had kept to the edges of village life – much like their cottage, the last on the road out of the village and set apart from the other houses. Alice had dipped into the community only when necessity had dictated, and then out again as soon as it was possible. She had managed to earn a living in the safety of their own home from various market research and sales jobs that required only a high boredom threshold and a functioning computer. But once Mattie had started school, they were inexorably drawn more closely into the village. Mattie made friends and Alice made acquaintances of their parents. They had helped out at village fêtes and Mattie had joined the Cubs and now the village football team. In recent years, Alice had even joined the local WI and made some tentative friendships.

But now, looking back, she wondered if she had ever done any more than skate across the veneer of a social life for appearances' sake. She hadn't even told anyone else about her cancer, preferring instead to drive herself or take taxis to her hospital appointments and chemo sessions. Perhaps some instinct for self-preservation had always held her back; and now she knew why. It had been her diagnosis that had triggered it. Her true past was a book that she had left unopened and on a high shelf for many years now; so long, in fact, that she had forgotten what was written on its pages. She had, instead, created her own reality, moulding and shaping it to fit her needs. But the shock of her diagnosis and the real possibility of her own death had knocked the book from its shelf and she had been forced to face the truth.

Alice switched off the laptop and went into the kitchen. She rummaged in the freezer amongst the frozen bricks of ready meals before deciding to make a proper dinner from scratch. Mattie deserved so much better than some processed rectangle of gloop purporting to be lasagne. Her cancer treatment was finished now, but the bone-dissolving weariness had yet to leave her. Her prognosis was still very uncertain. She had to make her peace, and not just with God. But most importantly she had to make sure that Mattie would be taken care of, whatever happened, and she still wasn't exactly sure how the truth was going to help with that. But even if he never forgave her or understood why, so long as he was safe and loved, it was a risk she had to take, and she would have to tell him herself.

And what about the other little boy?

Alice steadied herself on the sink and took a deep breath as her body threatened to convulse once more. Her heart broke when she thought about him. She had to give him a proper resting place at last. Father Peter gave her the advice that she had known he would. She had finally found the strength to make a full confession. She had spared him, and God, nothing. But, of course, God already knew. Father Peter had been so shocked that he had forgotten to allocate the 'Our Fathers' and 'Hail Marys', but Alice knew that no number would be enough. It would take a great deal more. If she died, she must face God's judgement; if she lived, then it would be man's. There could be no happy ending for Alice; she could only try to find one for Mattie.

Chapter Fifty-Eight

⁓

Masha

Today's pool temperature is 12.7 degrees and it is a beautiful spring morning. The sun is shining brightly with the promise of real warmth later in the day, and the flower pots outside the café are golden with daffodils. These days it is not only the Olympian who scythes through the water. I regularly swim fifty lengths, and in the water I feel free and invincible. It has become my friend. And so has the Olympian. Gideon is now my official, bona fide, publicly accredited boyfriend, and has been for six months now. It is a ridiculous word to use – I am not a girl and he is certainly not a boy – but it makes me smile. Edward still calls him my paramour of the pool, Kitty Muriel, of course, calls him my lover, and Epiphany calls him Daniel Craig. But to me he will always be the Olympian.

He is waiting for me in the café, and Flo has once again abandoned her counter and is standing chatting to him at the table where he sitting with two coffees and two slices of carrot cake. As I join them, she winks at me and grins.

'I'll leave you two lovebirds to it, then. Enjoy your cake.'

Gideon pushes my coffee towards me. 'How was your swim?'

I help myself to a slice of cake. 'Exhilarating.'

'Do you want me to come with you on Monday?' he asks, taking a sip of his coffee.

Monday is the day of Dad's court case.

'I'd love you to come with me, but to be honest, I don't know if it would be the best thing for Dad.'

Dad had liked Gideon as soon as they met. 'About time you got yourself a good man!' he said to me as they shook hands. But tomorrow is going to be a difficult day, and I'm not sure how Dad is going to handle it.

I try to explain my fears. 'Dad will be full of bravado, of course, but I know he'll be worried and maybe the fewer people he has to pretend in front of, the better.'

The truth is that he stubbornly clings on to his alpha male pride, despite the impediments of his age and physical decline. Gideon is a stark reflection of what he no longer has – a body and brain in peak condition to buttress his dignity and bolster his self-respect. Dad is not a man who is comfortable with old age, but instead fights it at every turn. Monday will not be a good day for him to face such a potent reminder that it is a battle he is already inevitably losing. Gideon places his hand over mine and threads our fingers together. Joined like this, our hands always remind me of the keys of a piano. I can almost hear Flo clucking with delight.

'Okay, that's cool. I'll meet you all in the pub afterwards with Haizum. I'll get the drinks lined up on the bar.'

I smile gratefully and steal the last piece of his carrot cake.

'We'll probably need them.'

That I trust Gideon with Haizum is probably the strongest testament to my feelings for him. Until now, Mum and Dad and Edward were the only people in this world to whom I would entrust the care of my precious canine. The fact that Haizum is besotted with Gideon and attempts to wrestle him to the ground each time he sees him, and that Gideon finds this both amusing and endearing, is all the reassurance that I needed. Haizum, like most dogs, is an excellent judge of character.

There is a commotion at the counter and we both turn to see Kitty Muriel and Elvis greeting Flo enthusiastically. True to her word, Kitty Muriel is now a regular swimmer at the lido, but she has yet to persuade Elvis to enter the water. He is, however, happy to watch his wife from the comfort of the café on a Saturday morning if he's not working, and have tea and toast waiting for her after her swim. When Kitty Muriel sees us, she leaves Elvis to place their order and hurries over to our table. She kisses each of us in turn and asks if they can join us.

'We'd be offended if you didn't!'

Gideon pulls back a chair for her and makes room on the table for the tray that Elvis is now carrying. Kitty Muriel is her usually glamorous self in a black trouser suit, white silk blouse with a huge bow at the neck and a black fedora. It is clear that she has not been swimming today.

'No time today, dear. We're on our way to auditions for the latest show, but we thought we'd have a quick cup of tea and a muffin to keep our strength up. Actually, I'm rather nervous. I should really like this part, but the director and I don't always see eye to eye and I don't think I'll be his first choice.'

'There is no other choice, my darling girl,' Elvis assures her as he arrives at the table with their tray. 'The part was made for you, and there's nobody else who'll be able to carry it off with your unique élan.'

Kitty Muriel takes his hand and kisses it.

'Bless you for saying that, but I think you might be slightly partisan.'

They have been married for seven months now and are clearly more in love with one another than ever. The old Masha might have found it embarrassing, but now I think it's rather wonderful.

'So, Elvis, are you auditioning too?'

He shakes his head in mock horror at my question.

'God forbid! I'm just going along as a good luck charm.'

Kitty Muriel immediately starts singing the first lines of the song of the same title that the other Elvis made famous and Gideon nearly chokes on his coffee with laughter. But that is the effect they have. When Kitty Muriel and Elvis walk into the room it's like the Blackpool Illuminations being switched on. They are a dazzling duo, exuding life, love and a healthy shot of bonkers. They just make people smile, and that's a real gift.

'My husband has a wonderful singing voice,' Kitty Muriel proclaims, 'but he is too modest to perform in public. I, on the other hand, am an inveterate show-off!'

Elvis smiles at her proudly. 'You, my darling, are an absolute star.'

'Well, let's hope the director agrees with you!'

Kitty Muriel checks her watch, and hastily finishes her tea.

'We must be off. It wouldn't do at all to be late.'

Elvis gathers their tea things back onto the tray, ready to return to Flo.

'What's the show?' I ask.

But my question is lost in the flurry of hugs and kisses that accompany their farewells.

'Break a leg!'

Chapter Fifty-Nine

'If they send me to prison, I'm going on hunger strike.'

Dad is wearing his best suit – charcoal grey, because it does for both weddings and funerals, which are pretty much the only occasions these days when he has to endure a suit. And court appearances. We are sitting in the dark, cavernous entrance hall of the Magistrates' Court, whose architect was obviously determined that all who enter here should feel the full gravitas, might and splendour of the English legal system embodied in both the design and construction of the building. The windows are all small, very high up, and are glazed in rich, jewel-coloured glass that allows very little daylight to filter through. There are yards of polished mahogany panelling and each of the splendid staircases that lead to the courtrooms has sweeping marble steps and mahogany balustrades. The acoustics are such that the softest of voices is amplified tenfold, and each footstep echoes sonorously throughout the hall. This secular cathedral was intended to be a place where secrets could not be kept. Every lie, every whisper, every movement would be witnessed and given up by the fabric of the building.

These days, however, the congregation do not appear to be remotely repentant for their sins, and demonstrate no reverence whatsoever for their hallowed surroundings. Dad is conspicuously overdressed. Low-slung ripped jeans, football shirts, trainers and baseball caps are evidently the new 'Sunday best'. One young woman has made an attempt at more formal attire, but the effect of the cheap brown skirt and jacket is somewhat marred by the fact that the skirt is several sizes too small, and the gold-coloured necklace she is wearing spells the word 'bitch'.

The witness for the prosecution and his parents are waiting on the opposite side of the hall to us in the seating area near the drinks vending machine. There is a woman with them whom I'm guessing is a solicitor for the Crown Prosecution Service. She is in her mid-thirties and wearing a navy suit and pearl stud earrings. Her hair is dark and glossy, and pulled back into an immaculate, no-nonsense ponytail. The woman has shot us a couple of curious glances and is now in animated consultation with her client and his loudmouthed father. But there is something about the youth that unsettles me. It is an ominous familiarity that I am not yet able to comprehend because I can't see his face, which is almost totally obscured by his hoodie.

Dad's solicitor has been recommended to him by a friend at his bowls club, Eric, who is here today to act as a character witness for Dad. Eric is wearing navy slacks with a dark sports jacket, dazzling white shirt, and a tastefully patterned silk tie. His cheery, round face is scrubbed, and he smells of aftershave and toothpaste. He is doing his best to distract Dad with a detailed report of last night's bowls club committee meeting. Mum's hands flit up and down to check that her wig is in place and her silent lips are moving furiously as she concentrates on counting the number of people in the hall. Dad's solicitor is called Justin Case and looks about twelve years old.

Finally the case is called and as I look across to where the enemy is mobilising, I realise, as he stands up, that the youth is

Deliverance Boy – bully and duckling murderer. Dad and his solicitor lead the way into the courtroom, closely followed by the lacrosse team captain, and then Mum and I. The witnesses, Eric and the youth (who is still being audibly coached by his father on what to say) take their seats in the corridor outside, where they must pass the time until they are called to give evidence. Eric swiftly engages the father in a hard stare-out with the confidence and composure of a man who was doing his National Service fighting in Egypt whilst the other was still in nappies.

The youth smirks cockily at us as we pass him, and I resist the temptation to kick him in the shins. But only just. The youth's mother shuffles into the courtroom and sits as far away from us as possible. She is thin and bony, and her skin is the texture of leatherette from too much sun and too many cigarettes. She looks hollowed out and exhausted, as though all the life has been sucked out of her. Her eyes dart backwards and forwards between the door and the courtroom, and she is nervously twiddling the zip on her handbag. I can't decide whether she is watching for the arrival of the magistrates, or planning to make a run for it. I shouldn't blame her if she did. She would have been pretty once, but somehow I doubt that anyone ever told her. Her eyes meet mine briefly as she catches me studying her, and then she quickly looks away. It is hard not to feel any sympathy for her.

Dad looks very smart in his suit, but perhaps for the first time I see him as a stranger might; an elderly man, active and upright with bright blue eyes, but physically diminishing, wary of the twinges in his joints as he sits down, and reliant on his wire-framed glasses to show him where he is. I feel as though I have returned, after an absence of many years, to a favourite childhood seaside resort to find that everything is smaller and a little more dilapidated than I remember. And for the first time I am afraid. I am afraid that this proud, decent, hardworking, honest (and admittedly sometimes obstreperous) man who is my dad will be let down by the law he has lived by all his life, and which is meant to protect him.

The clerk of the court announces the entrance of the magistrates, and the two women and a man take their places on the bench. The chairwoman sits in the centre and scans the room with a purposeful air. Her eyes rest on me for only a fraction longer than anyone else, but it is long enough for me to know that everything is going to be all right.

Chapter Sixty

❧

Mrs Rosamund Lewis and her colleagues on the bench took just ten minutes to return a verdict of 'not guilty'. Dad's solicitor was an absolute revelation. He may have looked like a twelve-year-old, but he had a deep, booming voice and the confidence of a leading man on the West End stage. He swashbuckled his way round the courtroom, commanding everyone's attention, and extracted testimonies from the witnesses like the conductor of an orchestra drawing performances from his soloists. He was indeed a virtuoso. For Dad, giving evidence was easy. He is a man who couldn't tell a lie if someone wrote him instructions. The lacrosse captain tried her best to trip him up, but her efforts were fruitless because he only had the truth to tell. Eric said his piece clearly and politely, and with a certain avuncular charm that seemed to disconcert her a little. Deliverance Boy, however, had a rather unreliable recollection of events, and his memories seemed to ebb and flow like drawings on an Etch A Sketch.

In her summing-up, Mrs Lewis described Dad as a decent and honourable man who had clearly made a useful contribution to society and continued to do so, even though he was now retired. She said that he had attempted to prevent an act of wilful vandalism that could have resulted in the loss of someone's life, without a second thought for his personal safety. She added that the tragic drowning of his own grandson, which had been alluded to by Dad's solicitor, lent a particular poignancy to the case and that, given the circumstances, Dad had acted with commendable restraint. She told the youth he should consider himself lucky that he was not appearing as the defendant himself on this occasion (whilst perhaps thinking to herself that it was only a matter of time before he did).

As we step outside, squinting in the bright sunshine of an early April afternoon, Dad looks an inch or two taller, and several years younger. His relief is palpable. Mum is holding his arm and smiling uncertainly, like someone who has just got off a particularly stomach-churning roller-coaster ride and might still throw up. Dad hugs her close with unaccustomed tenderness and declares, 'You look like you need a stiff drink, my girl.'

We thank Dad's solicitor, who blushes furiously and regretfully declines our invitation to join us in the pub. Gideon meets us there with Haizum, Edward and Lord Byron, and we toast Dad's vindication, the triumph of British justice, and the resounding defeat of the lacrosse captain. However, I warn Dad that today is his only day of grace. He may boast about his virtue, quoting Mrs Lewis's words of fulsome praise for one day only. After today, if he continues with such swaggering, I shall be forced to pinch his ears and confiscate his DVD of *Bridge Over the River Kwai*.

Haizum is allowed to share a packet of his favourite cheese and onion crisps with Lord Byron as a special treat.

After her gin and tonic, Mum says to me, 'I know it sounds silly, but that magistrate looked awfully like the woman we saw in Brighton who was holding hands with the man in the dress.'

As she gets up and makes her way to the Ladies, Dad whispers to me, 'Your mother never could hold her drink.'

Chapter Sixty-One

Alice

Away with us he's going,
The solemn-eyed:
He'll hear no more the lowing
Of the calves on the warm hillside
Or the kettle on the hob
Sing peace into his breast,
Or see the brown mice bob
Round and round the oatmeal chest.
For he comes, the human child,
To the waters and the wild
With a faery, hand in hand,
For the world's more full of weeping than he can understand.
From 'The Stolen Child' – W. B. Yeats

Alice had decided that a letter would be the best way. She couldn't bear to meet the woman face to face, or even speak to her on the phone. An email seemed too impersonal and yet, at the same time, too casual. Alice had sat for a long time, pen in hand, wondering how to begin. She didn't want to make excuses for herself, but she wanted the woman to know everything, so that she could at least try to understand. Before Mattie, Alice had never truly felt how annihilative it was to lose a child. All her babies had died, but she had barely known them. She had never fed them, felt their breath on her cheek or rocked them to sleep. She had loved them; of course she had loved them, but instead of allowing herself the time to grieve, she had replaced each death with a pregnancy. Until Mattie. And it was only now, with the prospect of her own death, that she faced the exquisite irony and agony of losing her precious boy. Alice would finally experience the grief that the other woman had endured for so long, even though her own child had never died.

Alice had called him Matthew because it meant 'gift from God'. When he was born, safe and well, she had truly felt blessed. It was hard at first, caring for him alone and in a new place, but he was always such a good boy, always so happy. And healthy; strong. The other babies were never forgotten, but the sorrow was papered over again and again by Mattie's first word, his first steps and his beautiful face. Every day, when she woke, she would hear him chattering to himself before she went into his room. He would press the button on the musical mobile attached to the side of his cot and sing along to the tune it played.

And then there was a morning when the music ended.

At first she thought that he was sleeping late. He was just one year and five months old. She couldn't let him go. He looked so perfect and God wouldn't do that to her; He wouldn't be so cruel. She had always wondered about her first-born son and what had happened to him. What if he hadn't really been dead? What if he had woken up alone and afraid? They had taken him away so quickly, too quickly for her to be really sure that he was dead.

It wasn't going to happen again.

She bathed Mattie and changed his clothes, talking to him all the time. She kissed his marbled cheek and stroked his soft curls with her fingers. She spent the day cradling him in her arms and singing to him. And the next day, and the next, and the next. This time she would keep him with her until he woke up. The days grew warmer and Mattie began to look and feel wrong, but still she couldn't let him go. It was too warm for him in the house, so she wrapped him in a cool, cotton sheet and took him down to the shed at the bottom of the garden, shaded by the woods beyond. She laid him down gently inside where he could sleep in the cool quiet until he was ready to wake up and then she locked the door to make sure that he would be safe and undisturbed.

She went to the river that day to walk and think. She couldn't remember getting there, but it was a bright, spring day and the river was sparkle-strewn in the sunlight. A flotilla of baby duck-lings bobbed past behind their mother and father, and Alice wished that she had brought some bread. She couldn't think straight any more and she was so tired. She had prayed and prayed so hard that God would return His gift to her. The water looked cool and soothing. She imagined what it would be like to slip beneath the surface and float away.

I have been half in love with easeful death.

She remembered a line from a poem she had learned at school. Would it be easeful? She was almost tempted to try. And then suddenly, there he was. A little boy, crying and alone. He had lost one of his shoes and was clutching a soggy piece of bread in one hand and a tiny white feather in the other. It was Mattie. It had to be. He looked a little bit different, but then he had been asleep for so long, and anyway, who else could he be? There was no one else around. Her prayers had finally been answered. She gathered him in her arms, dried his tears and took him home.

For weeks afterwards, she and Mattie hardly left the house. She watched over him night and day to make sure that he wouldn't fall into such a deep sleep again. At first he was strange and unsettled, as though he didn't recognise his own life, but gradually he became himself again. They picked up from where they had left off and carried on.

But the little boy she brought home wasn't Mattie.

His name was Gabriel. And for all these years, the woman, Gabriel's mother, had believed him to be dead, and the shed at the bottom of Alice's garden had remained locked.

Writing it all down crystallised the appalling truth for Alice. It was incredible that she had got away with it for all these years, but perhaps it was largely because she had been able to fool even herself into believing that it was true. And, of course, she had been lucky; she and Gabriel had the same colouring, the same common blood group. Luck had conspired with her to create her own truth, and her circumstances were such that it was never doubted by anyone else. She didn't shop in the village, preferring to use a nearby supermarket, and her doctor's surgery was a large practice in town, where she rarely saw the same GP twice. Her nearest neighbour was an elderly man who had little interest in anything other than football and horse-racing and spent most of the day in front of his television screen. By the time she was forced to engage in village life by enrolling Gabriel in pre-school, he had long been Mattie to both her and himself, so why would anyone else have reason to question his identity? Her head ached as much as her arm. The physical as well as the mental act of confession was exhausting and terrifying, but she was nearly done.

I am more sorry than I can ever express for the pain that
I have caused you and would not dare ask for your

forgiveness, but only beg that you try to understand. I have told Gabriel nothing. I have no idea what to tell him, but, as his mother, I must leave it to you to decide what should be done next. I can only tell you that he is happy and healthy, and that I have loved him as my own son, because for most of his life, however hard it is for you to accept, I truly believed that he was.
 Alice

Tomorrow would be the anniversary of the day that Alice found Gabriel. She had to post her letter today.

Chapter Sixty-Two

⁓

Masha

We shall find peace. We shall hear the angels,
we shall see the sky sparkling with diamonds
                    Uncle Vanya – Anton Chekhov

It is far too hot for May and I have climbed to the top of the hill in the cemetery in search of a fresh breeze. It was worth the climb. Here, the breeze is strong enough to fly a kite or lift an angel's wings. Haizum is sitting next to me with his nose in the air, catching each scent in his twitching nostrils as it wafts past. His long, wiry hair is ruffled by the breeze like a field of corn, and his ears are flapping gently, lifted by the wind. His soft, dark eyes are staring into the distance. I'd love to know what he is thinking. It will definitely involve food.

Edward and I meet less frequently in the cemetery now. He looks younger each time I see him. Love has rejuvenated him, but it is not love alone that has made him truly happy again. He has witnessed my resurrection, which in turn has set him free. I shall never stop dancing for Gabriel, but our little boy – for he did, in so many ways that really matter, belong to both of us – must now be allowed to rest in peace. And I have Haizum and Gideon and another chance to love my life and really live it.

On my way here I stopped to call on Ruby Ivy, Nellie Nora and Elsie Betty. They are pretty much redundant as my worry dolls these days; I rarely need to worry them. So instead I tell them all my gossip, which might not always be knicker-twistingly exciting, but I should hate them to feel neglected. Marble head-stones and granite chippings sparkle under the midday sun, and trees are tipped with fresh new leaves. A little way down the hill, a crow is grappling with a large twig. Nests are being built in tall pines all over the cemetery, and very soon there will be ducklings on the pond in the park. From my seat on this wooden bench, I can just about see Lily Phyllis, Phoebe and Charles, whom I shall visit on my way down.

Gideon has a friend who is a record dealer, and he managed to get me some early recordings of Phoebe singing Mimi from *La Bohème*, and Isolde from *Tristan and Isolde*. It is clear from her records that Phoebe had an extraordinary musical talent, which makes her recovery after its loss all the more courageous and remarkable. I have been able to play them on Kitty Muriel's gram-ophone. When they married, Elvis sold his house and moved into Kitty Muriel's flat. I am invited there each Thursday at 5.30 p.m. for cocktails and canapés. Haizum is also included, and although he performs on the polished wooden floors like Bambi on ice, he seeks refuge on the exquisite rug, and clings to it as though it were a life raft on a storm-tossed ocean. He is allowed four cana-pés. But only four. The pink walls of Kitty Muriel's flat are almost exactly the colour of the fondant fancies in my old nightmare, but Gilbert and George, art deco and Venetian glass are a far cry from the Formica-topped tables, plastic chairs and lurid wallpaper of the abominable Happy Endings home. Kitty Muriel, like me, has no children to care for her in her dotage, but she does have an adoring husband and is living a very happy, and frankly rather exciting, alternative to the old age I had envisaged and feared for myself. And so shall I.

As I look down across the Field of Inebriation it shimmers in the heat, and I remember Sally. I know I should call her Phoebe now, but I can't help but think of her as Sally. I don't think she'd mind. I miss her. But here, I always feel that she is somewhere close by. Some people leave an indelible imprint on your life, like the indentation of a fossil in rock. Sally was one of those people, and she made me realise that Gabriel never deserted me. He left an imprint on my heart that I have learned to cherish, instead of grieve that it is all that remains of him.

Sally would be delighted to know that Kitty Muriel is hard at work rehearsing for *The Merry Widow*, in which she is indeed playing the title role. Marcus, much to everyone's delight and rather mischievous amusement, has been cast as Count Danilo, her leading man. I am so looking forward to the show, but fear that I may have to be sedated beforehand if I am to retain any measure of self-control throughout the performance. Lady T, look away now. I am helping Kitty Muriel to learn her part. For this particular character she is channelling Zsa Zsa Gabor. I'm not sure it's quite what Lehár originally intended, but I'm confident he would have come round to her way of thinking. After all, the director has. Eventually.

Elvis also has a role to play in this production. He is doing make-up. Recently, I've noticed that Kitty Muriel's maquillage has undergone a rather flattering transformation. It is clearly applied with a lighter touch and from a subtler palette. I complimented her upon her new look and she proudly attributed it to her 'adorable husband'. Apparently, Elvis the undertaker has for years been providing an entirely complimentary service for dead people in his care. He performs a post-mortem mini-makeover for each client, with the help of the kindly receptionist, Mabel, who does their hair (if they have any), in order that they can look their best for friends and relatives visiting them in the chapel of rest. I couldn't see Helen accepting this as part of her job description – answering the telephone, filing, cut and blow-dries for corpses – but I do think it's a very kind and generous thing to do.

Kitty Muriel told me that Elvis and Mabel even do it for the ones who have no friends and family, because Elvis says that they deserve the same treatment as everyone else. In his book there's no such thing as a second-class corpse. They all leave his care with blushed cheeks, pink lips, neat, shiny hair and a touch of mascara. The ladies get eyeshadow (and some of the men do too, but only when Elvis feels it would be appropriate), but what they all get is the utmost respect and a clean hanky for their journey. I can absolutely see why Kitty adores this man and is delighted to have him working alongside her in *The Merry Widow*. And if the School-Girls' chorus in *The Mikado* was a fair representation of the dramatis personae, he won't notice much difference from his day job.

Haizum is beginning to get fidgety. The cool breeze has revived him after the hot and tiring climb up the hill, and there are squirrels and pigeons waiting to be chased. But I am reluctant to move. It is peaceful here, and the view is glorious. The whole cemetery is scattered with clumps of pale lemon primroses and drifts of sunshine yellow daffodils. From this place, high on the hill, I can see the graves of almost all my Family on the Other Side. But I am very much on the side of the living and I feel like the queen of the castle. The wind is growing stronger, and I stand up and stretch out my arms to feel it buffeting against me, as though I were a sail on a ship. I reach inside the pocket of my crumpled linen jacket and grasp a handful of the softness that is nestled there. It is almost too soft to feel. Closing my fist I take it out of my pocket and raise it high above my head like the marble angel on Lily Phyllis Phoebe's grave. And then I let it go. The air is filled with pure white feathers, dancing and spinning in the wind across the bright blue sky. I have finally taken Sally's advice and set my angels free.

Haizum has grown impatient and has set off back down the hill without me. He is taking his favourite route, off the path, through the Field of Inebriation. It must be a popular night-time haunt for the local foxes, as Haizum's nose has barely left the ground. As I start to wander downwards through the long grass, I am too warm in my jacket and have to take it off. Haizum's restlessness and excitement seem to be catching, and I can't bear the thought of having to carry anything, so I tie it round my waist with the sleeves. For some strange reason I feel as fizzy as a champagne cocktail. What begins as a fairly innocuous 'hop, skip and jump' soon develops into a full-scale impersonation of Anna dancing the polka with the king in *The King and I*, which, if you haven't seen it, is a heart-pounding gallop of a dance in a very puffy skirt (Anna's, not the king's). Haizum has stopped what he is doing and is looking at me with the expression of a teenage boy who has caught his mother wearing a boob tube and mini-skirt in public. I pause for a moment and plant a huge kiss on the top of his head, and then challenge him to a race down the hill – an activity that meets with his approval a great deal better than my dancing does. As we career together through the long spring grass, I am shrieking and tripping and stumbling and barely in control of my legs; and Haizum is leaping and bounding across my path, barking with excitement.

Somewhat inevitably, we end up in a tangled heap amongst the primroses, somewhere near the bottom path. I am breathless, covered in grass stains and have tears of laughter streaming down my face, and Haizum is kindly washing them away with his huge, rasping tongue, whilst trying to sit on top of me. When I am sufficiently recovered, I glance round furtively, to see if anyone has witnessed our high spirits and is speed-dialling the local mental healthcare team. I can see one cemetery worker, mercifully some distance away, but I recognise him, and know that he has seen me here many times before and will not be in the least bit surprised or concerned.

We stop to say hello to Lily Phyllis, Sally/Phoebe and Charles, and tell them about the forthcoming production of *The Merry Widow* and its rising stars. Charles and Phoebe's grave is covered in violets, and I pick a small bunch (I know they won't mind) to take to Epiphany's this evening. Epiphany and Stanley have invited us all to dinner. Today is the anniversary of Gabriel's death and we are all going to remember him. But we are also going to celebrate the lives that we still have. Roni is bringing her new boyfriend, Jericho, who is a call centre manager and part-time shaman. We can't wait. Helen predicts that he'll have a ponytail and a glass eye, and Edward predicts that I'll be choking on my Sauvignon Blanc within two minutes. Lady T is surely hoping that we remember our manners and strive for graciousness. I fear she may be disappointed.

Haizum and I head home. The post is waiting on the doormat and, as I pick it up, I am vaguely curious about the handwritten envelope on top, but I am running late and it will have to wait. I dump it on the dresser unopened. Haizum pushes ahead of me through the front door and trots off to the kitchen, his nails clicking on the floor. He greedily slurps half the contents of his water bowl, and deposits a generous quantity of water and slobber across the kitchen tiles in a precise distribution designed to ensure that I tread in it as many times as possible whilst collecting a mug from the cupboard and switching the kettle on. I hastily shove the violets into a tumbler of water, and, taking my tea with me, skip upstairs to shower and change. I only have half an hour before Gideon arrives to collect me. On my way out of the kitchen I hear Haizum slump noisily to the floor with a sulky sigh. He knows I am going out and wishes to make his disapproval clear. Barely thirty minutes later the doorbell rings, and as I run down the stairs to greet Gideon, Haizum gallops along the corridor to join me. Hanging limply from the corner of his mouth is a solitary purple flower. Bugger. He has eaten the violets.

Chapter Sixty-Three

⌒

Alice

Through this holy anointing may the Lord in His love and mercy help you with the grace of the Holy Spirit. May the Lord who frees you from sin save you and raise you up.

Alice's mind was feeling very still. This was the closest thing to peace that she had known for as long as she could remember. She wasn't sure if it was the prayers, the drugs, or a combination of the two. Father Peter had anointed her with oil and blessed her with the hope of God's forgiveness. She no longer felt part of the flesh and bones that lay on the bed. In the end it was such a relief to simply let go.

Epilogue

In the cemetery fallen leaves swoosh and swirl in a dance choreo-graphed by the fitful wind. As the afternoon slips away into a Titian-tinted autumn twilight, a woman, a wolfhound and a teenage boy carrying two orange chrysanthemums walk together amongst the angels, crosses and headstones. Where the path begins to meander uphill they turn onto the grass and head towards a new grave still brown with freshly dug earth. Beside it is a smaller grave, less recent and clearly that of a child. The woman hangs back, respectful and perhaps a little uncomfort-able, but the wolfhound stays close to the boy, nudging his free hand with his nose. The boy stands staring at the dirt mound that has yet to settle. Then he crouches and gently lays down a flower each for mother and son. His fingers rest for just a moment on the cold marble cross that marks the smaller grave, and then he stands and wipes his eyes with the back of his hand.

The wolfhound presses himself close against the boy's side and pushes his head under his hand. The woman waits. A solitary crow flies overhead and lands on a stone cross, watching the three of them with beady, blackcurrant eyes. The woman reaches into the pocket of her long coat and throws what she finds for the crow. He snatches his prize and gobbles it down before taking flight once more and disappearing into the highest branches of a towering pine. The wolfhound barks, just once, and the boy turns away from the graves towards the woman. She smiles at him with infinite tenderness and takes his arm.

'Let's go home,' she says.

Author's Note

When I began writing *The Particular Wisdom of Sally Red Shoes*, I wanted it to be a book about hope and living life to the full. But I'm with Dolly Parton when she said, 'If you want the rainbow, you gotta put up with the rain', and so I also wanted to tackle some more difficult and painful issues.

Life has a habit of throwing you a curve ball every once in a while, and there's nothing you can do about that, but you can always choose how you deal with it. You can lie down and roll over, or you can stand up and fight. But you don't need do it on your own: there are people who can help. All you need is the wisdom and courage to let them.

When I discovered a lump in my breast I told no one (in fact, I was even reluctant to write this sentence!) At first I didn't even tell my husband; I went to my GP who referred me to the hospital, and then I told him. But I made light of it, *it's probably nothing*. Once I was diagnosed with cancer, I didn't want anyone else to know: I didn't want to deal with other people's reactions, I just wanted to get on with what needed to be done. I thought that if I only had surgery and radiotherapy, I could probably get away with telling only a handful of my closest family and friends. But the side-effects of other treatments are much trickier to hide; a few weeks after my first chemotherapy I was completely bald, and, quite frankly, past caring who knew.

And I was foolish trying to hide it from friends and family who loved me and wanted to help: they came with me to chemo, and organised rotas to take me to radiotherapy; they sat in hospital corridors and waiting rooms with me, and one friend (who happens to be a vet) even prompted the diagnosis of my crashed thyroid by suggesting to my consultant that I had all the relevant symptoms and perhaps he should order some blood tests. (He did – she was right, and the next day he jokingly offered her a job!)

But it's not just friends and family who can help, there are also amazing organisations that can provide support and information when you most need it. I wanted to include the contact details of three of them here, ones that are most relevant to the storyline of my novel.

Macmillan Cancer Support
At Macmillan they know how a cancer diagnosis can affect everything. They provide support to patients and their families, and help them to take back some control in their lives. Macmillan can also help with money worries and advice about work, and if you just need someone to talk to, they'll be there.
macmillan.org.uk

Cruse Bereavement Care
Cruse Bereavement Care is the leading national charity for bereaved people in England, Wales and Northern Ireland. They offer support, advice and information to children, young people and adults when someone dies and work to enhance society's care of bereaved people.
cruse.org.uk

The Lullaby Trust

The Lullaby Trust is an organisation that is working to reduce the number of SIDS (Sudden Infant Death Syndrome) deaths, and supports bereaved parents and families.

lullabytrust.org.uk

Acknowledgements

For most authors their second book is a tricky beast and so it was for me: I worried that I'd already used my best plot, most engaging characters and cleverest phrases. But once *The Keeper of Lost Things* was published, something wonderful, and to me completely unexpected, happened. Readers from all over the world started sending me messages. They told me how my words had touched their lives; they told me about their own experiences with cancer; they sent me pictures of their rescue dogs, and one lady even sent me a picture of her rescue donkey. And they told me how much they were looking forward to my next book (no pressure!)

So, the first people I want to thank here are my readers – for all their support and encouragement, and for sharing small but important parts of their lives with me. You have all inspired me to keep telling my stories and, hopefully, to keep getting better at what I do.

I'd also like to thank all the booksellers for their wonderful support. Thank you for allowing my readers to find my book: it is very much appreciated.

I want to thank my parents for their shameless publicising of 'Their Daughter, the Author'. My dad is always bringing me copies of my books for me to sign from people he meets dog walking, and my mum has pinned every single PR photo I've had taken on their living room wall. Well, I suppose it saves them redecorating . . .

Thank you to my brilliant agent, Laura Macdougall for her wisdom, straight talking and for always being there when I need her, and to the teams at Tibor Jones and United Agents for looking after me so well.

I want to thank Fede, my fabulous editor, who makes editing so easy and fun, and always knows how to reign in my writing excesses with tact and humour. Working with him is a joy.

Thanks also to the team at Two Roads, particularly Auriol Bishop, Kat Burdon, Sarah Clay, Hannah Corbett, Nick Davies, Rosie Gailer, Ben Gutcher, Lucy Hale, Alice Herbert, Lisa Highton, Jamie Hodder-Williams, Lizzi Jones, Jess Kim, Maiko Lenting, Grace McCrum, Peter McNulty, Emma Petfield, Susan Spratt, Ellie Wheeldon, Ellie Wood, and everyone at Hachette Australia and New Zealand. Thank you to Amber Burlinson for her awesome copyediting skills, and to Diana Beltran Herrera and Sarah Christie for their incredible work to produce another beautiful cover.

When I was writing *The Particular Wisdom of Sally Red Shoes*, I spent a lot of time wandering and pondering in Bedford's Foster Hill Road Cemetery, and also Highgate Cemetery. The upkeep of these beautiful places is dependent on volunteers and I should like to thank Sue and Rowan and all the other Friends of both Foster Hill Road and Highgate cemeteries for doing such an amazing job.

Peter at The Eagle Bookshop in Bedford continues to be my writing buddy and has even sold (new!) copies of my book alongside his antiquarian stock. He still hasn't finished writing one of his own books yet, but I live in hope.

Acknowledgements

Once again, I want to thank the staff at Bedford and Addenbrookes hospitals, and particularly the staff at The Primrose Unit for their care and support.

And finally, I want to thank Paul and my beloved dogs, Duke Roaring Water Bay and Squadron Leader Timothy Bear, for so many things, but mainly just for being there.

Bedford, September 2017